COAST TO COAST

VANCOUVER VICE HOCKEY 5

MELANIE TING

CONTENTS

INTRODUCTION

Coast to Coast: When a player skates the puck from one end of the rink to the other.

When Lily Larson goes to Sweden on exchange, she loves everything: the university, the town, and her new friends —especially one tall and grumpy Swede. Lily's sure that Gabriel Olsson's gruff exterior hides a caring heart.

But when Lily returns to Vancouver, it's up to Gabriel to bridge the distance between them. He'll have to cross oceans and continents, but it's his family ties that will be hardest to break.

If Gabriel succeeds, he'll find a place in the sport he's loved and lost *and* win back the woman of his dreams. Can he go the distance?

1

LOST IN LUND

THESE COBBLESTONE PATHS AND STONE buildings are quaint and adorable, but what I really want is a good old-fashioned street sign. Or a map app that works.

This is supposed to be the first day of the best semester of my whole life. I begged to go on exchange in Sweden, over my mom's protests that I'm too scattered and disorganized to cross a street alone, let alone a continent and an ocean. I battled and now here I am—all by myself in the middle of the Lund University campus.

And I'm completely lost. I have no freaking clue how to get to my first class. The map I got from the exchange office is either wrong or unreadable. Oh, and legible signs on the buildings would be a nice touch, people.

Well, lost is not a problem, right? My Swedish sucks, but everyone here speaks English, so all I have to do is ask someone for directions.

My first target is this guy who is tall, dark, and gorgeous. Just because I'm lost doesn't mean I've lost my senses. I smile and try to catch his eye. But he motors past me before I can even get a word out.

Okay, I'm going to have to be faster. Target number two is also tall and gorgeous. Honestly, this place must be ground zero for model recruiters. Guys *and* girls all look incredible. Since I'm tall, I appreciate being able to look people in the eye instead of seeing the tops of their heads. I've seen more crooked parts than Christoph Waltz.

This time, I'm sure the guy sees me, but he looks away and veers away onto the grassy lawn. He's walking so fast that I can feel the breeze of him passing.

Maybe I'm scaring off the guys for some reason. I look normal by Vancouver standards: denim mini, cardigan, and a floral print top. But here I'm the only one wearing colour in the middle of Club Neutral. And everyone—male and female—is wearing a uniform of ridiculously skinny jeans, t-shirts, and cotton scarves, even though it's August. Despite my blonde hair and half-Swedish genes, I look foreign.

Two women walk by and I say hi, but they ignore me completely. Ditto a woman on a bicycle who suddenly goes all Tour de France when I raise a hand to stop her. Remind me to check to see if an open palm means something disgusting here.

An entire group of guys pass by me like I'm a statue. Even an older man, who's probably a prof, averts his eyes when I smile at him. What the hell is going on?

Standing in the middle of the path, I notice that people are detouring around me. I'm in a plague bubble. They are deliberately avoiding me. Why on earth would they do that?

I check my phone. If I don't figure out something soon,

I'm going to be late for my very first class, then the prof will hate me and fail me. My mother will get to say she told me so. I'll have to go to university for an extra year, and I'll graduate in a recession and never get a good job and end up living on the street. My whole horrible future flashes before me, and tears well up in my eyes. I open them wide so I don't cry. I can't remember if I wore water-proof mascara this morning, and adding black smears to my face won't help me look sane. I have an overwhelming urge to call my dad. I'm not sure exactly what he could do since he never went to university here, but at least he's Swedish. Hearing his voice would calm me down and comfort me which is exactly what I need right now.

Buck up, Lily. I look down at the stupid map again. It doesn't make any more sense when it's blurry. I sigh in frustration but it comes out more like a sob.

"Do you want me?"

The voice is right beside me. Someone has penetrated my plague bubble! I turn and look up.

He's sort of cute. Mature cute, with dark blond hair, a trimmed beard, and pale blue eyes. His face is long and slightly freckled. But he looks stern and his brow is creased. His words sound like a lame pick-up line, but it's only a lost-in-translation thing. If he were interested, he'd at least smile.

Do you want me? Oh yes, I want you. Lust and relief rush through my body, but relief wins out. I'm grinning mania-cally, and words start tumbling out of my mouth.

"Thank you so much for stopping. I thought I had cooties or something. I'm looking for the Lux building."

"Which one?"

Aargh. There's more than one? I fumble with my

3

schedule until he takes pity on me and removes it from my shaking hands.

"*Ja*, Building C. I go there as well." He tilts his head slightly and begins to walk down the path. I take this to mean I should follow him.

My knight-in-shining armour is apparently the strong, silent type, but my verbal diarrhea continues.

"Ugh. Does the fact I can't even find my first class mean that my whole semester is going to be a disaster?"

"You should say *termin*."

"Excuse me?"

He continues without a sideways glance. "*Semester* is like holiday here. Your *termin* will be a disaster."

Thank you for that prediction, Mr. Dictionary. Still, he's the only person to even offer to help me, so I'm determined to make this friendship work.

"Right, one terminal *termin* coming up. If I can even find my classes."

"Lund campus is not large."

"Well, it's big enough for me to get lost on my very first day. I'm Lily, by the way."

"Gabriel Olsson." He finally stops and looks directly at me. And then he extends his hand, and we shake because we're suddenly on Planet Old Business Guys. This feels both awkward and hot. His hands are warm, calloused, and large—and we all know what that means, ladies. I stop myself from verifying that fact by checking out his tight jeans. The warmth of his flesh is triggering something inside me, a zing of attraction. But it's a one-way street, because he's giving me zero back. Given the many attractive people around here, I won't be winning the Miss Lund crown any time soon, but I'm cute. And since I'm definitely attracted to him, you'd think he'd get the vibes I'm sending his way.

We resume walking at Olympic speed. Being late is no longer a worry. His strides are so long that I have to trot-walk to keep up. I'm tall, but he's taller. Tall is something I like.

Although there's apparently a tax on words here, I keep trying. "I'm from Canada. Vancouver. I'm only here for the semester, I mean, *termin*."

"I know."

"You know? How could you know I was from Canada?" So far, everyone I've met assumes I'm American.

Gabriel points to the tiny Canadian flag that my sister pinned to my backpack before I left.

"Oh. Duh. You must think I'm a total idiot, right?"

No response. There must be a tax on smiles too. This conversation has become a challenge. I love challenges. I'm going to *make* him converse with me.

"Well, Gabriel, you're the first Swedish person I've met in five days. I'm in residence, so I've only met other exchange students so far. I have to ask you: am I doing something wrong? It seems like whenever I try to talk to someone, they avoid me. Maybe it's just my imagination. I mean, they don't even know me. And I look harmless, don't I?"

He sneaks a look at me. "*Nej*, er, yes."

I take this to mean I look normal. "So, what am I doing wrong?"

There's a long pause before he replies. "We do not like to talk to strangers."

"What? That's crazy. How do you make new friends then?"

He shrugs. He seems proud of this fact, as if only pushy countries need normal social interactions.

Now representing the extroverts of Canada, Lily Larson. "Well, when you're plunked into a new place like me, if you didn't talk to strangers, you'd die of loneliness. Everyone is a stranger. You must be from around here, Gabriel."

"Ja. Lund."

"You're so lucky," I say. Not only have I loved Sweden my whole life, but now that I'm not lost anymore, Lund has regained its picturesque charms. It's straight from a fairy tale. "I'll have to get advice from you on all the good stores and restaurants."

He struggles to come up with retail advice, which lets me stare at his face. He's not conventionally hot; his eyes are a bit small, his nose is too long, and his mouth is very wide. But everything put together looks great. And it certainly doesn't hurt that he's tall and built: his long arms are sinewy with muscle and, thanks to his tight jeans, I can see his bulging thighs. I'm starting to appreciate this particular fashion trend.

Finally he mumbles a couple of names that I can't understand at all.

"Maybe you can write them out for me," I suggest.

"Do you not speak any Swedish?" Finally, a question. Ladies and gentlemen, we have a conversation.

"A little," I say. "My dad's from Malmö. We used to visit his family in the summer and my *farmor* made me practice my Swedish. But being able to ask my grandmother for cookies isn't going to help me at university."

The corners of his mouth turn up a little. More success.

"Why did he move to Vancouver?" This is a topic I want to avoid, but Swedes always wonder why anyone ever leaves their land of gender equality and social democracy. However, this exchange is my chance to get away from the huge shadow cast by my famous father. Or maybe it's more of a chance to figure out who I really am. Whatever, it's a fresh start.

"For work," I reply vaguely. Luckily, he doesn't ask anything else. Gabriel is a good listener.

"We are here," he announces. We're at a building that combines steel and glass in the front with ancient red brick in the back.

"Oh great." I fumble for my battered schedule, but Gabriel is miles ahead of me. Well, kilometres ahead actually.

"You go in here. Your classroom is that way." He points, to ensure I won't get lost now that he's gotten me ninety percent of the way here.

"Thank you so, so much for your help."

He ducks his head and turns away. But before he can set a new speed-walking record, I grab his arm; there's solid muscle under his sleeve.

"Wait. Gabriel, you're the nicest person I've met today. Would you like to go out for *fika* after school?" I'm pulling out all the friendliness stops here, by offering the one thing I know Swedes love the most: a coffee break.

Again he looks at me with zero interest, like I'm a bug on the sidewalk. I'm rethinking the whole gender equality thing, as I get ready to be shot down.

Then he speaks, "Ja, okay."

"Good, good. We can meet here. I'm done at 3:00—I

mean 15:00." I beam up at him. "This day is turning out great!"

"You are very cheerful." He smiles, and the smile changes his face completely. His eyes crinkle at the corners, and his full lips part to reveal straight white teeth. I lost my breath. Gabe is so delectable that I'm ready to skip coffee and move right into a delicious dinner —featuring Swedish meatballs.

2

MUST LOVE COFFEE

GABRIEL

SHE'S ALREADY five minutes late. Typical for a foreign student. Maybe it's not a big deal for her, but here we like to be on time. Or early, as I was.

I should leave. It's ridiculous to wait here. It's ridiculous to agree to meet a stranger and waste what little free time I have. I'll wait five minutes more then leave.

I sigh. There's no way I'll leave. Lily is very compelling, and my feet are glued to the pavement by the sheer force of her naive expectation that I will be happy to spend time with her. She reminds me of a fairy tale princess whose clothes are brought to her by birds each morning.

"*Hej*, Gabriel."

It's my friend, Johan Nyborg.

"You want to come for *fika*?" he asks.

"Ja. But I have to wait for someone."

"Come now, they can meet us there," he urges me.

I shake my head. "She doesn't know where it is." And she's likely to get lost finding it.

"Who is it? Eva?"

"Nej. Some exchange student."

Johan pretends to be shocked. "You work fast. The first day of class, and you already have a date."

"It's not a date."

This is too difficult to explain. When I first saw Lily this morning, standing in the middle of the footpath and twisting her campus map around as if a new direction would give her a clue, I felt sorry for her. She was so clearly lost and even though she's quite pretty, nobody was stopping to help. I too passed her, but then I made the mistake of looking back.

There was a fleeting expression of poignant sadness on her face. As if she expected the worst and was unsurprised that it happened. And that momentary sadness propelled me to turn around speak to her.

But Lily turns out to be the opposite of a waif. She's brash, confident, and talks far too much. She's relentlessly happy in that North American way where everyone smiles constantly and talks about goal setting and self-actualization. In short, she's the type of person I avoid.

Yet, for the first time in months, I have no idea what someone will say or do next. My life is predictable. I have a routine and responsibilities. And I have no desire to become a tour guide for a chatty Canadian. Still, I cannot refuse her. It's a mystery.

Johan shrugs and leaves. I continue to wait. The sunshine is pleasant on my face.

"Gabe, Gabe!"

Lily runs towards me across the quadrant. She glitters

in the sunlight because her top has metallic threads. Even without the glitter, she would be noticeable because her top is a bright blue pattern. My eye is drawn to her blouse: it's a sheer fabric, and underneath is a thin blue top and under that are the straps of a purple bra. I've never known a woman who wears a purple bra before.

"Phew." She blows a strand of blonde hair from her forehead. "Sorry I'm late. The prof from my last class wanted to talk to me afterwards."

"That's fine." I turn and start walking.

"Is it okay if I call you Gabe?" she asks, after having done so twice.

I nod, and then she's off. "My first day turned out great —once I found my first class. Everyone is so nice here, and I only got lost one other time. It's all thanks to you helping me out this morning."

She turns my one good deed into a task equal to a Herculean challenge.

Lily is tall enough to keep up with my normal stride. She trots along beside me. She is as trusting as a baby lamb, and that makes me worry.

"Should you go off with someone you've just met?" I ask.

Lily snorts. "It's daylight, we're in the middle of town, and besides..." she eyes me up and down, "I think I could outrun you."

I doubt that, but outside challenging her to a race, I'm unsure how I could prove it.

"You have to take chances to have adventures," she adds.

"Is that your life philosophy?" My tone is more sarcastic than I intend, but Lily doesn't notice.

"Haven't you heard the saying: live each day like it's your last? That's what got me here."

Of course I'm familiar with that ridiculous cliché, but no one can live that way in reality. Not only does she walk too close, but she invades my mental space as well. She comments on the various shops and buildings as we pass. Apparently, Lund is "adorable," "crazy historic," and "the coolest."

"So, what's this great coffee place you promised me?"

For one moment, I'm tempted to take her someplace different, someplace where my friends are not already gathered, someplace where we can be alone and truly converse. But I promised to take her to the best place.

"Love Coffee," I reply.

"Oh, me too. I am a scary dragon in the morning before I get my coffee."

I shake my head. "No. That's the name: Love Coffee."

She tips back her head and laughs so loudly that a passing lady stares. Lily's laugh sounds like someone sitting on a goose, yet it's so joyous that I can't help but smile. Her laugh is simultaneously ridiculous and something I want to hear over and over.

"I knew I was going to misunderstand a ton of stuff here, but I didn't think English would be a problem," says Lily. We arrive, and I pass through the entrance and hold the door.

"Looks cool," she proclaims.

We get our pastries and coffees. Mine is a dark Columbian roast, and Lily's is a latte.

"What a beautiful swan." She admires her cup and then compliments Thor, a jaded hipster barista from Stockholm. I wait for his sarcastic response, but instead he thanks her. I have never seen him smile before this moment. More proof of Lily's magic.

We make our way out to the back patio. My friends are in the corner, and I lead the way to their table.

"Mårten, Johan, Beatriz, this is Lily," I say. "

"*Hej*, Lily," they chorus back.

We sit at one end of the table. My friends resume their discussion about classes, but now in English. Lily sips her latte, closes her eyes, and the tip of her pink tongue emerges and licks foam off her lips. She seems to be having a coffee orgasm. "Oh, this is delish."

"Is there anything you don't like?"

Johan leans towards Lily. "Don't mind Gabriel. We're used to his rudeness, but you may not be."

"I'm only truthful," I protest.

Lily waves a hand dismissively. "It's okay, I'm not offended. Gabe's a total sweetie who helped me find my classes, and now he's introduced me to the best coffee place in Lund."

Mårten laughs. "A total sweetie? Yes, that's exactly how we describe him."

Lily cannot be insulted because she's so positive. She compliments me because she cannot imagine a darker side, and I'm oddly flattered.

"Where are you from, Lily?" asks Johan.

"Vancouver. In Canada."

He nods. "I love Vancouver. My father took me and my brother there when I was about ten. We had the best time, and everyone was so friendly."

"Oh, that's great!" Lily leans towards him. "Did you go to Stanley Park?"

"Ja, ja, ja. The big park in the city? Yes, and the aquarium. But the best part was that we went to a Vancouver Millionaires hockey game. My first NHL match. That was so exciting."

For once, Lily doesn't respond enthusiastically, instead taking another sip of her latte. Perhaps she doesn't like hockey.

Johan continues, "Actually, one of the reasons we went was to see Jesper Larson play. He's a very famous hockey player from near here, from Malmö. Have you heard of him?"

"Yes, I've seen him play," Lily answers. Her smile is gone, and she looks quite flushed. Perhaps she's getting too much sun. I manoeuver the table's umbrella with my knee so she's more shaded.

"Well then, you know how good he is. He was captain of the team then, and my brother's favourite hockey player. What an experience it was. I'd like to return to Vancouver someday."

"I want to visit there too," says Mårten.

"You should," she replies. With a return of her animation, she and Mårten begin discussing outdoor activities and a music festival. I should have taken Lily somewhere private. Mårten Blom is inevitably drawn to the most attractive woman in any room.

I am only half-listening as they continue to discuss Vancouver and travel in general. What's more interesting is Lily's relentless optimism on any topic. How does a person become like that?

When I check my phone, it's already 16:45. I stand up.

"I have to go now."

"Oh really? Already? Where are you going?" Lily rises too.

"Home," I reply. "You can stay."

"No, I'll go with you. Nice to meet you all." My friends nod and smile at her.

"You can't follow me home," I tell her once we get outside.

She laughs. "Gabe, you *are* a grouch."

We walk down the street in unexpected silence. We stop at the corner where she goes back to the university. Lily lays her hand on my arm as she did this morning. Normal personal boundaries don't exist for her, but like her laugh, I am both repelled and attracted.

"Am I bothering you? Do you want me to leave you alone?"

I open my mouth to say yes, but no comes out instead. "I have a lot on my schedule. But you can message me if you have any more questions."

"Okay, thank you."

We exchange phone numbers.

"What's your last name?" I want to file her correctly.

"Larson," she replies.

"One 's' or two?"

"Um, one." I wish she would look at me, but she keeps fiddling with her knapsack.

"Oh, like the hockey player."

"Yes," she says. "It's a very common name in Canada though."

"And in Sweden," I reply.

There's a brief silence, then Lily says in a subdued voice, "I miss my family. Things here are harder than I thought."

Once again she is the bewildered person I first spotted.

I put my hand on her shoulder and feel the warmth of her skin through the gauzy fabric.

"Everything will be fine," I say. Now Lily looks up at me. When her brilliant smile returns, I release her. Still, that hidden sadness within her is more compelling than the sunny exterior.

3

BUN SALUTATIONS

LILY

"IT'S TOO bloody early to be awake," grumbles Sally as we trudge our way through the empty campus. Sally Lloyd is an exchange student from Manchester who lives down the hall from me. Our bond was formed by her sarcastic asides during an hour-long presentation on residence recycling.

"To meet Swedes, you have to join clubs," I say. That's the advice we keep getting from the university. "You're always complaining that all our friends are exchange students."

Sally's stated purpose for studying in Lund is to "shag a Swede," and I've been watching her progress with interest. She's very direct.

A grunt is her only response. Sally is not a morning person, but I've been up for an hour getting ready. Besides showering and blow-drying my hair, I practiced a few phrases of greeting in Swedish. Because what I've failed to tell Sally is that I already know one Swede in the yoga club: Gabe.

So far, he's been pretty elusive. I've suggested that we meet up for various events, but he always seems to be busy in the evening. And when we do get together for *fika* after class, he has to leave early. Maybe he's a reverse vampire who has to get home before dark. And dark keeps getting earlier around here.

Any normal girl would have given up by now, but I really like Gabe. I enjoy his straightforward, no B.S. ways. And he's patient each time I message him with questions about life in Lund.

Of course, the fact that he's gorgeous and way taller than me doesn't hurt. "The heart wants what it wants" as Emily Dickinson said. Or was that Selena Gomez? What-ever. My heart wants Gabriel Olsson.

Sally stops. "Oh hell, are we supposed to have our own mats? That's the way it is back home, people scared out of their tiny little minds that they're going to pick up germs if they lay a pinkie on a used mat."

"I have a mat for you," I reply, patting my carrier tube.

"Christ, you are organized." Sally squints at me. "And you look too bloody good for this time of day. You're not one of those morning people, are you?"

I don't cop to this, but I am the kind of person who gets up early and goes for a run or a workout. I have a lot of energy, and if I don't burn it off, there's no way I can sit through hours of class without going crazy. My little brother and father are the same.

We finally find the room where the yoga club meets. It's a lot smaller than I expected, but Sally is amazed that anyone at all is here.

Gabe is already here. He's standing at the side of the room doing neck stretches. He's wearing long shorts and a thin waffle-weave Henley. His legs are long with sinewy muscle, his shoulders are broad, and his rounded ass is worth waking up early for.

Sally exhales audibly and mutters something complimentary about Sweden.

I manage to stumble over only one yoga mat on my way towards him.

"Oh, *god morgon.*" Does my good morning sound casual enough, like I had forgotten he would be here?

Gabe turns. He seems unsurprised to see me. "*Hej,* Lily."

I continue in Swedish, asking how he is. But I've mangled it somehow, because the woman beside Gabe smirks. She's a cute blonde with a messy topknot. This isn't his girlfriend, is it? I've tried to suss him out about girlfriends, and he doesn't seem to have one. Unless— horror of all horrors—he actually lives with a girl and that's why he's always rushing home. But wouldn't he just tell me that whenever I try to finagle him into meeting up?

"Hiya, I'm Sally." She reaches out and shakes Gabe's hand. I was too busy visiting Worst Possibility Land to introduce them.

"Gabriel Olsson." He doesn't introduce the blonde, which I take to mean that he doesn't know her. Hooray!

"I'm beginning to understand why Lily is so keen on

yoga," my tattletale friend says. When Gabe turns, I stick my tongue out at her. Then I realize that he can see me in the mirror. Damn.

The instructor claps her hands and says something that clearly means get into place. Sally and I unroll our mats behind Gabe and his not-girlfriend.

The instructor is a tiny woman with black hair, one pierced nostril, and an arm decorated with intricate black floral tattoos like a Japanese woodblock print. There are so many types of Swedish cool around here, and she's yoga cool. She eyes us and adds in English, "If you are new, please talk to me after."

Fortunately, it's not too complicated to follow along. I can't understand a word she's saying about breathing, but mimicking her movements is a breeze.

My only distraction is Gabe's magnificent ass. It doesn't help that Sally keeps giving me these exaggerated winks and raised eyebrows that are the equivalent of an elbow nudge. Luckily, he's oblivious to both of us. I'm not sure that's a good thing though. I didn't blow dry my hair and wear my cutest Lululemons to be ignored.

We move through poses quickly. Morning yoga wakens your body, but if I get any sweatier I'll have to take a second shower. Gabriel must be getting warm too because he pauses from his posing to peel off his Henley in one graceful motion. Underneath he has a loose tank top.

I swallow. Gabriel's broad shoulders are sculpted and golden. His upper arms are more muscular than I would've expected. When he stands and raises his arms in a sun salutation, I can see the hedge of his feathery underarm hair. Seriously, I'm getting excited about underarm hair. But he's so luscious. I want to tickle him there, bite the flesh of his shoulder, and lick the sheen of sweat off his body.

"Don't forget your box breathing," Sally purrs. I will deal with her later.

I close my eyes. When I open them again, I have to scramble into a seated position.

In front of me, Gabriel is already seated with his legs spread. He can actually do the splits. *I* cannot do the splits.

"Fuck," breathes Sally. In that one curse word, she manages to express everything we're both thinking: what would it be like to have sex with someone that flexible?

The rest of the class goes by in a blur. I'm feeling very energized, but I'm not sure if it's the yoga or the repressed sexual desire. I've already spent way too much time fantasizing about Gabe. But my imagination never conjured that athletic build. From our conversations, he's more a poet than a jock.

At the end, the instructor offers us all praise and encouragement, judging from her smile and hand motions. The blonde casts one forlorn look at Gabriel as she rolls up her mat and then leaves. Buh bye, sweetie!

He turns to us. "How was that for you?"

If Sally hadn't snorted with laughter, I could have kept it together. But instead we both giggle like schoolgirls while Gabriel watches us in bewilderment.

She's the first to recover. "The view was amazing."

He glances around the white cinderblock walls. "Ja? Well, I must go now."

Then he leaves without a backward look.

"Ouch," says Sally. We go over to chat with the instructor. I am ready to sign up for the yoga club, but Sally is ambivalent. The instructor, whose name is Ingrid, suggests that Sally come to a couple more sessions and then decide.

"You didn't like it?" I ask her on the way back to residence.

"I thought yoga was supposed to be relaxing. I didn't know I'd have to sweat my arse off."

"Morning yoga energizes," I explain.

She shrugs. "Besides, haven't I already served my purpose?"

"What do you mean?" I ask.

"Let me see if I've got this right. You bought two yoga mats, two sets of towels, woke at the crack of dawn to shower and primp: all to 'accidentally' bump into your crush. I was the excuse to get you in there without looking a complete numpty."

I've never heard the word numpty before, but I must be one. "Do you think I'm being an idiot?"

Sally rolls her eyes. "Well, he's not exactly trying hard, is he? You did all that work for a minute of chat."

"I enjoyed the yoga," I reply sadly.

"Oh, chin up, Lil. Next time you go to yoga, you get in front of him. Then he can spend the whole class watching *your* arse."

The mere mention of his ass has me fantasizing again. "Did you see how flexible he is?" I moan.

"Couldn't miss it, could I? If you do get to boff him, you have to report back. How did you meet him?"

"He helped me on my very first day of school when I was completely lost."

Sally shakes her head. "You're completely lost now. I had no idea you were such a sap, Lily."

Is it sappy to be so attracted to Gabe? I'm already attracted to his serious personality, and it's encased in such a lovely—and flexible—body. The more I learn about Gabe, the more I like him.

4

ALL ABOUT EVA

GABRIEL

I'M SITTING on the grass with Eva and Johan during our lunch break. It's the first day of September, but the weather is unseasonably warm. Being outside in the sunshine feels good.

Lily is across the concourse. She's easy to distinguish because of her height. And also because she's so animated: her hands fly everywhere as she talks to her friends. I recognize Sally, but not all the guys surrounding them.

When I think she's looking, I raise a hand but she doesn't wave back and I'm left feeling like a fool.

"Nice try." Johan mocks me. "Do you have a crush on her?"

"Who are we talking about?" Eva asks. *Helvete.* I really don't want to discuss this with her.

Johan motions lazily. "Lily Larson. The Canadian exchange student."

Eva squints. Lily is laughing, and I can hear that odd honking noise.

"Oh, her, the princess. *Glider på en räkmacka,*" says Eva, suggesting Lily has always had it easy. "Don't be stupid, Johan. Gabriel would never date her."

"Why not?" Johan's offended.

"Because she represents everything he doesn't like: she's rich, superficial, and here to party."

"She's also hot," he mutters, but Eva is not listening. She is busy on her phone.

"You should not judge people by their appearance. Just because she's attractive doesn't mean she's not socially aware." I have no idea whether Lily does any type of advocacy work, but I don't like Eva making assumptions about Lily. Or me.

Eva puts down her phone and turns to me. "But I do know. First, look: she is wearing leather boots." Lily is wearing low boots and shorts. I find it hard to disapprove of this look, but Eva would never wear any animal product.

"Second, Bettina was in her room, and apparently it's been professionally decorated."

Johan scoffs. "Nobody would get a decorator for a dorm room."

"I haven't seen it," replies Eva. "But I hear it looks like a Snowflake showroom." Snowflake is an expensive store in Malmö that my Aunt Freja loves, but I have no idea what their goods look like.

"Imagine wasting money on your dorm decor. She even

has designer underwear. What a rich bitch," Eva concludes.

Designer underwear? Like the purple bra she was wearing on the first day? And would there be a matching lace thong too? Eva wears plain bras and briefs that are made from ecologically certified organic cotton.

"How do you know what underwear she wears?" I ask. It's a subject I've spent time reflecting upon, but I didn't realize anyone else had.

Eva rolls her eyes. "She messed up her laundry booking and everyone saw her stuff. But enough about her, are you two coming to the eco march on Saturday morning?"

"What are you protesting now?" Johan asks.

"Did you not hear? There are several large manufacturing companies in Malmö who are trying to skirt the new zero waste regulations." She takes a pamphlet from her backpack. "Here are all the details. I don't have time to explain because I have to catch Helmut before class. We'll meet in the main square at 9:00." And she strides off without another word.

Johan crumples the pamphlet without reading it and releases a loud breath. "How in hell did you go out with her for six months?"

"It happened."

Eva and I hang out in the same crowd. She is very smart and active in social reform, and I admire that about her. At first, we spent a lot of time talking, and the sex part evolved. It's hard to say exactly when we started going out and when we stopped. But Eva decided everything.

"Does she stop talking when you're having sex?" Johan asks.

"Women talking during sex is a good thing," I reply.

"Ja, it's good if they're saying, 'Spank me, I've been a bad girl,' but maybe not comparing solar and wind power generation."

I laugh. Johan jerks his head towards Lily. "She's the opposite of Eva. Which could only be good, in my opinion."

Is it strange that no particular type of woman attracts me? Perhaps dating is a scientific process of elimination. My first girlfriend, Susanne, was also the opposite of Eva. She was quiet and artistic, and we shared interests in poetry and music. But we were both too introverted, so eventually our relationship became boring.

Eva's intelligence and outspokenness attracted me, but became too intense and tiring. Perhaps it's true that Lily is more superficial than the type of women I usually enjoy conversing with. But there's a sheer joy about Lily that I admire. She's full of feelings, and she stirs emotion in me.

"Dating an exchange student is about sex anyway," says Johan.

"Why would you say that?" Not that I'm opposed to having sex with Lily.

"Well, they're gone in a couple of months. And you can't really communicate with them because of all the language and cultural barriers."

"We can both speak English."

Johan nods. "I guess. But it's not quite the same."

That is true. There are so many unspoken standards to living in Sweden, which I don't notice until Lily accidentally breaks the rules. Then I have to explain why we do things in a certain way. But it's also refreshing to see everything through new eyes.

At first, I found Lily a little too much—too much emotion and enthusiasm. But it's hard to resist her puppy-dog friendliness. And I'm now accustomed to the way she veers from subject to subject like a hyperactive insect. She is a welcome distraction to the routine of my life.

"Gabe! Hey, Gabe!" Lily has spotted me now and she's coming over. Her bare legs are long and surprisingly muscular. Perhaps Eva is right that Lily is rich, but she's not a princess. She's too energetic to be lying around and eating bonbons.

She sits down beside me. "Hi, Gabe. Hi, Johan. How are you guys today?"

"I suffered from allergies yesterday, but today my sinuses are clear," I reply.

"We're fine." Johan shakes his head at me, and I remember that North Americans don't mean it when they ask how you are.

Lily smiles regardless. "Isn't it gorgeous out?"

"Yes, enjoy it while you can. Tomorrow it will be normal: cold," I say.

"Really? Well, I am enjoying it."

"I see you have mastered Swedish small talk," says Johan.

Lily's blue eyes crinkle in delight. "What do you mean?"

"We must discuss the weather first in any conversation. So you did that."

"*Tack så mycket.*" She thanks him in her terrible accent.

"Wow. *Pratar du Svenska?*"

"Nej, nej." Lily laughs. "That's all I can say. I want to practice my Swedish, but everyone here is so perfectly bilingual that they switch to English when they hear me struggling."

"Maybe they want to practice their English," Johan says. "Tell me what Canadians are like."

"We cut down trees, drink maple syrup, and eat poutine. Beauty, eh?"

Johan laughs and winks at me. He appreciates Lily's sense of humour, all the more because he has complained about Eva's lack of one. "When I listen to Canadian hockey players in interviews, they always finish their sentences with '*eh*.'"

"When they're not talking about giving one hundred and ten percent or winning one shift at a time," Lily adds.

"Ha. You know a lot about hockey," Johan says. "Are you a big fan?"

"Not really. I have a complicated relationship with hockey."

"What does that mean?" I ask her.

She lifts one shoulder and shrugs. "Everyone makes such a big deal about hockey players. They're just people."

"She's not going to be impressed when we tell her we play hockey," Johan says to me.

Lily's eyes widen. "You play hockey, Gabe? I am surprised."

"Why?" I ask.

"I don't know. You seem more a poet than a jock."

"People can be more than one thing," I point out.

"I guess. And if you're playing rec hockey, it doesn't take much time."

Johan shakes his head. "Now a Canadian is insulting

our hockey ability. I believe we've beaten you at Olympic and World Cup levels."

"Oh, I have a healthy respect for Swedish hockey players," she says. "What positions do you play?"

"I play defence," says Johan. "And Gabriel plays goal."

Lily turns to me. "You're a goalie. That makes more sense."

"What do you think of goalies?" I ask.

"Goalies are weird. Everyone knows that."

Johan chuckles. "That's true. Particularly for him."

But goal suits me. To be part of the team, yet be able to control my play, that's what I enjoy.

"Will I get to see you play sometime?" Lily asks.

I shake my head. "It's not an important team." I'm not embarrassed about the team, but I know what good hockey should be. We're a casual university team, and I asked to be the backup goalie since I can't attend travel games.

"Okay, whatever." Lily is very easy going, another way she differs from Eva or Susanne. She turns to me. "Our residence floor is organizing a potluck dinner tomorrow night. I was wondering if you guys would like to come."

Tomorrow is Thursday, so I have to be home to make dinner. Besides, the event itself does not appeal to me. "No, I'm busy."

Her face falls. "Oh, okay. That's too bad."

"I can come," Johan announces. "If you still want me without Gabriel."

Lily's smile returns. "Of course. It's always nicer to have someone Swedish around. Otherwise we end up asking questions that nobody knows the answers to." She pulls out a little notepad from her purse. It has a mauve leather cover, and she writes in it with a silver pen. Eva is right about one thing: everything Lily owns looks special. "Here's our address and the time. Bring whatever you want."

She stands and brushes grass off her shorts, which only draws my eyes to her rounded ass. "Okay, well, I've got class now. See you later."

I watch those long legs stride away.

"You might want to encourage her," Johan says.

"What are you talking about?"

"She likes you. And I'm pretty sure you feel the same way. But if you keep treating her like an ant at a picnic, she'll move on."

A guy with curly dark hair is walking beside Lily now. He was eyeing us the whole time she was sitting with us.

"I'm being normal with her," I protest. What would be the point of acting different to attract someone?

"Your normal state is fuck-right-off," Johan says. "That's fine for people who know you, but strangers might not appreciate it."

"I have never been able to lie or pretend. Besides, I don't think she likes me." Why would Lily like me? She is a heroine straight out of a movie, and I'm a regular guy.

"You're clueless about women, Gabriel. You always have been. That's how you end up with women like Eva, who do all the work." He shrugs as if I'm a lost cause. "The least you could do is go to something when Lily invites you."

I don't bother to answer. Johan doesn't know Lily. She is friendly and sociable. People gather around her like bees around sweet clover. It's ridiculous to think that she is asking me out.

5

I HEART LUND

Lily

I LOVE, love, love Sweden. Or Lund. Or maybe just my life here.

I love the old buildings at the university, some dating from before Canada was born.

I love the anonymity of not understanding what people are saying around me—I can imagine that they're talking about books or philosophy even though they may be complaining about their boyfriends or discussing a football match. I love being free from other people's expectations of who I should be.

It's three weeks in, and I'm completely adjusted to my new life. I know where all my classes are. I'm on top of all my assignments so far. My mother has finally calmed down enough to stop sending me daily emails recounting the dog's digestive issues and pleading for minute-by-minute updates on my new life. If I message her as much as she wants, I won't have enough time for a social life. Especially my agonizingly slow progress with Gabe.

"Isn't life great?" I ask Sally as we walk back to our residence. It's sunny. I have no homework. What more can you ask from a day?

"Nauseating, that's what you are." Sally shakes her head. "So, do you want to come to the *systembolaget* with me? I'm buying some booze for the pre-party tomorrow night." Drinking here takes planning since the state liquor store closes early and it's the only place that sells alcohol.

"Can't. I'm meeting Gabe for *fika*."

Sally raises a disdainful eyebrow. She has the most expressive eyes and emphasizes them with a wide swath of eyeliner and thick false eyelashes. "Gabriel, again? Lily, give it up already. Why don't you go out with Jakub? He's got a big crush on you." Jakub is an exchange student from Prague who is also on our floor. There's nothing wrong with Jakub, except he's not Gabe.

"Things are progressing," I say.

"Because he speaks to you for thirty seconds after yoga instead of fifteen? He's a conceited prick, and you could do better."

"You're just saying that because you don't know him well. Why don't you come to *fika* with me?"

Sally lifts her black amoeba of an eyebrow. "Right. Why on earth would I want to do that?"

"Well, Gabe's friends join us. He's always running into people he knows. Swedes." Lund is not a huge place, and Gabe has lived here for his whole life.

"Are they as attractive as he is?" Sally wonders.

"Almost."

"Undoubtedly with better personalities." I ignore this.

We drop off our school stuff in our rooms and head to Love Coffee.

"I love that you can sit with one coffee all day, and nobody minds," I say.

Sally snorts. "They should make you head of the tourist bureau. Name one thing you don't like about Lund."

I offer up the number one student complaint: "It's very expensive here."

"It is that," Sally agrees.

Gabe is already there. He's out back in the sunshine with his head back and eyes closed.

"Hi, Gabe. You look like a lemur." I demonstrate by closing my eyes, stiffening my body, and turning my palms up.

Gabe smiles at me. "*Hej,* Lily." I love the way Gabe pronounces my name, Lil-lay. It sounds musical and soothing.

"*Hej,* Sally," he adds. My spidey senses can detect nothing different in the way Gabe greets either of us. Maybe my random animal impressions aren't as sexy as I thought.

"*Hej du,*" Sally says. We leave our jackets on the chairs beside him and go in to get our coffees.

"*Jag tar en kaffe och en kanelbulle,*" I say proudly. After multiple trips to this coffee shop, I can order my coffee and cinnamon bun in Swedish with no miming. Whoopee.

"Look at you, speaking Swedish," says Sally. She's been studying Swedish for the past year and is already fluent. I've been visiting Sweden since I was a baby and know about ten phrases unrelated to coffee.

By the time we rejoin Gabe, he's talking to a cute guy. I nudge Sally. "I told you."

Gabe introduces us. "Lily, Sally, this is Robin."

"*Tjenare*," Robin says. He has an angular face and a jagged shag haircut. To Sally's delight, he's quite charming. He goes to Lund University as well.

"How did you meet Gabriel?" Robin asks me.

"On the first day, she forced me to help her find her classes," Gabe replies.

Sally sucks in her breath, but I laugh. "It's true. And now I force him to meet me here. I save up all my questions about Sweden."

"Nej, you SMS me with questions frequently," Gabe points out.

Sally snorts. "God, you're a real charmer. Don't worry. I'm sure Lily will soon get the hang of life here and stop bothering you."

"It's not a problem," Gabe replies in a matter-of-fact way. It's funny that Sally finds Gabe rude, since she is equally blunt. But I like them both. I've spent too long dealing with hypocrites.

"How are everyone's classes?" Robin asks.

"Easy peasy," Sally says. She's a complete brainiac, who is doing a full year here instead of only one term like me.

"It's weird here. Everything I've taken for granted is flipped," I say.

"Like what?" Robin asks.

"Hmm. Okay, you guys love group work. I've always hated it because I get stuck with slackers who make me do everything."

The guys stare at me as if I've suggested clubbing baby seals to death.

"Group cooperation is the best way to get things done. Shared knowledge and agreed goals are ideal," Robin says.

"But what if people don't agree to do things the right way?" I ask.

"Your way, I assume," says Gabe. Without even looking, I know that Sally is rolling her eyes.

Robin leans towards me. "There is value in compromise. Perhaps the solution will not be one hundred percent good for you, but it will be eighty percent good for everyone in the group."

He's blowing my mind. I've always led the groups I'm in because I know how to get things done and get good marks. But I may have stepped on a few toes along the way, and now I feel guilty. In Sweden, consensus is more important than being right.

Sally checks her phone. "Ugh. I need to get to the *systembolaget* before it closes."

"Do you need help to find it?" asks Robin.

"That would be brilliant," declares Sally, and they leave.

"Did you not buy liquor with Sally last week?" Gabe asks.

"Um, yes," I confess. Sally has been to the state liquor store at least five times since she arrived here. But perhaps hipster Robin will become Sally's first Swedish leg over.

Gabe doesn't ask any more questions, but I read disapproval in his silence. This is how well I know him already. I too prefer people who tell the truth, but sometimes people act out of character when they're attracted to someone. And I'm Exhibit A.

"Do you want to practice your Swedish?" he asks.

"Ja, *tack*," I reply. Improving my spoken Swedish is one of the goals I've set, but I seem to lack an ear for languages. Also, he's not really teaching me Swedish; I say things, and then he corrects me. Gabe is kind of weird, and I wonder if I would like him if he weren't cute. And so tall!

"*Hur lång*, um," I'm trying to find out how tall he is, but the whole phrase escapes me. "Oh, *hur lång är du?*"

The corner of his mouth turns up. "You want to know how long I am?"

I inadvertently glance at the bulge in his tight jeans, and my cheeks flame. "Oh my God, is that what I said?" I know that *lång* means long.

"I'm joking. You are correct. I am 193 centimetres."

"That's very long." I crack up. Finally, a Gabe joke. Or yoke, as he says. And kind of sexual one. Maybe there's a Swedish leg over in my future too.

But right on the dot of 16:45, Gabe rises to go. For the millionth time, I wonder what he does and why he's never available on school nights. He's a private person though, and I respect that.

I'm not giving up though. "One of the Student Nations is having a dance club on Saturday night. Are you going?"

He hesitates for so long that I'm sure he's going to say no.

"Ja. I'll go."

My tummy is doing backflips, but I calmly reply, "I'll see you there, then."

6

TRAPPED

GABRIEL

"Åh, your mother hasn't come back from her walk." Britt-Marie, my mother's caregiver, greets me at the door with this news.

I check the time. My mother has a routine, and she usually walks in the afternoon and returns before suppertime.

Britt-Marie continues, "I went out looking for her, but she's not on her usual route."

I pull out my phone. "We can trace her on her phone."

"Nej. She forgot to take it." Britt-Marie pulls the phone out of her pocket. "I'm sorry, I usually ensure she has the phone, but she was in a bit of a mood when she left."

Britt-Marie's face is creased with worry. She is a kind soul, much nicer than the younger woman we had before. In the six months she's been here, she's been very gentle and patient—even through my mother's increasing testiness.

"How long has she been gone?" I ask.

"Three hours. I was just going to call your Aunt Freja." Although she loves walking, my mother gets tired and ninety minutes is her norm.

"Ja, maybe you should do that. Meanwhile, I'll go out on my bike. I can cover more ground that way."

I begin by biking along her usual route. I try to imagine what would attract her off her usual path. In the old days, it would be an unusual plant or intriguing architecture. But now, I have no idea what would attract her. The voices of children? A small cat or dog?

I cycle up and down streets at a frenetic pace then realize that I would miss her if she had stopped somewhere. I slow down, but my body is pumped with adrenaline. I cover her usual route twice over and the side streets as well.

I decide to check out the botanical garden, which used to be her favourite place. It is full of winding paths and impossible to cover in a systematic way. Each time I double back, my worry increases. The formal ponds resemble drowning traps to me. And what if she's wandered into a forested area? The evening is getting colder, and she could freeze to death. A thousand awful possibilities swirl in front of me.

I almost miss the hunched grey figure on a bench by a pond. Surely that's too small to be my mother, but her coat is that colour. When I get closer, I see that the person is all curled up. Her knees are up to her chin, her hands are clutched in front of her face, and her face is hidden behind the collar of her coat. She's a tiny huddled ball, trying to be as small and invisible as possible.

"*Mamma?*" I call out, but there's no response. I drop my bike and run over.

It's her.

"*Oj, mamma,* I found you. We've been so worried." I sit down beside her and wrap my arms around her coiled body. She's shaking slightly.

She lifts her face to look at me. I can tell she's been crying. Her expression is that of a frightened child. She blinks at me.

"Ah, Magnus. You came. I got lost." She begins to cry again—the tears coursing down the lines on her cheeks. She's lost in so many ways. The first time she called me by my father's name, I angrily corrected her, but it keeps happening. She sees the past, and the young man that I am now looks more like her husband than her son. Still, each time is painful and uncomfortable.

"I am here now." I keep my arms around her, and she leans her head against my shoulder and continues to cry. We sit there for a long time. I know I should call Britt-Marie and Freja, but comforting my mother is more important.

The crying stops, and she pulls away from me. Her face is a mask of suspicion now.

"Who are you? Why have you taken me here?"

"I'm Gabriel, *mamma.* Your son."

Her eyes narrow. "Nej. My son is a little boy. What have you done with Gabriel?"

The evenings are the worst time with my mother. She becomes paranoid and lashes out at everyone.

"Okay, Milla, please calm down. I will take you home,

and you can see your son." I have to spout this nonsense to calm her down.

She reluctantly joins me. I make a quick call to Britt-Marie, and then we walk home. It's less than half a kilometre to get home, but one block off her usual route is all it takes for her to get lost.

Both Freja and Britt-Marie are there when I get home. They hug my mother and hustle her off to get changed out of her damp clothes.

I sit in the living room and try to empty my mind. But memories keep rushing in. My mother used to be so smart, decisive, and strong. I remember running to keep up with her as she strode up a hiking trail.

"Coffee, Gabriel?" Britt-Marie materializes beside me and holds out a steaming cup.

"*Tack*." I lift the cup to my face and feel the heat. When I finally take a sip, it still doesn't warm the chill inside me.

"I'm so sorry. I've tried to walk with your mother," she explains. "But she prefers to go by herself."

I work up a smile. "Please, don't worry. I understand. She's always needed solitude." How much of my mother's real personality is still there? Because it would be torture for the real Milla to be under constant supervision. But if we don't watch her, events like today can happen.

She nods. "Ja. Well, there are other things we can do. Instead of her phone, we can attach a tracker to her clothing. Then she can never be lost. Or maybe consider restricting her walks."

She's already trapped in her mind. Do we have to imprison her in the home as well? But I don't say this. Britt-Marie is a very kind woman, and we're lucky to have her.

Freja walks in the room and sits across from us.

"She ate a sandwich and went straight to bed. Britt-Marie, you've stayed way past your time. You should get home now."

The caregiver smiles. "I would not have been able to do anything else while Milla was lost." She gathers up her things and leaves.

Freja and I go to the kitchen. It's too late to make a proper supper. I make myself a sandwich, and she heats up some leftovers.

"Do you have to go back to work?" I ask. She works flexible hours and stays late to make up for her late starts. We have a system: Freja gets my mother fed and ready each morning until the caregiver arrives. And I come home when Britt-Marie's shift is done and make dinner.

"Nej. I'll finish up at home." She motions towards her bag, which is stuffed with papers. The microwave pings, and she sets her plate down across from mine. "Gabriel, we need to discuss what happened today."

"After dinner," I suggest. She's going to repeat her plan to put my mother into a care facility. I went with Freja to visit the place she's recommending. It's a nice place, with a large property and gardens. The staff seemed nice as well. But the other patients! A wizened old woman grabbed my arm and asked if I was her grandson, then followed me for several minutes nattering away. I could hear an elderly man shouting down the hallway. I couldn't imagine my mother among them. She is so much younger. She hates strangers.

Freja politely waits until I've finished my sandwich and drink.

"If your mother can't walk, she'll be very frustrated.

The place we went to see, they have grounds for the patients to walk around."

I shake my head. "It's a matter of technology. Britt-Marie mentioned something to wear. Then if she forgets her phone, it makes no difference. We'll be able to track her immediately."

"At the facility, they have programs as well. Your mother could be stimulated by having things she can do—"

"Why now?" I interrupt her spiel. "Why are you raising this subject now?"

Freja reaches across the table and takes my hand. "Because she's much worse. I am happy to stay with Milla as long as I am making a difference, but the Alzheimer's has taken away so much of her real self. She is increasingly upset and frustrated, and I believe that being in a proper facility could relieve her stress."

It's funny to think about my mother's life as stressful. She was once a brilliant biodiversity researcher at the university, and now someone babysits her day and night. And my aunt is right: each day a little more of my mother disappears. She's becoming a statue, pebble by pebble. Soon everything I love about her will be locked inside a granite prison. Her life is brutally unfair. But I still believe that being at home brings her pleasure, so I'll keep resisting my aunt's suggestions. Freja is too kind-hearted to force the issue.

I owe my aunt so much. I was only seventeen when my mother was diagnosed with early onset Alzheimer's, and we could not have managed if Freja had not come to live here.

My imagination escapes to my time with Lily. And

seeing her on the weekend at the dance club will mean a completely new experience for us. We've walked and had *fika* together, but never anything this social. I'm oddly nervous.

I mention this to Freja. "I'm going out Saturday night, is that okay?"

Freja's whole face lights up. "Of course! I told you that you should go out more on weekends. Get drunk like a normal university student. Kiss pretty girls." She blushes. My aunt is an incurable romantic. "Is there someone special in your life, Gabriel?"

I squeeze her hand back. "Nej."

But the image of Lily glows golden in my mind's eye.

7

DANCING QUEEN

Gabriel

"Gabriel! You're here?" Robin is shocked.

"Obviously." I stand beside him in the loud and busy club.

"Wow. You don't usually, I mean, I'm more used to seeing you at—" Then he laughs. "This is exactly where you should be." He holds up his beer, and we clink glasses.

But he is correct. I haven't been to a dance club in years. Eva never wanted to go to clubs, and Susanne hated crowds. But what do I want? Perhaps only to stay safe, not to do things that challenge me. I have enough to deal with in life without leaving my comfort zone. But I am foolish and driven by thoughts of one person.

Lily is standing four metres from me. Tonight she wears a pretty flowered dress. She has high-heeled ankle boots on, which make her even taller. Her height makes her stand out more than usual. With her straight blonde hair, fair skin, and wide-eyed gaze she looks more Swedish than anyone else in the room. Except she isn't. Perception over reality.

And as always, there are many people around her: her exchange friends and a couple of guys I know.

It's too noisy to talk much, and my eyes keep returning to Lily. She's talking, motioning, and making everyone around her laugh. What if Johan is right, and she is interested? I've come all this way. I should go over and talk to her, but I'm not good at this kind of thing. The only way I can tell if a girl likes me is if she tells me so. Period.

Indecision swamps me. This is another emotion I'm not used to. I drink my beer. Maybe I'll finish it and leave.

"Don't."

I hear Lily's voice despite the loud music, the shouted conversation, and the general roar of this club. Her flat accent rises above the undulating Swedish voices.

And something about that "don't" sets off alarms. I turn and see Gustav Persson pulling her by the wrists. We played competitive hockey together, and he's overly aggressive on and off the ice. He's not my favourite person to begin with, and he's rapidly descending. He needs to get his hands off Lily.

Robin turns to see what I am looking at. "Ah, of course. The lovely Lily Larson has your attention. It's all making sense now."

"Persson's an idiot. I'm going to make sure she's okay."

He laughs. "Yes, go and be her knight in shining armour. You could save a lot of effort if you ask her out yourself. Sally told me Lily's interested."

But can I trust anything that Sally says? I know her to be a liar.

I walk over to them. He has finally let go of her, but is still too close.

"*Hej*, Lily."

She turns and beams up at me. "Gabe! You came!"

Up close, her face is flushed and her speech louder. She's not drunk, but she's been drinking.

"We're busy. You should fuck off home to *mamma*," Persson says to me in Swedish. He leans towards Lily and tries to freeze me out of the conversation. But she is scowling now; she understands either his words or his scornful tone. People are deceived by Lily's terrible spoken Swedish, but she understands a lot.

I continue, "Are you okay?"

He switches to English. "Lily's fine. She doesn't need you to babysit her." He snakes his arm around Lily, but she wriggles out from under him.

"No, Gabe promised he'd dance with me." She loops her arm through mine.

Persson snorts. "Gabriel Olsson doesn't dance. It's too superficial for him."

He can go to the devil. I follow Lily onto the dance floor.

How difficult can it be to dance? We're surrounded by people, so it's hard to move. I shift my body from side to side, feeling large and awkward. Persson is right, I don't dance. I don't hang out in clubs. Coming here was stupid and futile.

Lily watches me dance robotically. She frowns and without a word takes both my hands and places them on her hips. My palms feel the silken softness of her dress, and underneath the heat of her skin. The reality of her stirs me. Touching her makes me want so much more. I want to learn the sensuous details of Lily's body—if her nipples are the same colour as her lips, whether her legs feel as satiny as they look, and what will make her gasp and cry out.

She leans towards me. Her face is raised to mine at the perfect level for us to kiss. I can't tear my eyes from her lips, outlined in a deep pink stain. But her mouth moves past mine and speaks in my ear, "Feel the rhythm."

Ah, that's what this is. Not an invitation to make out, but a dancing lesson. Because her hips are moving with the music in a way that my body is not. Goalies can react though, and I relax the tension from my shoulders. I allow Lily's energy to flow through me and follow her lead. Now we're dancing together. We move to the pulsing EDM and, in the midst of jostling bodies and flashing lights, it's just the two of us. A wave of unfamiliar emotion rolls through me. I don't know Lily that well, but something between us feels monumental and magnetic.

"See, you're a good dancer. I knew you would be." Lily is smiling.

Only with you, I think, but I don't say that. I smile back at her.

"I'm glad you came," she says. "I wasn't sure if you would."

"I almost didn't." A tiny crease appears on her forehead, and I want to smooth it away.

Then the music slows. A few people groan, and the crowd disperses.

But this I can handle. I pull Lily's body close. We meet in all the right places: her hips against mine, her soft breasts against my chest, and our eyes almost level. I can feel the puff of her exhalations, and I match my breathing to hers. I could stay together like this for the rest of the evening.

"You are tall," I say. It sounds stupid the instant it leaves my mouth.

Lily nods; she never makes me feel awkward. "Yes. In Sweden, I get to wear heels. Another reason I love it here."

"We fit together well."

She doesn't answer, but instead moves even closer to me, leaning her head against my shoulder. A few strands of her hair tickle my cheek. She smells sweet and earthy, like a summer garden after a rainstorm. That wave arises in me again; it's the pure pleasure of being next to Lily.

We dance for a long time, fast and even better slow. We get drinks and talk a little, but it's too noisy to converse. Guys approach Lily to dance, but she turns them down and stays with me.

I sense her energy flagging, and she stifles a yawn.

"Are you tired? Would you like to go?" I ask.

She nods. "But we have to find Sally first."

"Why?" Sally appears more than capable of taking care of herself.

"Women need to look out for each other. Guys use alcohol or roofies to take advantage," Lily explains.

I had no idea that being a beautiful woman came with so many dangers.

Sally is busy dancing, and she waves us away. "I'm absolutely fine here. You two can take off." She and Lily whisper to each other while Anders and I exchange nods. He's an okay guy. The trouble with living in Lund is that we have all known each other for years. That makes new people like Sally and Lily even more desirable.

We zip up and go outside. Luckily, the light rain has stopped. The pavement glistens in the streetlight glow, but there are no stars at all.

"The weather here is exactly like home," Lily grumbles from behind a pink scarf wrapped around her neck. "Except the rain is even earlier."

"Then you will not be homesick."

"I'm not. I love everything about Lund." Lily "loves" more things than anyone I've ever known.

"Why did you choose to come here?" Because of my situation, Lund University is the only place I could choose.

"I wanted to get away. To be free to be me." She stops and spins around in a ballerina circle with her arms extended. Her light hair sparkles in the street lights. She whirls until she sways, and I catch her and straighten her up. She smiles up at me, and something inside me churns. I desire Lily in a completely new way—I want to know her body and her mind. Her uniqueness fascinates me.

Then we continue walking.

"What is your home like?" I ask. All I can imagine are the homes I see on American sitcoms: bright, cheery, and plaid.

"My house is so suburban, you know, long driveways and fences to keep out the undesirables. Every house all isolated, not like this." She motions towards the apartment buildings we were walking by. "And my mother never met a surface she couldn't accessorize. You would hate it."

"Why?" I wonder. We have never discussed aesthetics before.

"Because Scandinavian design is all about clean lines and natural materials, isn't it? What's your place like?"

"It's pretty minimal." We have wood floors and pale furniture. Here people try to bring as much light as possible into their homes. But my mother was never interested in decoration. It was my father who had cared how things looked. My mother preferred to be outside.

"You've never talked about your home or family before," I say.

"Kettle meet pot," she replies. It's not a saying I am familiar with.

As opposed to our ease in the club, our conversation is slightly strained as we walk home. I feel as if there's a script I haven't been given.

We were now at the main door of her building. Lily turns to face me.

"Thank you for walking me home."

"You're welcome."

Then she puts her arms around my neck. Her face comes closer to mine, and she closes her eyes. I keep mine open and focus on her slightly parted lips. When our mouths meet, that pleasure wave breaks over me again. Kissing Lily feels fantastic. Her mouth is soft and yielding, and she tastes so good—sweeter than all the Saturday candies I've eaten. I wrap my arms around her back and pull her tight to me. Thankfully, our coats are preventing her from feeling exactly how excited I am right now.

Finally, she pulls back and blinks up at me.

"Wow," is all I can say.

"Yeah." A tiny smile crosses her soft lips.

I release her. I certainly don't want to be one of those guys who take advantage of Lily when she's been drinking. And she's not quite herself.

Lily drops her chin, and we both look at the pointy tips of her boots.

"So, would you like to come up to my room for a nightcap?" she asks.

"What's a nightcap?" I wonder. It sounds exciting.

"A drink. I have booze in my room."

I shake my head. "No, thanks." I've had enough to drink tonight, and I have a hockey game tomorrow.

"Uh, okay then. Night." Lily whirls around without another word and marches into her residence.

"Good night," I say. But she's already gone.

8
_____

THE BATTLE PLAN

LILY

SALLY and I are having breakfast in the common room on our floor. It's Saturday, so we can relax. Well, for an hour anyway, and then I have to clean and do my laundry. Last week, I missed my slot on the laundry schedule, and now I'm getting desperate for clean socks. In Sweden, everything is scheduled, and the schedules are set in stone. Apparently I shouldn't have been sitting at the back giggling with Sally while the rules were explained.

I taste my *filmjölk* and muesli. The yogurt part is sour and horrible, and I make a face.

"Why do you cat that crap?" Sally asks.

"Because it's what the Swedes eat. Gabe told me he has this for breakfast each day."

Before I left, I vowed that I would try to integrate in Swedish life and not be that person who complains that "things are better at home." I glare at her two slices of stone cold toast. "What's the point of eating exactly what you eat at home if you're here?"

"There are better ways to immerse yourself in Swedish culture," Sally replies. She has an irritating smirk on her face.

"Are we talking about Robin again?"

"Robin was weeks ago. Tonight, I'm seeing Karl."

I shovel in another spoonful of cereal. "What's Karl like?"

She props her chin in her hands. "Gorg. He's got cropped brown hair and this incredible forehead."

"I don't think I've ever heard anyone rave about a forehead before. You're weird."

"Swedish men have amazing foreheads. I can't believe you haven't noticed. I think high foreheads are linked to intelligence. You know, the opposite of Neanderthals."

"Is intelligence even on your list of requirements? I thought two legs and a penis were enough." I'm a grump this morning.

"Spoken like a woman who has yet to experience the sword of a Viking in her sheath."

"God, that's gross. It's breakfast."

She laughs. "Really, Lily, you need to get out there. Swedes have the best attitude about sex. They believe it's a natural part of getting to know each other. And they're not judgemental if a woman wants to sleep with different men."

"Are they judgemental about that kind of thing back in Manchester?"

"God, yes. Sexism rears its ugly head. It's fine for boys to be on the pull, but let a woman try..."

"Yeah, that's like back home in Vancouver too."

Theoretically, being free to have random sex is liberating, but I'm not attracted to multiple guys at once. Exhibit A: my continuing crush on Gabe. Despite last weekend's rejection, he's still the star of my night time fantasies.

"There's a thing tonight at Lunds Nation. You're going, right?" Sally asks.

"I guess. Do you know who else is going?"

"Jesus, Lily, if you don't go because Gabriel is not going, I'm going to throttle you. How many times do I have to tell you to ditch that arrogant git?"

"He's not an arrogant git—whatever that may be." It's hard enough understanding Swedish without having to translate English too.

"Yeah, he is. He's so quiet but then when he does speak, it's something rude. At first, I thought it was an ESL-thing, but now I think he's a wanker. Besides, nothing's happening between you two. Go out with one of the lads who do fancy you."

But I like Gabe's bluntness. It's one of about a hundred things I like about him. He's thoughtful, he reads poetry, he's a good listener, he's smart, and he's reliable. I like the way he dresses and his perfectly tousled hair and trimmed beard. The way his beard circles his full lips. And his smile. Gabe's smiles are rare, and that makes them more beautiful.

"He's hot, I'll grant you that," Sally continues. "But there are a lot of hot guys around here. Interested hot guys."

At first, I wasn't sure if Gabe liked me. Then I thought he did. And at the club, we danced, we kissed, but then he turned down an invite to my room. And during the week, we met for *fika* again, and he acted as if nothing had happened. Talk about hot and cold.

Even his elusiveness is attractive. I won't admit this to Sally, but guys have never been a problem for me. Not to say that I could get anyone I want, but most guys—given the right amount of encouragement—are interested. But, here in Sweden, without my squad, without anyone knowing who my family is, it's just me. And maybe me alone is not enough.

"Nobody's asked me out lately," I protest. That's not the complete truth as Jakub keeps suggesting we do things, and I keep pretending he means with the group.

"Well, the fact that you're always linked at the hip to Gabriel doesn't help."

I finish my yucky cereal. Surely the fact it doesn't taste good means it's healthy, right?

Sally sighs. "Okay, it's obvious you have a one-track mind. I am now an expert on Swedish men, so I'll help you get a leg over with Gabriel and you can get him out of your system. Have you let him know you're interested?"

"Of course."

"How?" she demands.

"You know, the usual flirty stuff—sitting close, watching him while he speaks, hair flips." I don't mention the kiss. The kiss is something I keep to myself, like Gollum's ring. My precious. Besides, the after-kiss part was Gabe rejecting me.

"Well, I can see that life is much easier when you're a blonde Amazon." She rolls her eyes. Sally is my opposite: a short brunette with a curvy figure. Contrary to her complaint, she has zero problems attracting men. "Have you asked him if he wants to do you?"

"No." That idea floors me. In Lilyland, guys make the first move when it comes to sex.

"Swedish guys are very shy. It's bonkers because they're so tidy, but there you have it."

"Really?" I'm cracking the code of Sally's brand of English. "Tidy" does not mean that the guy put away his clothes before you had a "leg over," but that he's hot. Honestly, Canadians need more words for *hot* than just *hot*. And it is shocking that someone can look like a male model and yet be too shy to make the first move. Maybe they don't have to. They can stand there, look hot, and let women come to them.

She nods. "If you want Gabe, you're going to have to get him drunk."

I shake my head. "That doesn't seem right. What about consent?"

"Oh for fuck's sake, I don't mean get him so pissed he passes out and then you ravage his unconscious body. All I mean is enough alcohol to lower his inhibitions. Surely, that's happened to you?"

"Nope. One of my girlfriends had a bad experience back in grade twelve. We made a pact not to get that drunk again at parties."

"Whatever grade twelve is," mutters Sally. "You Canadians are so puritanical. If I stopped drinking after one black-out, I'd have no social life at all."

I smother a laugh. Sally is a huge drinker.

"Tonight's the night. I'll help you. We'll get Gabriel drunk, and then you can see what happens. But here's the deal: if he's still not interested, you have to move on."

I must be making a face because Sally adds, "You can still be friends with him. But you definitely can't leave

Lund without fucking a Swedish guy. It's one of the basic tenets of an exchange program—fuck a hot local."

Sally masterminds this plan like Churchill at Dunkirk. "We'll get some cool flavoured schnapps for the pre-party, and you can offer Gabriel shots. Then maybe detour back here instead of the club."

I nod.

"Body shots," she suggests.

"God, Sally, it's too early for this."

But the idea of Gabe's warm lips on my bare skin is very tempting. He's an amazing kisser—open mouth, no tongue, hot breath, and perfect pressure. He could teach kissing. *Class, any volunteers to demonstrate technique?* Me, me, me, choose me, Professor Olsson!

"Too early for what?" Jakub slides into the seat beside me.

"Would you like to do body shots off Lily?"

"God, yes." He eyes me like I'm going to whip off my t-shirt and produce a bottle of Jägermeister. It's way too early for this. I put my face down on the table.

Sally turns to Jakub. "Would you agree with me that Swedes are shy? And they need a bit of alcohol to get going?"

"No. The women here are very aggressive." Jakub sounds slightly disapproving. What man could be opposed to a gorgeous Swede letting him know she was interested?

"There you have it. In gender-balanced Lund, women make the first move. This is the life I've been waiting for." Sally cracks her knuckles like she's ready to get to work.

Jakub and I exchange furtive glances. This is definitely not the life we've been waiting for.

9

SHOTS SHOTS SHOTS

LILY

I KNOCK on the door of the apartment where the *förfest* is supposed to be. We always pre-party at someone's place because booze is so expensive at clubs.

Nobody answers my loud knocking.

"I can hear music," says Sally. "This must be the place."

The door opens inward, and I smack it right into the jean-clad ass of someone removing his shoes. He begins to topple, and I reach out to save him and end up grabbing his crotch. To be specific—his cock.

"Oh my God! Sorry!" I let go immediately. Luckily he balances himself and stands up tall.

It's Gabe. Of course it's Gabe. On a scale of pink to blood red, my blushing is at horrific crime scene level. I've made spectacular entrances before, but this is one for the history books, especially if the book is entitled *My Most Embarrassing Moments.*

He has a strange look on his face, but he says only, "*Hej.*"

"Well, now that the foreplay's over, you two can go straight to it," helpful Sally suggests.

"*Hej,* Sally," he says. His eyes are so pretty. He has very long eyelashes for a guy.

"I'm really sorry," I repeat as I remove my shoes.

"Don't worry," says Sally. "There are lads who would pay you to do that. Let's put this lot in the fridge."

She drags me along with her. I'd rather not leave Gabe, but she is saving me from apologizing for a third time since I can't think of anything else to say.

"Changed your mind about the shag now that you've felt the goods?" Sally asks.

Luckily I'm already so red I can't get any redder. "The goods feel more than adequate." I can't believe I have to keep defending Gabe.

She jams our booze into an already packed refrigerator. She uncaps two beers, hands me one, and then adds the bottle of schnapps and two glasses.

"Okay, little Red Riding Hood, off you go and turn Grandma into a wolf."

"Are you sure this is going to work?" I take a swig of beer for courage.

"If not, just grab the family jewels again. That certainly got his attention."

When I find Gabe again, he's talking to a cute brunette. They're in a very intense conversation that I can't understand. I hesitate and turn back around. I'm too chicken to interrupt.

"*Hej*, Lily," Gabe calls out. I do a one-eighty and return. I'm an idiot holding two bottles and two glasses. All I need is a sign on my forehead saying, "I'm going to get Gabe drunk so I can even have a chance with him."

"Hey." I try to smile, but my lips stick on my teeth.

"This is Eva," he says. She nods, but doesn't say a word to me. She continues talking very seriously to Gabe, but he doesn't appear too interested. She keeps touching his arm to punctuate her sentences. I wish I could do that. I drink Sally's beer instead.

"*Hej då*," she says as she leaves.

"What's that all about?" I ask.

"She wants me to join her plogging group."

"Uh, plogging?" It sounds like an English word.

"Ja. You pick up garbage while you are jogging. *Plocka upp* and jogging."

I snort with laughter, but Gabe doesn't respond. Apparently, he's serious. I'm happy that it wasn't something more personal than that, but I got an intimate vibe off the two of them. "Are you dating her or something?"

"Nej. Not now."

Oh. An ex-girlfriend. "I feel like I don't know anything about you."

His forehead creases. "That is what we prefer, yes? We discuss what is important."

"I guess." I don't mind not knowing about his past, but I wish I knew more about his present. His emotional present.

"Why do you carry two bottles with you?"

"Oh." I hold out a glass. "Want to do shots with me?"

"Ja, sure." His expression looks more puzzled than excited. "You don't drink much usually."

"It has to be in the right circumstances." Like when I'm trying to seduce tall, shy Swedes. Still, being the sexual aggressor is new to me. I swallow the nervous lump in my throat.

My hand shakes as I pour out shots for both of us.

"*Skål!*" I lift my glass and clink it against his. There's a burning warmth as it coats my throat. Strong alcohol is perfect in this cold weather.

"You should look at me," Gabe says.

Well, sure. I enjoy that all time, second only to accidentally feeling him up. He looks great as usual. He's wearing a navy sweater and a pale blue shirt that's slightly frayed at the collar. The shirt brings out the bluish circles under his eyes, and I feel a rush of concern. I want to put my hand up and caress his face. Okay, it's concern plus lust.

Gabe continues, "In Sweden, it's bad luck not to look in the eyes when you toast."

"Oh." So, not a prelude to sex, but a culture lesson. Discouraged, I refill our glasses. What if this doesn't work? Should I take Sally's advice and move on?

This time I look him in the eye, and we clink the glasses together. Then my gaze gets caught on his mouth. His lips are so oddly full on his angular face. I remember how good it felt to kiss his pillow-soft lips. And his beard was soft, not bristly. Impulsively, my hand reaches up and touches his chin.

Gabe starts slightly. The tip of his pink tongue darts out and then he swallows. "What are you doing?"

"Sorry. Your beard feels soft. Like you," I say.

His blue eyes widen. "You think I'm soft?"

I lift my chin. "Yeah, I do. I think you act gruff, but

inside you're all soft and sweet—like a chocolate lava cake."

He shakes his head. "You don't know me."

I pour us another shot. We toast and our eyes meet. Each time we do this, it's hotter because I feel more connected to him. I tip back the shot. The heat travels through my body. Soon my toes will be warm too, because hardwood floors and thin stockings don't match.

"I do know you," I protest. "You said we know each other, like the essentials. You said that about five minutes ago."

"Ja, but there many things you don't know about me."

"There's nothing you could tell me that would change the way I feel about you," I say. The people next to us stare. Oops, my voice is a bit loud.

"You are full of enthusiasm. Like a child," Gabe says. But he looks sad as he says this.

"And you're so busy being an adult, you never relax."

Something shuts down in Gabe when I say this. The curtains close on the window of his face, which wasn't expressive to begin with. I regret snapping at him, but I hate being called immature. Which only proves I am immature.

"I'm so sorry," I say. Apologies are my main theme tonight. Gabe isn't looking at me, I'm not sure if he even hears me. I put my hand on his chest, exactly as I wanted to earlier. His sweater feels soft, but his muscles underneath are tensed. I can feel his warmth and the lift of his breathing. I've broken that shield around him, and there's a palpable tension between us. Now his eyes are on me, and he looks... upset or angry.

I pull my hand away as if it's scorched and pick up the

bottle from the table. But when I lift it towards the glass, he puts a hand on my wrist. "Slow down."

"Why?" I roll my eyes. "I can handle it. Look how big I am."

He obediently looks me over, and I almost shiver under his scrutiny. All my yearning is so close to the surface.

"You are not so big as you think," he says. The gentleness in his voice is soothing, but there's that gap again. His words seem to carry more meaning than I can understand. Does he just mean that I'm smaller than he is, or does he understand that I use bravado as protection?

He steps closer to me. When I look up at his face, I'm hyper-aware of all his features: his narrow nose, his dark brows, his combed-back hair, and his pale skin.

I hear myself blurt, "I'd like to count the freckles on your face. And then lick every one of them."

"What?" I've finally shocked Gabe.

"Nothing," I mumble. There's a bowl of crispbreads on the table, and I eat one. Then, against his warning, I pour us more shots. No toast this time, I just knock it back.

I realize the flaw in Sally's plan. Gabe is way bigger than me. I may have good tolerance for a woman, but there is no way I can keep up to him in a drinking contest.

"What do you weigh, anyway?" I ask.

"Around 95 kilos." My brain is too fried to do the math, but it's over 200 pounds.

"What is that in real..." I don't even finish the question before I feel queasy. Not throwing up queasy, but not good. I mumble something about fresh air and push my way through the crowd to the front door. Once outside, I breathe in. I feel better, but I'm also freezing. It's only September, but the night is pretty cold.

Maybe it's the sudden change in temperature, but now I *am* nauseous. I stumble down the stairs and throw up. Not a full-blown there-goes-my-dinner vomit, but more that horrible sensation when you're dry heaving and nothing is coming up. I feel like absolute crap.

"Lily." Gabe's deep voice is right beside me. He wraps an arm around me. "You okay?"

I swallow and all I can taste is that vile bile. "Ugh. Not really."

He squeezes me tighter, and I realize that I'm shivering. Gabe pulls off his sweater and offers it to me.

"I might get sick on it." He shakes his head like that doesn't matter. I pull on the sweater. Awesome, instead of getting into his pants, I'm getting into his sweater. And instead of sexy, I'm lame. Team Lily is going down for the count.

"Wait here," he says. I nod. I can't do anything else.

Gabe goes back into the house and a few minutes later returns with my coat, purse, and shoes. He's already wearing his coat.

"I'll take you home. Can you walk okay?"

"If I say no, what are you going to do, piggy-back me?" Despite my queasiness, I'm a sassy drunk.

"I could carry you," he states.

"You wish." I snort. I'm the furthest thing from a tiny damsel in distress who can be swept off her feet. But I am unsteady, which means that Gabe keeps an arm around me. This is not the worst feeling in the world, despite the nausea.

"It wasn't supposed to be like this," I complain.

"How was it supposed to be?"

"I'm supposed to get you drunk. Well, no. Lower your

inhibitions." I swing my arm through the air. "And then I'd get to feel your Viking sword in my sheath. Sally promised."

I can feel the vibrations of Gabe's internal shaking. But he's too polite to laugh out loud. He's being so nice, and I feel stupid and embarrassed. At this point, I wouldn't sleep with me either.

We get back to my residence. I fumble for the outside door fob.

"Okay. Thanks for walking me home. You can go back to the party now."

"I will see you to your room."

I shake my head. "It's okay. The cold air sobered me up." But a loud hiccup shows I'm not right yet.

"Please, Lily. Let me make sure you're all right."

His polite protectiveness is breaking my heart. How could I even have thought about getting such a nice guy drunk so we could have sex? It's way wrong. I've zipped through the stages of drunkenness, and I'm already reached the feeling sorry for myself part.

We go up to my room in silence. Well, silence is Gabe's normal state, so that's not a surprise. Me being quiet is unusual though. When I unlock my door, he follows me in. I tidied my room, hoping that we might end up here. Now we have, but it's not as I'd imagined.

"Do you still feel sick?" he asks me.

"No, I'm okay now." I peel off my coat and throw it on the floor. Then I return his sweater. "I'm just going to lie down." Preferably with a giant duvet over my face. I'm going to hibernate like a bear. Wake me up in the spring when I'll be over my humiliation.

"One moment." Gabe disappears and reappears with a

plastic bucket. I don't know where he got it, but it's probably a good idea. He puts a glass of water on the bedside table. I eye it sadly.

"You should drink lots of water," he says. He gets up and goes to the door, where he puts his boots back on.

I manage a faint smile. "Thank you for everything, Gabe. You'd make a great doctor."

Then I close my eyes. Things will be better in the morning, mainly because they couldn't be worse. But another wave of nausea comes over me. I get up, pull back my hair, and lean over the bucket.

Just before I barf, I catch a glimpse of Gabe's horrified expression.

Best. Night. Ever.

10

HASTA MAÑANA

Lily

I WAKE up and open one eye. It's dark, but that doesn't mean anything around here. I'm wrung out, my mouth is dry, and as a bonus, I have a headache.

But I'm not alone. Gabe is asleep in my chair, with his head cradled in his arms on my desk. He doesn't look very comfortable.

I sit up in bed, but as I swing my legs out of bed I knock over a plastic bucket. It's empty, but for some reason it's giving me bad vibes.

Gabe raises his head. "Ah, Lily. Are you okay now?"

"Yeah, even though I kicked the bucket." Yes, folks, I wake up like this.

He doesn't even smile. He rubs his eyes, and I can't help noticing how good he looks for someone whose face was squished on a wooden surface for hours. Even his hair is in place. I'm sure mine is sticking out in multiple directions.

I search for my phone on the bedside table and find nothing. "Um, what time is it? And, er, what are you doing here?"

He pulls out his phone. "7:30. I stayed to make sure you are okay."

"Excuse me a sec." I make my way to my bathroom where I pee and then reload my bladder by drinking an entire glass of water. I look awful. Also, my hair smells kind of vomitty. Did I throw up in front of Gabe?

I poke my head out. "I'm just going to take a—"

Gabe is already gone. Damn. Who can blame him though?

I hop in the shower anyway. I wash my hair and get all the yucky whatever out of it. I compose my to-do list for the day. It includes apologizing to Gabe and figuring out exactly what I did last night. Also, going back to that store Sally showed me with the extensive array of Lelo vibrators, since I won't be having sex on this side of the Atlantic Ocean.

I dry off. At least my headache is lessening. Another glass of water helps even more.

When I emerge from the bathroom, Gabe has rematerialized in his chair. I'm wearing a terry robe and a towel on my hair, so once again, I'm bringing sexy back.

"Is that coffee I smell?" I ask. I comb out my hair, and hope I don't resemble a drowned rat.

"Ja, I got you coffee and juice." He sips his own coffee.

"God, yes," I whimper. I drink the orange juice first, and it's an IV to my bloodstream. My energy returns, and my headache is completely gone.

"If there's a pastry around here, my life will be complete."

"Nej." He offers me a bag that contains yogurt and a fruit cup.

"*Tack* very much." I sit on the edge of the bed and taste the yogurt. Delish. "So, you stayed to look after me?"

"Ja. You were not too good last night."

"Um, what exactly did I do?"

"You drank shots. After beer. I have never seen you drink so much."

"Yeah, well, it happens. So, did I say anything embarrassing?"

"You cannot remember?" Gabe asks me. He's not smiling, but he doesn't look upset either.

"I sort of remember," I lie.

"You did not say anything embarrassing," he says.

This feels like a word game, and my brain is not operating at full capacity. I resist an urge to smack the person who brought me life-giving elixirs. "Okay, if I didn't say anything embarrassing, what did I say?"

He is trying hard not to smile. "You said something interesting."

"Damn it, Gabe. What did I say?" I jump up and try to whack him on the shoulder, but his hand flashes out and catches my wrist. My robe gapes open and nearly reveals my breasts. Gabe sees this. Hell, he sees everything.

He pulls me over by the wrist until I'm close enough to feel the heat of his breath. His other hand is around my waist, holding on to the belt of my robe.

"You said that you were trying to get me drunk so I would not be shy. Then you asked me to have sex with you."

The room suddenly feels really hot. Or maybe that's just me. We didn't actually have sex, did we? I do a mental check of my body parts. This does not feel like a body that had sex. Not memorable sex anyway.

I bite my lower lip. "And what did you say when I asked that?"

"Nej."

Oh man, that's disappointing. Apparently, no amount of alcohol will make him want to have sex with me.

"I'm so sorry." I try to back away, but he won't let go. Gabe is watching me with blazing intensity.

"When we have sex, I would like you to remember it," he says.

Not *if*, when. Halle-freaking-lujah! My whole body flushes with excitement and a touch of nervousness. My hopes are finally being answered.

"Well, I feel good now. One hundred percent conscious for anyone that's wondering." This may be my worst seduction line ever, but I have a hunch it's still going to work.

Gabe's mouth curves up in a smile. I can't stop looking at his mouth: his pale lips and his straight white teeth. I move closer and straddle his lap. I can feel the strength of his thighs flexing under me.

"Ahhh, Lily." His hands move over to the sash of my robe and undo the knot. The terry fabric opens and pools at my hips where I'm on top of him. He leans forward and plants a warm kiss on the exposed place between my breasts. I breathe in and enjoy the hot sensation of Gabe's mouth on me. The heat spreads in ripples across my body like a pebble in a pond.

I bend my head down, and our mouths meet. This kiss

is a million degrees hotter than our first kiss; it's hard, messy, and wet. I kiss the parts of a face I've been fantasizing about: his soft beard, that sprinkling of freckles across his nose, his prominent brow. And he's kissing me back, fixing his full lips on any part of me he can reach. Finally my doubts are gone. Gabe wants me as much as I want him, and that's a huge turn-on.

I slip my hands under the hem of his prickly wool sweater, and lift it off, then unbutton his shirt. The first buttons unveil the prominent slope of his chest and the dark fuzz of hair.

All the times I imagined him naked, I didn't imagine the chest hair. But that's the surprise of sweaty, wonderful reality. And it's one more signal that he's more mature, more man than anyone I've been with. I run a hand over the curling hairs that end abruptly under his pec muscles. When I trace the perfectly round circles of his nipples, Gabe tilts back his head and groans. He likes having his nipples touched, knowledge I file away.

I continue to unbutton his shirt and reveal his deeply outlined abs. I part his shirt and his waist is ridiculously small. And there's another line of hair that splits him right down the middle of those concave abs. My breath shortens as I admire the excellence of his torso.

"You're gorgeous. This body, unh," I mutter. We roll onto my bed. I kiss his throat and then move down. I linger on his round, dark nipples, swirling my tongue round and around them as he strokes my hair. As I move my mouth down the sculpted surface of his taut abs, he drops one hand to clutch the duvet. He's an innie, and I tongue the tiny dent of his navel.

Gabe swears quietly in Swedish, and he lifts his pelvis

in an unconscious plea for attention. I run my finger down his happy trail. There's an intriguing bulge in those tight jeans.

I unzip his pants, pull them open, and pull them down as much as I can but his thighs are too big. His cock strains to be freed from the grey cotton of his boxer briefs. I kiss the pulsing fabric and inhale his scent: clean, earthy, and all Gabe.

He's raised his head to watch me, but there's a tension between us, like we are in uncharted territory.

"*Hur lång är du?*" I ask as I stroke his cock through the fabric. Because I'd like to know how long this pulsing beast is. It takes Gabe half a beat to understand my terrible Swedish joke. Then he laughs, and everything feels comfortable again.

He sits up and pulls off the impossibly tight jeans. Omigod. His legs are amazing too. Not a surprise though, since I've been checking them out at yoga club. They're endlessly long, shaped with sinewy muscle, and covered in golden hair.

"You have too much clothes," Gabe tells me, and pulls off my robe completely. He freezes for a moment as his eyes travel over my body.

"Wow." He extends the word to two syllables: wu-ow. Gabe's subtle exclamation of flattery means more to me than flowery compliments. His hands stroke my sides, and his touch is tentative and almost ticklish. It wakens every molecule of my skin, and I'm on fire. I need to feel more, so I lean towards him and I guide his hands towards my breasts. He circles them almost lazily, beginning at my ribs and slowly moving towards the centre. My nipples crinkle as his fingertips near them, and when Gabe lifts his head and finally sucks on one, it feels incredible. His mouth is gentle at first, but each time he alternates between nipples he goes harder.

"Unh, that's good." My hands are busy too, tracing the definition of his thighs and the indents on his hips. His muscles are steely hard. And that's not all that's hard. I stick my thumbs into his briefs and pull them down. His cock springs free and nudges my thigh in a happy greeting.

"Hey, buddy," I say, and stroke his width. He's uncut, and his foreskin glides in my hand.

"Do you talk to my penis?" Gabe asks.

"Of course. He's going to make me very happy soon."

Gabe chuckles. "You are very different. And I want to make you happy."

"*Very* happy," I correct him. His hands are sliding down to my hips now, and he deftly flips me onto the bed. Then he ducks his head down and kisses my tummy. Then lower. Maybe it's not only Gabe's cock that will be making me very happy.

His hot breath on my skin is sexy, and even better are the moist kisses he's planting all over my inner thighs. He spreads my legs, and then I feel his mouth on me. His tongue nudges my clit, and my whole body arcs in response. Seeing Gabe's head between my legs is almost as hot as what he's doing.

I moan as he teases me down there. This one tapping motion practically sends me off the bed.

"Oh God, yes! That's good," I whimper, which encourages him to do it more. And more. I start to come in a rippling wave. When it's done, I open my eyes and Gabe is watching me.

"You're very beautiful," he says. I'm not sure whether he means all the time or post-orgasm.

"That was effing incredible." He moves up my body, and he kisses my forehead, the tip of my nose, and then my lips. I caress his cock again because even after coming, I urgently need him inside me.

"Do you want me to use a condom?" he asks.

"Yeah. I mean, I'm good health-wise, but of course," I reply. Apparently orgasms deprive me of my ability to speak English.

"I am healthy too," Gabe replies.

He reaches back into his jacket and pulls out a foil packet. I help him put it on, because I'm just that eager.

Then I lean back onto the bed. Missionary would be good because I really want to watch Gabe's face. He eases the tip of his cock inside, and I relish the feeling of him entering me slowly. Then pulling out, and back in.

The sex feels incredible, but beyond that there's this connection between us that I've never had before. Our bodies are in sync with each other, moving in the right ways and directions without a word.

"Unnnh, yes," I grunt. It's so good.

Gabe's stoic at first, but the longer it goes, the more he loses himself into the sex. He's sweating and straining and feeling it all. I can't keep my hands off him, touching his defined chest, his sculpted shoulders, his narrow waist —every part of Gabe that I've fantasized about is right here. Here in the bed where I've touched myself and imagined us doing exactly what we're doing right now. I slip my hand between us so I can hurry the second orgasm that's building up in me.

He stops his thrusting. I feel his hand on mine.

His voice is far away. "Let me do it, Lily. I want to make you come."

And then his finger replaces mine. He watches my face to see what pressure and speed I like and then begins the exquisite friction again. Fully inside me. Pulling back so far, I'm afraid he'll fall out. And then in. So deep. I send a silent prayer of thanks to the flexibility gods.

"Oh. Unnh." My breaths shorten, and my body stiffens as I come again. And then I feel Gabe's body relaxing as he allows himself to come as well. He falls onto me, and we lie together as one sweaty, satisfied mess.

11

THE RULES

LILY

"HOW MANY TYPES of meatballs do they make in this country?" Sally wonders as we get our lunch in a campus café.

"I'm having fish meatballs today." That sounds like a contradiction in terms. Neither Sally nor I are good cooks, but one of the few bargains in Lund is the daily lunch, which includes a hot dish with salad, bread, and water. So we eat like kings at lunch, storing food like greedy squirrels.

We sit at a table in the bright atrium. The student cafés here are really nice, more restaurants than cafeterias.

"Is student dining this nice in England?" I ask.

"Are you mad?" Sally launches into a description that sounds more like a nineteenth century prison. Lunch is just another thing that the Swedes get right. Living in another country means I take pleasure in the simplest things—this delicious lunch for example. I pop a piece of bread into my mouth and relish the crunchy freshness.

"Hello, may I join you?" It's Frida. She's an exchange student too, but she's from Denmark so it's almost home for her, although she's keen to distinguish Danes from Swedes at every opportunity. I pull out a chair for her. Instead of pigging out like us, she's having a fancy salad.

"Lily, are you humming as you eat?" Sally asks.

"Oh sorry." My foot is tapping too. I'm full of energy.

"Someone's in a good mood today." Sally continues. "Did my plan work?"

"Your plan failed miserably," I reply. "I'm the one who ended up getting drunk and puking. So attractive."

Frida smiles. "Lily, you're always getting into scrapes. Like Anne of Green Gables." Frida studies children's literature, and she's disappointed by how little I know about L. M. Montgomery and that I've never been to Prince Edward Island.

"I'm sure that Anne never barfed in an attempt to seduce Gilbert," I reply.

"No, but she did get Diana drunk once," Frida says.

Sally interrupts our journey to Avonlea. "You're not supposed to match him drink for drink. Any moron would know that."

I'm not any moron then, but I'm still happy.

Sally watches me from under thick bangs that are streaked with crimson this week.

"Hmmm, still you're awfully cheery. What did happen?"

"Wouldn't you like to know?"

But my perma-grin is telling Sally everything, and she

makes a victory fist. "Oh, well done you. Hope it was all you dreamed."

To top off my happy day, I see Gabriel and Johan walking towards us. They have their lunch trays.

Our eyes meet, and he smiles at me—his gorgeous, angelic smile that turns me into Liquid Lily.

"Someone must have a magic fanny," Sally says. "I don't think I've seen him smile before."

"*Hej, hej,*" he says as they approach us.

Then he keeps on walking.

He never even looks back. I know this because I'm watching the whole time. I'm sorry, is this the same guy who I got naked with yesterday morning? And now we're back to "*hej*"?

"Too bad he can't see those sad puppy eyes," Sally remarks. "I'm sure he'd melt. I'm melting, and I'm only a bystander."

"What are you talking about?" Frida asks.

"Lily. She's just experienced her first Swedish post-coital rejection."

"Ahhh," Frida replies, like she understands. But I don't.

"What are you two talking about?" I ask.

"It's something that North Americans don't realize," Frida says. Her know-it-all voice is really bugging me. Also, I hate being lumped in with an entire continent. I'm an individual, damn it, and I'm tired of this EU superiority complex. "Sex is not a big deal for the more... sophisticated countries."

I resist an urge to yank on her sophisticated cotton scarf. "I think you have it wrong. Sex is a big deal."

Frida raises a casual shoulder. "Let's say you're

attracted to someone, then you have sex, and it's awful. He's not a good lover. You don't want to be stuck with him because you had sex once."

"The sex is probably bad because you don't have an emotional connection," I reply. What happened between Gabe and me was a real connection. Wasn't it?

"In Sweden, sex is separate from dating," Sally explains. "You have sex, then maybe you get together after for *fika*. Maybe you have sex a few more times, then you decide if it's a thing."

"How do you know all this?" I ask.

"Well, something similar happened with Robin," Sally says. "But now that I've got the hang of it, I prefer the Swedish way."

"So it's not like this back in Manchester?" I ask.

Sally shrugs. "No, not exactly. You have fuck-buddies in Canada, don't you?"

"Here, they're called KK. *Knull kompis*," Frida adds.

"Add one more K and you're in trouble," I snipe. Ugh. This is so disappointing. I liked Gabe before we had sex, and to me, the sex brought us even closer together. But of course there's a Swedish procedure for dating. Relationships have to be scheduled like laundry.

I'm not someone who needs to be in a relationship all the time, far from it. But Lund has been a big change for me. I don't have my friends, my family, my normal routine. Gabe and I fit together so well. I can talk to him about anything. It's painful to think that everything sweet and intimate that happened meant nothing to him.

Sally rubs my arm. "Chin up, Lil. I'm not saying that things aren't going to work out the way you want—only that Swedish guys are on a different agenda. If he can't make the first move to have sex, imagine how big a deal a relationship is."

"Ugh. This is not the kind of culture shock that I prepared for." But I feel better. Gabe wasn't giving me the cold shoulder like some hook-up who doesn't want to acknowledge you at school the next day. It's normal here.

"If he wants to see you more, he will invite you for *fika*," says Frida. Good grief, they have rules for everything here.

I pull out my phone, and there's already a message from Gabe. He asks me to meet for *fika* after class today.

"That's more like it." My perma-smile is back.

Sally nods sagely. "Is it *fika* later?"

"Yes. He's even given me a nickname. Puss." I crinkle my nose. I'm not really a nickname person, and I'm definitely not a cutesy animal nickname person.

Sally and Frida both laugh.

"Lily, you silly cow," Sally says. "*Puss* means kiss."

"But *puss* is a good sign," Frida says. "It shows affection."

I try to turn down the voltage on my smile, but I can't. *Puss*, I repeat silently and think about Gabe's soft mouth on mine. Because regardless of how he's acting, he's also thinking about us kissing—again. Soon.

12

TAKE A CHANCE ON ME

GABRIEL

WE SIT down with our coffees in a little café off campus. Lily suggested we go somewhere new, and I sense she wants us to have privacy. I'm glad to be alone with her as well.

She takes a big bite out of her cinnamon bun and scatters crumbs all over the table. She does everything with enthusiasm. I swallow as I remember her licking her way down my chest.

"Mmmm. *Kanelbulle*. So good. I need to take a hundred of these home with me. Maybe I can find the recipe somewhere."

"Are you a good cook?" There are many little things I want to know about Lily.

She laughs her huge laugh. I admire the joyful ease of her emotions.

"I am a terrible cook." She finishes the *kanelbulle* in

four bites and wipes her mouth with a paper napkin. "Luckily, I've only lived at home or in residence. But my time is coming. When I get back, I'm moving in with my girlfriends. I foresee a lot of pizza in my future."

"They don't teach you cooking in school?"

"Yeah, in Home Ec. But it's not really about meals. More like a bunch of dishes. Lots of cookies."

"What are you good at?" I ask.

"I'm coordinated," she says. This is something I've observed in yoga club.

"Do you do sports clubs?"

"Yes, of course. In high school, I was on all the teams. But in university, I just do intramurals. I run, hike, go to the gym, you know, the usual stuff."

I enjoy being outdoors as well. "We should hike together. I know the best trails here."

Lily props her chin on her hands. "That would be great. I always feel good out in the fresh air. But the weather's been so sucky lately."

"Here we say, 'There is no bad weather—'"

"Only bad clothing," Lily finishes along with me. "My *farmor* used to say that too."

"Do you have rain clothing?"

"Of course. I'm from the rain capital of Canada."

"Then we will go next weekend. Regardless of the weather," I say.

She fidgets with her coffee spoon. She wants to discuss something, but for once she's not being direct.

"When you said *puss* in your message, I thought you had given me a cutesy nickname like pussycat. But it means something else."

I smile. "That is not the nickname I would give you."

Lily's eyes crinkle in delight. "So you already have a nickname for me?"

"Ja. I call you Canada goose."

"Why?"

"Because you are from Canada, and your laugh sounds like a goose."

"Oh. My. God." Lily tilts her head back and laughs her huge, honking laugh. I can't help but laugh along with her. And now the tension is broken.

"You know, some people might find that insulting."

"Why?" I ask.

She shakes her head. "You amaze me. You just say whatever you're thinking. I'm surprised you never get beaten up."

"I'm not trying to offend you. Why is honesty a problem?"

"It's not. And I should be honest too." Lily sets down her coffee and smiles at me. "Sunday morning was awesome."

I can feel my cheeks warming. I nod. It was awesome. Lily is very open about sex. I don't have to worry about what she wants because she speaks up. As any normal guy, I think I'm more than adequate in sexual matters, but it's nice to know my partner is enjoying things as much as I am.

"Well, um, I don't know if this is true, but Sally tells me that Swedish guys are on a different agenda." Lily searches for the right words. "But I'm Canadian, and I'm not here for that long. All I wanted to say is that I really like you, Gabe. I like hanging with you, and I really liked sleeping with you, so..."

She pauses again. As usual, I have zero idea of what she will say next.

"All I wanted to say is: if you want to go out for real, I'd be good with that. Um, whenever you're ready. I know you like to take your time."

She turns back to her coffee cup and looks into its depths.

The silence is profound. It's my turn to say something, but I must consider this. Going out with Lily is a possibility, but it's too soon. We've seen each other a lot, but it has only been a month since we met. My nature is to be cautious, to wait until I'm completely sure of my decisions.

What would it be like to date Lily? With Eva, dating wasn't that different from being friends. We already socialized with the same people, participated in marches and campaigns for social justice causes, and had much intense conversation. The only difference was that we had sex. Eva considered traditional dating to be old-fashioned and patriarchal. And that was perfect for me too. Eva's independence meant there would be no extra emotional burdens in my life.

Lily's expectations are more conventional. Johan describes her as "high maintenance." So dating her will be like dating in a Hollywood movie. I will have to make romantic gestures and invent exciting activities. That will take too much work and energy.

"*Hej, hej.* What are you two doing here?" Beatriz pulls out a chair at our table and puts her coffee down. "How was your weekend?"

"Mine was great. Very satisfying." Lily winks at me. "How about you?"

Beatriz talks about a shopping trip to Malmö. Lily is enthusiastic about Beatriz's new jeans, which look like every other pair of jeans to me.

Lily is right. She will only be here until December. We can't do the usual courting dance where we sleep together some more, go out some more, and evolve into a relationship. If I want something to happen, I must decide soon.

An old friend, Mohammed, now joins us, and I introduce him to Lily. He works as an apprentice to an electrician, so he's not around as much as my university friends. Lily chats easily to him. Eva and Johan were wrong; Lily is not a snobby, high-maintenance princess. Even if I have never seen her wear the same outfit twice and her underwear is very beautiful, she is herself: friendly and open to everyone. Dating Lily will not be a labour. She reacts delightedly to the simplest things in life here and makes me appreciate them more. Spending time with Lily is the highlight of my day.

It is ridiculous to imagine I'm not emotionally involved with Lily. She's constantly in my thoughts, and even more since we were intimate.

When I check my watch, it's already time.

"I have to go now." I rise.

"Ah. How is your mother?" Mohammed asks me in Swedish.

"Much the same." It's nice of him to inquire. When we were boys, he often played at my home.

Lily and I walk out of the café. She doesn't reintroduce the topic of our dating. In fact, she's unusually quiet.

We come to the corner where we part.

"Bye, Gabe. See you tomorrow." Lily turns to cross the street without even looking at me.

"Wait."

She turns around. Lily's eyes are curious, but she's not smiling, and she's almost more beautiful in repose.

"What we were talking about before—" I begin.

"Yes?"

"I want to be with you," I blurt, my words sounding not quite correct.

Lily's eyes widen. They're the exact colour of a summer sky. "Oh Gabe, really?" She wraps her arms around my neck and plasters herself against me. "I'm so happy!"

Then she kisses me. Her mouth is soft, and she tastes like *fika*. My arms wrap automatically around her, and her body—as always—fits perfectly into mine. I can feel the swell of her breasts, the strength of her shoulders, and her happy energy. Her kisses warm the very core of me.

I was wrong all along. Lily is not a princess; she is the prince battering at the walls of the cold fortress I've erected around myself. And now that's she's inside the castle, my spirit is awakening. Lily's joy has become mine too.

13

SWEET

LILY

DAMN, it's dark here. Early afternoon looks like night. Early morning looks like night too. And night looks like night, so it's all night all the time. I pull up the hood of my Arc'teryx jacket because it's drizzling too. So naturally, Gabe and I are going for a walk.

I don't really mind. We both enjoy hiking so much. He's always in a better mood during and after a walk. We've been going out for almost a month now, but his reactions are so low key that I have to really pay attention to read him. I'm getting the hang of it though. He likes the outdoors, exercise, coffee and... sex. And hey, me too.

"*Hej*, Lily."

Gabe materializes beside me. He's a vision of handsomeness in his black jacket, grey cowl scarf, and knit toque.

"Hey, you." I raise my face and put my arms around his

neck. He tilts his head and kisses me. His soft beard tickles me, and his lips are welcoming. I can feel his kisses warm my body right down to my toes—with a big detour in the panty area.

"Your kisses get better every time," I say afterwards.

Gabe takes my hand, and we head off. He knows every path in Lund.

"Where to today?" I ask, but I don't really care. These times alone with Gabe have become my crack. I can confide in him about anything since he's un-shockable. Not that I have anything crazy to say, but it's the relaxation of not having to edit myself. The freedom to blurt.

"Today I have a surprise for you," Gabe says.

"Really? What kind of surprise? Is it food?"

He has a smug smile on his face, and his lip is zipped.

I keep guessing. "Mmm, maybe something cultural?" Gabe took me to a museum last weekend. "Oh, is it something sexy?"

This makes Gabe laugh. "It's a little cold for that."

"Who knows? Maybe you have some hotel room reserved with rose petals strewn across the bed."

He frowns. "Is that what you want?"

"No. All I want is you strewn across the bed." I raise one eyebrow. "Naked."

Now he's content again. Then I wonder—is he taking me home? I'm not prepared to meet his family. Besides, that's not the kind of thing we share. Neither of us talk about our families, and frankly, that's fine with me.

For the next few minutes, we don't speak much. Gabe walks so quickly, I have to push the pace to keep up with him.

"We are here," he says. There's a small green space and a little pergola. There's a wooden bench but it's wet.

Gabe takes off his backpack. He brings out a small blanket and arranges it on the bench.

I plant my butt on the blanket. "You're very organized."

Gabe sits beside me. "Today is a holiday in Sweden."

"No way. We had classes and everything. Nobody told me."

He shakes his head. "It's not a school holiday. It's *kanelbullens dag.*"

"Wait, those are two words I know: cinnamon bun day? That can't be right."

"It is." Gabe smiles, and I melt. Blissful cause and effect.

He reaches into his backpack and pulls out a thermos, cups, and a plastic container.

He fills a mug with steaming coffee and hands it to me. "*Oj.* I forgot your milk and sugar."

"It's okay. I'm trying to be like you and go without. But the coffee here is so strong." I take a sip and hide my inner shudder.

"Better for you." Then he opens up the container, and the delicious scent hits me. He pulls out two perfect, golden coils, dotted with fat grains of sugar.

"Oh wow, those smell amazing. " I toast my coffee cup against his. Then I take a bite of the cinnamon bun. The pastry is buttery and flaky, sugar crumbs melt in my mouth and combined with the cinnamon, it's a celebration in my mouth. "Mmmmmmmmmm."

Gabe looks quite pleased with himself. It's adorable that he planned all this.

"It's so good." I manage to spray a few crumbs on his black jeans. Lily, queen of gracefulness. "So, what's it all about—*kanelbullens dag*? Eating more cinnamon buns? Because everyone already does a lot of that."

He frowns in the way that people do here whenever I ask them to explain some Swedish tradition. Things have always been done in certain ways, and nobody seems to know the exact reasons.

"Maybe first, it was to get people to bake together as a family. Home-baking."

I take another amazing bite and wave the half-pastry in the air. "Well, they failed here then. This may be the best *kanelbulle* I've ever had, where did you get it?"

"I made it."

At first I think he's B.S.ing me, but Gabe's tone is so casual that I realize he's telling the truth. I look down at the remains of my cinnamon bun. It's perfectly rolled and evenly baked. I feel guilty for digging in without the proper reverence.

"By yourself? Or did your mother help you?"

Gabe turns away slightly. "It is sexist to assume that only women can bake."

Uh, oh, he's pissed. His reactions are so subtle, but I've insulted him.

"I'm sorry. I'm not used to the perfection of Swedish guys."

That brings out a tiny smile. "This is what you should say to me after we have sex," he replies.

I laugh loudly at that. "I will next time."

Gabe smiles and sips his coffee. He's happier and more relaxed these days, and I like to think it's because of me—or us being together.

"Can I ask you a question?" I say.

"You just did," he replies. Sometimes it's like conversing with a robot.

I barge on. "Remember that night we went to the Nations club? You know, when we danced together and... had our first kiss." I don't know why mentioning a kiss is making me blush, when we've been having athletic sex since then.

He smiles. "Ja. That was nice."

"Well, when I invited you up to my room afterwards, how come you said no?"

His brow furrows as he thinks back. "Oh, right. Because I didn't want to have another drink."

"What?"

"You asked me to come up for a drink. I didn't want to be hung over the next day as I had hockey."

I'm stunned. "Are you serious? You didn't want to come up because I offered you a nightcap? What if I said, 'Do you want to come up and have sex?'"

"I would have said yes, of course," he replies.

Gabe doesn't understand why I'm smacking him in the chest. He holds onto my wrists.

"Why do you hit me?" he asks.

"I'm hitting you because you're an idiot. I know 'nightcap' is a ridiculous, sixties word, but it's a euphemism. Asking you up to my room for any reason means I want to have sex with you."

He chuckles. "You are repressed about sex. Not like Swedes."

I try to hit him again, but he won't release my wrists. Good thing, because he's in mortal danger right now.

"Repressed? Seriously? What about last weekend?

Remember, first we did that standing up position, and then we used that Lelo thing between us, while we were, you know. That is *so* not repressed."

"A good example. You cannot even say the words."

My eyes narrow. Is he being serious? I growl.

Gabe shakes his head. "I am supposed to decode your talk. If you say, 'Gabe, help fold my laundry,' it means you want to have sex. Very puzzling."

I know he's teasing me now, and I laugh. He laughs too. "My little Canada goose." It's the worst nickname in the world, yet I love it.

He releases my wrists, and I kiss him on the nose. "Gabe, will you come back to my room and help me fold my laundry?"

He glances down at his phone and does some mental calculations. "Ja, I think we have time for laundry."

Gabe begins packing up our *fika* fixings at light speed. As we rush back to my place, I remind myself to call him the perfect Swedish guy—once we're finished making love.

14

PERMISSION

GABE

I WALK HOME from Lily's place. It's early morning, and the campus is deserted. It's still dark out and very chilly. How much better it would be to stay in bed with Lily, feeling the heat of her naked skin against mine. She is as generous with her body as she is in all parts of her life.

Att skiljas är att dö en smula. That saying comes unbidden into my head. Because each time I part from Lily, something in me does die. All too soon, we will be permanently parted. I try hard not to think about that.

When I enter my home, I can hear Freja cajoling my mother.

"Please, Milla, eat a little more breakfast."

"*Godmorgon,*" I greet them as I walk into the kitchen.

My mother starts at the sound of my voice and then smiles. "*Godmorgon,* Gabriel." The normalness of her greeting delights me. She's always better in the mornings.

"Are you having a good day?" I ask her. I don't expect a response, but she nods at me and now I'm really pleased.

"Yes, we're going to do a bit of gardening today," adds Freja.

By gardening, my aunt means tending the windowsill herb planter we set up. My mother used to be an avid gardener with a plot in a communal garden, so we hope that getting her hands into the soil is a reminder of that.

"The garden light seems to be flickering. Maybe you could fix that today," my aunt says.

"Sure." I've rigged up a grow-light for the herbs. So far, they're quite spindly, which is either the fault of the lighting or because my mother digs them up regularly. But if she enjoys herself, that's the main thing.

"There's coffee," Freja tells me. I prepare my cereal with *filmjölk* and sit down at the table with the two of them.

"You're going out this morning, right?" I ask my aunt.

"Yes, I'm meeting Emma for *fika*. Thank you for remembering," she replies.

I nod and continue to eat.

"So, you've been staying out all night," Freja says. Her voice is bright with curiosity.

"Just on weekends." We have a weekday routine to care for my mother, but weekends are more unscheduled, so my aunt encourages me to go out and have what she calls a normal life. But my life is not normal.

She passes me a cup of coffee. "I'm not complaining. I'm glad you're out more. And you know, well, you're welcome to have your friend stay over here anytime."

"Okay." Poor Freja, what she really wants is to meet any woman I'm dating.

It's been a long time since I've had anyone over to our place. When my mother first began to get sick, she had fits of irrational anger. It was far easier to meet friends elsewhere than take that risk. Once she was diagnosed, her condition degenerated quickly. We ended up protecting her from strangers. New people disturb her, but it's more than that. She's a proud woman, and we didn't want to expose her to the pity of others.

I grew up in a household where debate and challenge were welcomed. One of our family habits was pouncing on each other's mistakes in fact or logic. I feel shame now that I drew attention to her many small errors in memory before her diagnosis. And I realize that her anger was triggered by helplessness at seeing her mind slipping away.

But I won't bring Lily here. Everything between us is a temporary escape. She's leaving in forty-one days. It's unnecessary to introduce her to my complicated home life. I'm not ashamed of my mother, but I do feel the gap between Lily's life and my own. Lily accepts me as I am, but like my mother, I don't want pity. And Lily's confidence only underlines the fact that her life is easy. She expects good things to happen, and they do. I'm not even certain how I came to be one of the things she wants, but I'm glad of it.

"Do you have a girlfriend now?" Freja cannot hold back any longer.

"Ja." I hesitate, but then decide to satisfy my aunt's curiosity. She watches me expectantly. She still looks youthful with her light brown hair and pale complexion. I begin cautiously, since one answer will lead to many more. "Her name is Lily. She's an exchange student from Canada."

"Ohhh." My aunt releases a contented sigh. "What is she like?"

"She's nice. Very friendly and talkative. She's lot of fun, and she—" I hesitate. I'm not sure how to describe Lily's magnetic quality. She's not a leader, but she attracts people. You want to be around her because things will happen. You want her to notice you because her attention is a benediction. For me, the best part of being with Lily is that she takes me out of my introspective mind. She is a constant surprise. And now that we are having sex, it's even better. There's a closeness that I didn't even know I was missing. But I can't express all this to my aunt, so I finish with an insufficient shrug.

Freja's expression is blissful. This news satisfies her romantic soul. She pats my mother on the hand. "Isn't this exciting, Milla? I told you something was going on with Gabriel."

My mother nods and smiles. I know she's reacting to Freja's tone rather than her words, but it's good that she's listening and sensing moods. I have spent a lot of time trying to estimate my mother's level of consciousness. At best, she's become a child who reacts to the adults around her. At worst, her brilliant intellect is trapped inside the irrevocably frayed synaptic connections of her brain. That's what I fear the most: the consciousness of knowing what is lost. Because of course, this could be my future too.

"Is she pretty?" my aunt asks.

"Of course." I laugh. What kind of guy would say his girlfriend wasn't pretty? But Lily *is* beautiful in a fresh, energetic way. She glows. Lily is made of energy and light.

"What do Canadian girls look like?" Freja asks.

"Well, Lily actually looks Swedish. She's tall and blonde. Her father is Swedish." When we are out in public, people don't notice that she's a foreigner until she begins to speak.

"Oh, what's her surname?"

I hesitate. Freja will probably search for Lily on Facebook once she knows her full name. But what's the harm? A real life soap opera is much better than the dramas my aunt binges on. Besides, Lily's surname is a common one. "It's Larson."

My aunt laughs. "You're afraid I'm going to look her up online now, aren't you? Well, you could save us both time by showing your mother and I a photo of Lily."

I smile back at her. It is nice to have something pleasant to talk about around here. We spend too much time like coworkers at a hospital, exchanging information on what my mother did all day. I pull out my phone and scroll through it. I'm not one for selfies, but Lily took a photo of us with my phone for a joke. The photo is typical of us: I look like a stunned moose while Lily is lovely and animated. I pass the phone over to my aunt.

She leans against my mother so they can both see the phone at once. "This is Lily. Gabriel's girlfriend."

My mother stares at the phone, but has no response. I'm not sure how much technology works for her. She watches television, but smaller screens don't hold her attention.

But Freja is enraptured. "Ahh, you both look so happy. No wonder you've been in such a good mood lately."

Have I been? I'm not one of those people who wastes time measuring his level of happiness. But with Lily, I forget my larger worries and live more in the moment.

My aunt continues. "I am happy to see you lighter, acting more your age." She slowly hands the phone back to me, but doesn't tear her eyes away from the image. "She's lovely. And she looks like she cares for you very much."

I look down at the tiny image. Lily is leaning against me, but beyond that it's difficult to see how Freja can read more into the photo than that. "She goes back to Canada at the end of the year."

Freja sighs. But even she can't argue once Lily is gone—thousands of kilometres away from here—everything will end between us.

15

HOLLY JOLLY

LILY

SALLY and I are at the Christmas market in Jakriborg, which is a faux medieval village near Lund. It may be fake, but it looks adorable with the lights and market stalls. And it's a great chance for me to get my Christmas shopping done.

"I wish there was snow," I say. The only way that Lund has disappointed me is that the weather is exactly like Vancouver: rain.

"You should have gone farther north then. Did you do any research before you came here?" Sally says.

"I did a ton of research," I reply. But all of my weather concerns were wardrobe-related.

We pause to look at some crazy, handmade felt animals. My sister might like the cat one, so I buy it for her. I put it into my environmentally-approved tote bag with the botanical soaps I got for my mother, the knit caps for my dad and brother, and local chocolates for my aunt.

"Are you getting Gabe a gift?" Sally asks.

"Yeah. I already ordered a funny goalie t-shirt." It's a kind of a joke gift, but I think that's the right tone. Gabe remains elusive in a very basic way, so I'm trying hard not to be *that* girlfriend. Anyway, I'm leaving in a week. Now is not the time to get serious.

We stop to get hot drinks and then continue to shop. Sally has bought nothing so far. Apparently she'll be doing all her shopping at Marks & Sparks when she gets home.

"Do you always get everything you want?" Sally's words are visible in the chill evening air.

I shake my head. "No, I have no clean socks. I missed my laundry time *again*. I thought Maja's head was going to explode when I tried to do a wash later."

Sally waves that away. "I mean everything important." She begins ticking things off on her fingers. "You decide— for reasons I cannot fathom—that you want Gabriel. And thanks to me, you get your leg over."

When I start to protest, she interrupts. "Let me finish, Lil. Then when Gabe gives you the post-shag brush-off, and I explain the facts of Swedish dating life to you, you're all sad and dejected... for about ten seconds. Next time I see you two, you're looking all loved up and blissful."

I'm not sure if it's the cold air or thinking about kissing Gabe, but my whole body is tingling now. "We skipped the usual stuff because I'm on exchange. Besides, this is how we date back home."

She's not even listening to my protests. Sally-on-a-roll is a bulldozer. "But of all the magic you've performed, the biggest trick is that Gabriel is now the perfect boyfriend.

A flowers, poetry, cover-you-with-his-umbrella kind of boyfriend. That sour statue of a man is now sweet and adorable. How in hell did that happen?"

I laugh. This is Sally's real beef. She thought that he was a jerk, and I turned out to be the better judge of character. "He's kind, I told you that." For a tall, hunky Swede, Gabe is surprisingly like an old-fashioned grandmother. He likes to look out for me.

"He only opens his mouth to insult people. How you discerned kindness from that is beyond me." Sally snorts.

Gabe has a serious exterior, but he's a good person. He sounds rude because he's honest and abrupt. But his honesty is one the best things about him. I don't have to waste time trying to figure out what he really wants. And underneath the surface, he yearned for more connection. That was something I could see in him right from the start. He was shy. And now that we're past that, he is the sweetest boyfriend.

Sally continues to shake her head. "Maybe I should get you to pick my next boyfriend."

"Robin Bergström," I reply with zero hesitation.

She raises a penciled eyebrow. "Why him? I've already ridden that pony."

"You two fit well together. You're opposites, but in a good way. He's easy-going and optimistic."

"Whereas I'm a cynical cow?" Sally demands.

"He's also sane," I add, and we both giggle. But I can easily see Sally and Robin together, and I'm sure I'm right. "Seriously, think about it."

I wonder if she'll take my advice. Just one more thing I'll miss when I leave Lund. I've already bargained with my parents to extend my time here: I'm going to spend

Christmas with my Aunt Karin in Malmö, but I leave right after that.

"I don't want to leave," I tell Sally. She's going home before Christmas of course, but then the lucky thing will be back for next term here. "I can't bear thinking of you guys here having fun while I'm stuck back in Vancouver."

"Stuck? You're the one who's all 'Mountains, ocean, natural beauty, blah, blah, blah.'" Is that a trick to get me to visit?"

I laugh. "It is wonderful. I only wish that I could magically transport all my friends from here back there."

"Were you unhappy back home?" Sally asks me. She's alarmingly perceptive at times.

"No. I have a great family and good friends too. It's just that in Lund, I've been able to really relax and be myself." It's hard to explain without a ton of background, but in Vancouver, I do play a bit of a role.

"That must be tough. You're not exactly the model of restraint," Sally says.

I laugh, and Sally joins in.

"Hey, would you like to come to a hockey game with me?" I ask.

"Not really. Isn't it all fighting?"

"No, of course not. Besides, Johan and Gabe are playing."

"Gabe is playing? Well, of course I'll go then." Sally punctuates her sarcasm with a dramatic eye roll. "Actually now that he's the perfect boyfriend, I'm planning on shagging him once you're gone. Does that insane ability to do the splits translate into a sex position?"

"Sally!" I can only manage one indignant word of protest. Thinking about Gabe dating anyone else is a kick in the stomach. I know we're going to break up, but it's so painful that I've been a complete ostrich.

"Lil, you numpty. Gabe only has eyes for you. He'll be a complete Heathcliff, pining on the moors once you're gone."

I can't help smiling. "Do you think so?" Gabe never mentions the future. And while he does pay me the sweetest compliments, we've never even gotten close to the L-word.

"So, when do these ice gladiators throw down?"

"Friday night."

Sally shakes her head. "Nope. That's the last night I'm here. I'm going to be out drinking and carousing."

"Please. You can do both, we'll go to the game first and then go out."

"The things I do for you, Lil," Sally complains.

I swirl around and hug her. "I'm going to miss you too, Sally."

She extricates herself from my arms. Luckily she doesn't notice the tiny bit of cider I spilled on her. "Ugh. I will not miss all that Canadian hugging though."

"You will," I say. But I'm almost tearful imagining everyone going on with their lives and having fun while I'm not here. And when it comes to leaving Gabe, I'm the little girl humming with her fingers in her ears. I'm pretending it's not going to happen.

16

NAME OF THE GAME

LILY

"HOCKEY IS the most boring game on the planet. Give me a little footy anytime. Easier to follow, and you can see how hot the guys are," Sally says as we settle into the almost empty arena.

I ignore her complaining. It's her first game, and once she sees how fast and exciting it is, she'll change her mind. I pull my turtleneck over my nose. "It's cold here."

"Yes. That may be on account of all the ice." Sally is wearing a fur-trimmed parka. I was president of the animal rights club at my high school, but now I'm too chicken to challenge Sally on whether that trim is real or faux.

"We had to come. It's the first time Gabe's ever invited us to see him play," I tell Sally. Well, *invited* may be too strong a word as I practically had to torture him to get the game time. Maybe I should have tried withholding sex, but that would have been a worse punishment for me than Gabe.

Robin comes over and joins us.

"*Hej, hej.*" He sits beside Sally, and they exchange a very casual kiss. Sally told me he's a fabulous lover who went down on her for ages, which makes me blush whenever I look at Robin's mouth.

"Have you seen Gabe play before?" I ask Robin, keeping my eyes glued to the ice.

He nods. "Ja, we played together as kids. But he never mentions hockey now. I am surprised he invited you."

"I insisted," I reply. Maybe he's a terrible player, which is why he didn't want me to come. My perfect Swedish boyfriend may have flaws after all.

The Zamboni finishes its work, and the players skate out. Gabe is gigantic with his skates on. His team wears red jerseys with some kind of logo. It might be an advertisement, but I can't read it. Living here is humbling since I miss half of everything that's going on.

"Is that them? *Hej*, Gabriel. *Hej*, Johan." Sally stands and waves both arms. It's hardly necessary since there are so few people here. Johan explained to me that it's some kind of make-up game, which is why it's happening so late in the term.

Johan waves. Gabe raises his stick in the air. Then he pulls down the front of his helmet and skates into the goal, dumping his water bottle on top of the net.

The game starts and within ten minutes, two things became clear:

1. Gabe's team is terrible.
2. Gabe is very good.

He's the only thing keeping them in the game. The

yellow team comes in waves, shooting from all angles, and Gabe makes stop after stop.

"Why are the teams so unbalanced?" I ask Robin.

He shrugs. "Some players have already gone home for the holidays."

"Still, the yellow team is much better," I point out. The whole game has been played in the red team's end.

"They are the top in the league. But Gabriel is the equalizer."

Still, Gabe can't score goals, so the best they can do is tie. "Maybe he should be playing at a higher level then."

Robin laughs. "Ja. Talk to Gabriel. He dropped out of competitive hockey years ago."

"If I played as well as Gabriel does, I'd invite the whole world to come to my games," Sally declares.

"What do you think of hockey so far?" I ask her.

"I'd like a goal so we could stand up and cheer. Anything to warm up. Can we sing a song while the game is going on?" Her eyes widen as she looks behind me.

"Hi Lily." The familiar low tones of… my father!

I turn in total shock. Is there a law that the moment I enter a Swedish hockey arena, my father magically appears? I jump up and hug him. There's a surge of pure joy. I missed him, but I didn't know how much until this very moment.

"Oh my God. What are you doing here?" I kiss him on both cheeks, and he envelops me in an enormous hug. My dad's hugs are the best.

"I wanted to surprise you," he says.

"Whoa, you sure did. I can't believe this. Did you come just to see me?"

"Yes and no. Chris was complaining that his team

didn't have its own scouts to watch players at the World Juniors, so I volunteered. But it was really an excuse to see you." Chris Luczak is my dad's best friend and works in hockey management. It's all making sense now.

"How did you find me at the rink?" We sit down, and I wrap my arm through his. I can't believe he's here.

"One of the girls at your residence told me. I drove straight here from the airport."

Sally leans over me and introduces herself.

"Oh sorry. Sally, Robin, this is my father."

"Jesper," he says, shaking both their hands.

Robin gives his head a dramatic shake. "*Oj!* Jesper. Jesper Larson? Lily, you never told me who your father is."

"Um, you never asked me." I examine my boots closely. My personal house of cards is about to collapse.

Sally notices Robin's over the top reaction and turns to my dad. "What? Are you from ABBA, or something?"

"I played a little hockey." If you look up modest in the dictionary, my dad's photo will be there.

But Robin isn't done. "A little hockey? He is the greatest hockey player ever to come out of Malmö. He was captain of the Vancouver Millionaires. He won the Norris Trophy."

Not that this means anything to non-hockey fan Sally. But Robin's fanboy act is enough to convince her that my dad is a big deal, and she shoots me a you've-got-a-lot-of-explaining-to-do look.

"He's probably the best Swedish hockey player ever," Robin adds, since his previous compliments haven't gotten any response from my embarrassed father.

"Foppa might have something to say about that," I chime in.

"Not a big deal? It's Jesper Larson!" Johan scoffs. "Wait. I remember I told you how much I admire him. You didn't say a word. Why not?"

I don't know what to say. I'm not ashamed of who I am, but I really wanted to be accepted for myself. This exchange was a test for me.

And I almost made it through the whole semester without anyone knowing, but now Robin and Johan will broadcast this news to everyone. People will be more interested because I haven't said anything. Damn.

Gabe reaches out and takes my hand in his large warm one. He squeezes firmly. "Guys, shut up. It's clear that Lily wants her privacy. So don't go talking everywhere."

I feel better instantly, but Johan still looks forlorn.

"I'm sorry, Johan. I'll get you an autographed something, okay?"

"Okay. Thank you so much, Lily." I can tell by the tone of his voice, he's already treating me differently. Being nicer, just in case.

We stop outside at the bike rack.

"I have my bike here. I'll take my gear home and meet you guys after," Gabe says.

"What? You brought your goalie gear on your bike?" Everyone rides bikes here, and nobody drives. Still, I can't believe that Gabe brought his huge goalie bag on a bike. And now it's snowing.

"Ja. I built this rack to hold it." He motions towards a metal contraption on his basic black bike.

"Look, why don't you put your gear in my room. It's closer and you can pick it up after."

"Okay," he agrees.

"We'll meet you two there then," Robin says.

"Wait," Sally says. "I want to say goodbye to Lily."

"What do you mean? I'll see you soon," I reply.

"Bollocks. Once you two are alone in your room, I know exactly what's going down."

Sally is hilarious. Although she is going home tomorrow, I'm the only one leaving for good. I hug her, and we all part.

17

SPARKLE LIKE DIAMONDS

GABE

WE WALK to Lily's residence. It's deserted along the pathways because most people have gone home for Christmas.

"You're a really good goalie," she says.

"*Tack*." But I'm not as good as I used to be. As her father said, I should be playing at a higher level, but there are too many games and practices. I play as a substitute goalie when I have time. And right now, Lily takes up any extra free time.

"Do you enjoy playing?" she asks.

"Yes. It's a place where my mind can focus completely." Hockey is an escape for me, and the familiar sensations of the arena instantly centre me.

Thankfully, she doesn't ask the next question: why don't you play more hockey? Lily is curious, but she never pushes me. Tonight I understand why.

It's odd to find out that Lily's father is Jesper Larson. I'm not sure if it explains more about her or less. It's odd that we know so little and yet we know each other's personalities so well.

"Thank you for not making a big deal about who my father is."

"It doesn't change who you are," I reply.

Lily sighs. "It does though. Everyone treats me differently once they know. You saw Johan and Robin."

She's right. And I do feel different, but not in the way she thinks. Her famous father doesn't matter to me, but seeing their warm relationship and hearing them speak of love so freely moved me. Lily's life is full of good things. And for the past few months, I too have been warmed by her golden halo. But that is almost over.

We get to Lily's floor. The whole residence is oddly quiet and empty.

"Creepy, right? It's like we're in a horror movie." Her smile is lopsided and teasing. "Two college students sneak away to an empty dorm to make out. But just when they're going to do it, out pops this weirdo in a goalie mask with a chainsaw, and—rrrraaawrrrrr—they're hamburger." She dissolves into crazy laughter.

"That was a chainsaw noise? It sounded more like a tiger with a sore throat." I ponder whether making love to Lily would be worth death by chainsaw dissection. Likely yes.

"I should have my Canadian citizenship revoked because Lumberjack is my middle name. Besides, I've already got my weirdo in a goalie mask." She squeezes my hand, and I tickle her side in return.

There are various Post-its stuck to her door, saying good-bye and promising to keep in touch.

"My fan club," Lily says, sweeping all the notes off and stuffing them in her purse. "This is what happens when I stay out on the last day."

There's also an envelope shoved under her door. Lily peeks inside and her cheeks flush.

"What's that?" I ask. But I'm pretty sure I know the answer already. There's a Czech exchange student who has a big crush on Lily. I feel both kinship and disdain for him.

"It's nothing." She tosses it into the garbage.

Her room is in an upheaval. Her many clothes are piled on every surface. She's taken down all the posters from the walls. Her bed is still nicely made, with its bright linens and pillows, but there are piles upon it. A sense of melancholy comes over me. We have spent so much pleasurable time in her cozy room, and now it looks like every other dorm.

She shoves some of the clothes aside and sits down, arranging pillows and then leaning against the wall. I sit in her chair.

"I found a bottle of vodka in my drawer. Do you want to pre-party before we go the club?" she asks.

"Nej." I'm not going to be drinking much tonight. Tomorrow is Christmas Eve, and I'll need all my energy to get through the day.

My hockey bag stinks, and I apologize.

Lily laughs. "It's not a big deal. I'm used to it."

Then a shadow falls across her face. Her expression reminds me of the first day I saw her: lost and forlorn. I've not seen this expression since we've been together. Have I made Lily happier?

"Lund was a chance for me to be me. Not someone's daughter. Is that dumb?"

"Nothing you do is dumb," I reply.

"It is dumb to go to the one place where everyone knows who he is. If I did an exchange in Australia, I wouldn't have to hide anything."

"Did you have bad experiences?"

"Am I still showing the psychic scars?" Lily jokes, but she's upset. She jumps up from the bed and weaves through the jumbled room. "The first time, I was about ten. I overheard my two best friends saying their dads made them hang out with me. That way their dads could get to know mine. He was still playing then."

She throws clothes into an open suitcase with violence. "And that was only the beginning. Of course, it's better now that my dad doesn't play anymore, but I'm still choosy about who I hang out with."

I stand and take her in my arms. I hug her tightly and feel her tension dissolving. She gives me a brave smile. "It's been much easier here. I have such nice friends."

I smile back at her. "Come. Sit with me."

We make a nest among the clothing piles on her bed. I keep an arm around Lily, and she puts her head on my chest. Silken strands of hair tickle my chin, and I kiss the tip of her ear. Is there a place on Lily's body I haven't kissed yet? This is my last chance.

"Why did you choose Lund?" I ask.

"Well, I looked at Uppsala too, but my mother was so worried about me going far away, that we decided on

Lund. My aunt lives in Malmö, so I can call her in case of emergency." Lily shakes her head. "My mother is nuts."

She says that with affection though, in a natural way that she couldn't have if I had told her about my mother. Everyone who knows my situation is very careful around me. I don't like feeling excluded in that way.

Lily moves around so she can see my face. "Can you imagine if I had gone to Uppsala? We would never have met."

"You would meet someone else. You keep saying how good-looking Swedish men are."

Her mouth drops open in mock surprise. "Gabe! Is that what you think? That I'd go out with any Swedish guy?"

I smile. "Well, perhaps I'm the only one who can tolerate you."

She shoves me. She's quite strong and almost topples me off the bed. "I'll have you know I had plenty of chances to date other Swedish guys."

I'm certain of that. Among the many things we haven't discussed are her ex-boyfriends, but I'm sure there are many. Who could resist Lily?

"Would it be okay with you if we don't go out tonight?" She cuddles back into me. "This is our last chance to be alone together."

"It's what I prefer too."

She raises her beautiful face. I kiss her, completely aware that it's all ending soon. I relish the feeling of Lily's soft body next to mine. I run my hand over her breasts, then lift her sweater to reveal pale skin. Tonight's underwear is another surprise: her bra is sheer with sparkly flowers covering her nipples. I poke one flower with my forefinger and it prickles.

"Ah, *paljetter*," I say.

"Is that the word for sequins?" Lily asks me.

"I guess. Is this designer underwear?" For some reason, Eva's remark has come back to me. I rest my hand on Lily's bare stomach, and her soft skin feels electric.

"Sort of. I order all my stuff from a company in Cali: For Love and Lemons. Weird name, right?" She giggles. "I do silly things to make myself feel unique."

"But you are already unique." Lily is like no one I have ever known. Her joy, her humour, her generosity, her beauty, they all combine to make someone so special. And more than that, someone who complements me—who makes me whole.

"Am I? Or am I unique because I'm a Canadian in Sweden?"

I watch her expressive face to see if she is really as melancholy as she sounds. "You have the most beautiful soul. Anywhere."

Lily raises herself to kiss me on the nose. "How do you always know the right thing to say to me?"

Then she stretches out full length on the bed, knocking her clothing piles to the floor. I unzip her jeans and pull them off. Her tiny thong has a flower as well. When I touch the flower, Lily giggles. I stand and pull off my clothes. I pile them beside hers: our two outer selves side-by-side like our real selves.

She raises herself on her elbows to watch me. Her lingerie sparkles in the low light, and I position myself between her legs. I run my finger over the warm silk of her tiny panties. Lily lets out a guttural moan and I rub harder in response. Then I pull off her underwear, lower my head, and raise her knees. The earthy scent of Lily stiffens my cock. My tongue probes at her pink folds, and she raises herself to meet my mouth.

"Oh yeah," she breathes. Her low voice is almost as potent an aphrodisiac as her scent. My cock hardens as I hear her react to the touch of my mouth on her clit. I form my tongue into a point and make the flicking motion she likes. Soon, she's arching her back and pushing herself onto my mouth. When her body freezes, she's coming. We know each other's bodies so well.

"God. That felt great." Lily melts into the bed. She's still wearing her sparkly bra. It looks kind of sexy, so I don't take it off. Instead I push the cups aside and free her breasts. Lily's nipples are already hard and pointing up. I gently pluck at them until they stiffen even more.

She opens her eyes and reaches up to pull me down for a kiss. "My turn. I want to taste your delicious cock."

My face flushes. Lily's openness about sex is startling, but most enjoyable. She rolls on top of me and moves down my body. The next thing I feel is Lily's hot mouth enveloping my cock. I lie back and feel it all. I have no idea exactly what she does with her tongue and hands, all I know how good it feels.

"Stop, Lily," I finally groan before I come in her supremely talented mouth.

She wipes off her mouth with the back of her hand and smiles at me. "Aww, you can come if you want."

"Nej. Not tonight." This is our last night, and I want face-to-face sex. I roll away from her and open the drawer where we keep our condoms. Lily's room has become our haven. There's a shard of unhappiness, as I remember all the times we've made love in this room and now this is the last.

I roll on a condom, sit on the edge of the bed, and pull Lily over.

"Oh, this way. I like it this way." Lily straddles my lap and lowers herself onto my cock. Fuck, she feels so good. I trace the side of her soft cheek with my hand and then kiss her beautiful face. We keep kissing as my painfully hard cock rocks in and out of her.

Lily puts her hands on my chest and pushes me down onto the bed. I manage not to slip out of her, and she rides me with erratic strokes. We rock our bodies in slow unison, and the speed feels achingly good. Lily's eyes are closed, and her pale lips part to release panting breaths. I move her knees apart until I'm even deeper.

"Yes," she gasps. "Like that."

My hands play over her body, along her arms, tweaking her hard little nipples, tickling her stomach, and caressing her legs. She responds to every touch; her soft flesh seems to quiver and rise to meet my hands.

"Gabe." My name sounds tender and intimate from her lips. She touches my soul.

Sensations are building in my cock, and I can't hold back much longer. Yet I never want this to stop. When I look down, past her trimmed pussy hair, I can see her tiny clit glowing like a bright pink rose. I rub her there with gentle circles until her eyes squeeze shut and she cries out.

"Yes, yes, yes." Lily is louder tonight, freed by the lack of neighbours to really let loose. "Unnnhhh."

She wriggles on my aching cock, and I give in and stop holding back my own orgasm. My release feels incredible.

Lily collapses onto me, and we remain tangled together. The room is warm, but I pull the covers up to keep her cozy. I'm falling asleep, when I feel something wet on my arm. I open my eyes. She is staring at me and crying.

"Ah, Lily, what's wrong?"

She sniffs. "This is our last time here. I'm so sad."

"I'm sad too."

"You always look sad," she says. "You smile less than anyone I know."

"I have resting sad face."

Lily finally smiles. "Was that a joke? Oh Gabe, I've converted you into Mr. Happy."

I smile back at her, but then she starts to cry again. I wrap my arms around her and squeeze her to me. Lily's emotions lie close to the surface.

Finally, her sobs turn to sniffs. She snuggles against my chest.

"Once I leave, I wonder when we'll see each other again?" Lily asks.

The answer to that question is difficult. If we do see each other again, it will never be the same. Our relationship is a matter of perfect timing. Even if she came back to visit next summer, she would have a new boyfriend by then. How could anyone resist her whirlwind?

"I don't know," I reply. "Maybe never."

"I hate your honesty. Why can't you say the polite thing?" Lily is silent for a while. I peek to see if she has fallen asleep but her eyes are wide open.

I interlace my hand with hers.

"There is this poem by Tranströmer. Two people are separated, but their thoughts rise up and meet—like watercolours blending together." To quote poetry now feels wrong. I curse myself for not being able to express my emotions as Lily does at a time when she needs comfort.

But Lily smiles. "That's beautiful, Gabe. So that's us, and we'll be together—no matter where we are."

She nestles into my side with a contented sigh and I hold her close. I have comforted her, but only because she reads my intent with generosity. She makes me feel a better man.

"Yes, we'll be together," I echo. I try to swallow, but my throat feels too narrow.

Lily will move on, but I will remain here, dreaming of her.

18

CHRISTMAS CRAZY

LILY

GABE LEAVES early in the morning, but he promises to visit me in Malmö. Still, it's wrenching to watch him go. My room is our sanctuary, and this is the end of all that. Once I'm alone, my tears leak out and drip randomly onto my packing. My luggage is sealed with a sob.

I'm squishing down my final suitcase when my dad arrives to pick me up. I've eradicated all traces that Gabe spent the night here except for the faint scent of eau de hockey bag. But after years of hockey change rooms, Dad's nose must be immune. He knows that I have sex, but we're both happier pretending I don't. Robin told me that parents here allow their teenagers to have their girlfriends and boyfriends sleepover at home. Clearly my father's not that Swedish.

"Did you have this much stuff at the beginning of the

year?" my dad asks after our third trip to the car. Spoken like a man who travels worldwide with only a carry-on.

"Well, some of it belongs to Aunt Karin. She's the one who helped me decorate the room when I got here." I didn't do a ton of shopping while I was here other than hitting H&M with Sally, so the clothes are all originally mine.

He grunts and finishes loading up the trunk. Everyone's gone but me, so there's nobody to say goodbye to. I shut the door on my little dorm room for the last time, and a few tears slide down my cheeks.

My dad reaches over and squeezes my shoulder. "You okay?"

"Yeah." It's the only word I can squeeze out. Everything I'm going to miss is jumbled up in me—hiking with Gabe, school, living in Sweden, confiding in Gabe, all my new friends, and making love to Gabe.

We drive along in silence. The places I know so well disappear, and I realize it's the first time I've been driven anywhere in months. Everyone walks, bikes, or buses. I don't even know if Gabe can drive. How can I leave Lund when I don't even know this simple fact?

Then I begin to cry for real. Tears stream down my face and slide over my down jacket like tiny liquid skiers. I fumble for a tissue but my purse is too stuffed with all my crap to find a thing. I end up wiping tears and, euw, snot away with my mittens.

My dad totally panics. "Are you all right? Do you want me to stop?"

We're in the middle of a tricky roundabout as he asks this, so no.

"I'm fine," I sob. I take a series of heaving breaths that make me sound like an asthmatic turtle.

"Sorry," I tell my dad who has been driving in concerned silence. You'd think after living with my mother and me for so many years, he'd be used to tears, but they still get him every time.

"Is this about leaving?" he asks me.

One last sniffle, and I'm done. "Well, I love Sweden, but you know Gabe—the goalie from last night? I'm going out with him."

My dad nods. He knew, of course he knew. I'm the worst at hiding how I feel about anyone.

"Wasn't he an amazing goalie? I'd never seen him play before last night."

"Mmm," is all he says. No matter how much I like Gabe, my dad's hockey judgement will not be influenced.

But I know hockey too, and I know what I saw. Gabe is a talented goalie. It occurs to me that my father might have gone through exactly what I'm experiencing now.

"Did you have a girlfriend when you left Sweden?" I ask.

My father chuckles. "No, I was only sixteen then. All I thought about was hockey."

"So, Mom was your first girlfriend?" That's the family lore, but I've never heard my dad's side. My parents started dating when my dad played junior hockey in Kelowna.

"Well, kind of." He concentrates on the road. My dad is very honest, so I interpret this to mean he did date other women. And he doesn't want to discuss his dating past with his daughter. I am A-okay with that.

"Was it hard dating Canadian girls, you know, with all the cultural differences?"

He considers this. "Well, perhaps. But it was also easier. I could sit back and observe people."

I nod. "Yeah. I know exactly what you mean. Here I don't always understand what people are saying, so I look for other clues."

We ride along in silence for a few minutes.

"How did you know that Mom was the right person?" They got married when they were only a couple of years older than me.

"Your mother has always been one of the kindest, most nurturing people I've ever known. That was clear from the moment I met her."

What a weird role reversal—Gabe is also kind and nurturing. He is exactly what I needed being alone here in Sweden. Yet what I feel for Gabe is also more serious and real than any other guy I've dated. We're synced in a way that's so comfortable.

I finally locate a tissue and blow my nose loudly. Since Dad hates discussing relationship stuff—particularly mine —this car ride must be torture. I try to switch to a neutral topic.

"You know what's good? The transportation system here. You don't have to have a car, and everything is close."

Dad nods. "Sweden is very environmentally-minded."

And we discuss environmental policy for the rest of the ride. Frankly, I'm glad to have a chance to regain my emotional equilibrium.

When we arrive at Aunt Karin's place, I'm almost back to normal. There's still a hollow feeling inside me, but I'm also excited to experience my first Swedish Christmas. And I know Aunt Karin will throw an amazing party.

Sure enough, the moment we walk in the door, we are smacked in the face with the spirit of Christmas. Her spacious condo is decorated with evergreen boughs, red pattern fabrics, and candles flickering in every corner of the room. There's a Charlie Brown Christmas tree with homey decorations hanging from it. The whole place smells of cedar and gingerbread.

Her place always looks incredible because Aunt Karin is the Martha Stewart of Malmö. Literally. She has a life-style store, and that's how I scored all the great linens for my residence room.

"Welcome, Lily. I've missed you." My aunt embraces me. I've seen her every couple of weeks since I moved here, but the last month has been hectic with exams and leaving, so I've missed our regular dinners. But she's busy too and never guilts me about not seeing her.

"Is that Lily?" a familiar voice calls out.

"*Farmor!*" I run to hug my grandmother. "I didn't know you were going to be here." She squeezes me tightly. When I was little and we visited my dad's family, I thought *farmor* was the tallest woman in the world. But now we're the same height. Her blonde hair is silvery, but she's as vital as ever.

"*God jul, älskling.* Ja, when I heard that you and my son were coming for Christmas, you couldn't have kept me away."

"This is so great. But where is *farfar?*"

"That man, he's so set in his ways. He won't leave the house. Thought it was too much fuss and too expensive to take the train at Christmas." We settle down on the couch together. She squeezes my hand. "Never marry a man from Småland."

"I won't," I assure her. I wonder if she has any prejudices about guys from Lund. "It's so sad to think of *farfar* all alone at Christmas."

Aunt Karin hands me a warm cup of *glögg*. "He won't even notice. Some men enjoy solitude."

I take a small sip of the mulled wine. Aunt Karin's version is very strong. Then a revelation hits me. Gabe reminds me of my grandfather. *Farfar* is a man of few words, who is quite grumpy on the surface. But underneath, he's a sweetheart. He always insisted on taking us kids out for *lördagsgodis*, Saturday treat day. And he would pile extra candies in our baskets in the shop and enjoy the treats along with us. Maybe that's why I kept insisting to Sally that Gabe was really nice under the surface. And I was right.

"Have you been crying?" my grandmother asks.

My eyes must still be red. "I'm upset about leaving Sweden."

Farmor examines my face closely. She is scary-smart and not someone you can ever lie to. "Sweden or someone in Sweden?"

"Both. I have a boyfriend here. Gabriel Olsson." Even saying his name makes me feel a little sad.

Before *farmor* can launch into relationship questions, my dad joins us. He's got a cup of *glögg* too. "I've invited Gunnar Lundström for dinner," he tells Aunt Karin.

"Who's that?" I ask.

"He's a hockey executive here. He's going to update me on players."

Farmor begins speaking to my father in Swedish. She

says he's losing his mother tongue and he must practice. And she's complaining that he's not staying here long enough.

I turn to my aunt. "There's lot of food for the *julbord*, right?" I don't even have to ask. Aunt Karin could stage a formal dinner for twenty at the drop of a hat. There's already an incredible amount of food on her dining table, and it's not even time for our lunch smörgåsbord. And there will be supper later. "Could I invite Gabe over?"

"Nej." My aunt sounds shocked. "Christmas Eve is for families. Gunnar is all alone, so he is welcome, but your friend has a family, right?"

I nod. But Gabe has never mentioned his family, except to say his parents are divorced. Again, I realize there's so much I still don't know about Gabe, and now it's too late.

"Invite your friend another time. Tomorrow or the next day," *farmor* suggests. She can scold my dad and listen to our conversation at the same time.

"Okay, I will."

Although we visited my dad's family every year when I was young, that was always in the summer because of hockey. I'm so excited to spend Christmas here, and I can already see that everything's different. There's excitement and expectation in my aunt's usual calm home.

Aunt Karin still has some preparation to do, so I help her in the kitchen while Dad and *farmor* continue to talk. It's funny to see my father being lectured by his mom.

"Is there something you can't wait to eat at home?" Aunt Karin asks me.

I shake my head. Ordinarily at this time on a weekday, I'd be meeting Gabe for *fika*. "I wish I could stay here."

She reaches for a jar of pickled herring. There are

multiple jars labelled with the different flavourings she's used, and they are a somber rainbow all lined up. "Will it be Sweden you miss or Gabe?"

"Both," I confess. I've already told Aunt Karin all about Gabe at our dinners together. It's easy to confide in her because she's very relaxed. She's so busy and successful that she doesn't worry about me. She's the opposite of my mother, who is overly interested in my life.

My aunt gently squeezes my shoulder. "You must come back. You're always welcome to stay with me."

Our guests begin to arrive in the early afternoon. My father's friend is first.

"Gunnar, this is my daughter."

Gunnar shakes my hand. He's tall and stocky with dark hair. "Good to meet you. Your father and I played hockey together—way back."

They sit in the main room, and I join them.

"Gunnar is giving me background on some of the players I'll be seeing at the tournament."

"What do you do in hockey?" I ask him.

"Scouting and player development here in Malmö."

"I went with Lily to her friend's game last night," my father says. "He was quite good. Gabriel Olsson."

"Ah, the goalie," Gunnar said.

"You know him?" my father asks in surprise.

Gunnar nods. "At one time he was a prospect here, he played at the highest level. But then he dropped out."

"Why?" my father asks.

"I'm not sure, exactly." Gunnar's face creases as he tries to remember. "He left suddenly. Went down a level or two, so he didn't quit hockey. There's guys like that, who can't take the pressure of competitive leagues."

"He still looks really good," my father says. "He's stopping everything. But it's only low level, so who knows."

"How come you're scouting for a minor league team and not the NHL?" Gunnar asked.

Dad shrugs. "This is not my real job. Chris Luczak's running the Vancouver Vice now, and he asked me to do him this favour. I'm not even getting paid."

His friend snorts. "Money is not a problem for you, I'm sure. You wanted an excuse to visit your beautiful daughter."

"I can't deny I missed her. Our whole family did." My father puts a hand on my shoulder. "When I found out she was going to stay here for Christmas too, this was a good chance to see her a little early."

"I'm fine, Dad," I scold him. "I would have been home in a few days anyway."

"But now we'll get to fly home together." He drapes an arm over my shoulder and smiles at me.

I can't help beaming back. When he played hockey, he was away so much that having time alone with my father was like gold. It's still a treasure. In fact, having Christmas with his side of the family is a rare treat. I only wish there was room for one more person at the *julbord*.

19

SWEET SORROW

GABRIEL

BREAKING up with Lily is taking an extraordinarily long time. While I'm very happy to continue seeing her, it is painful to have to keep parting this way. She cried when I left her room two days ago, which made me feel helpless and sad. Yet here I am on a train to Malmö.

Predictably, Lily's aunt lives in the trendiest neighbourhood of Malmö, Västra Hamn. In a matter of hours, I have gone from knowing nothing about Lily's family to meeting her famous father and now her extended family.

The correct address turns out to be a building right by the water, and Lily's aunt lives on the top floor.

I knock on the door, and Lily throws it open.

"Gabe! Welcome." She gives me an enthusiastic hug. She treats absences of hours like they are years, and I can't resist her sweet affection. But right now, there are others waiting to meet me.

"*God dag*. Karin Larson." Lily's aunt holds out her hand. She's a tall woman with blonde hair pinned back. She looks a little like Lily but more stern.

"*Hej*, Karin." I hand her a jar of preserves. "Thank you for inviting me to lunch."

"Gabe, did you make that?" Lily asks. "He's an amazing cook. He baked these *kanelbullar* that looked professional!"

Karin smiles. "You see, Gabriel, to Canadian women, men being able to cook is quite miraculous. Here, perhaps it's expected."

I nod. "Your home is lovely." The place is spacious yet well lit and cozy. I recognize the colourful fabrics that enhanced Lily's small dorm room.

"Of course, it's amazing, Aunt Karin runs Snowflake. Do you know her store?" Lily asks.

"Ja. My aunt's favourite store." Suddenly, Eva's words about Lily come back to me, calling her a rich bitch. Eva was wrong because Lily's beautiful linens were a gift. But Eva was also right, since Jesper Larson made millions as a hockey player. Lily is accustomed to money.

We move into the main room, where Lily's father and an older woman are having coffee.

"Gabriel." He shakes my hand. "This is Lily's grandmother."

"Ava Lindgren-Larson," she says. I start at her familiar name.

"Like the child psychologist?" I ask.

She smiles at me. She is silver-haired with very upright posture. Her handshake is firm, and her gaze is searching. "Ja, that is me."

"My mother had your books," I say. I can remember

looking at them when I was young. They were about raising creative children, and the covers had geometric shapes on them. Clearly, Ava herself has raised two successful children.

"And did you turn out to be a creative adult?" she asks with a warm smile.

"Hmmm. Difficult to say."

I am not especially creative, but Ava must consider hockey an acceptable pursuit. However, I am not successful at hockey. One of her theories was to allow children to pursue in depth their interests. My mother was not a huge hockey supporter, so she encouraged me to combine sciences with hockey—the physics of puck movement or the psychology of games. My father enjoyed the games, although he complained that the goalie's father could never relax.

"Gabe reads poetry," Lily says. "He's very smart."

Lily should stop defending me in this way. I am an average person and not ashamed of this. She wants her family to like me, but they will make up their own minds in time.

We sit down for lunch. The food is excellent, and although Karin apologizes for serving leftovers, it's all delicious. The conversation veers between subjects and languages. Ava challenges her children and granddaughter to good-natured argument.

There's a marked contrast between this family and my own. While my mother was well, she enjoyed debate, but now there is mainly silence. Freja chats, but mostly about our days rather than issues.

The perfection of Lily's life strikes me. While I am interested to know more about her life, I feel an unexpected yearning for our bubble of isolation. Only a few days ago, we existed in a world of each other, school, and our friends.

"We had better get going to the arena," says Jesper. I rise up and automatically begin to take dishes to the kitchen. Lily does the same but declares, "You're making me look bad, Gabe."

Karin follows us to the kitchen. "It's clear that Gabriel has been raised right. What do your parents do?"

That question hangs in the air for slightly too long.

"Uh, my father works in shipping logistics. And my mother's specialty is biodiversity research." I craft my sentence carefully because I do not want to lie.

But Karin has already picked up on my hesitation and presses me no further. "Are you a big hockey fan?" she asks.

"Gabe's an amazing goalie," Lily brags. Again, I'm touched by her pride in me, but it's not warranted. After all, her father is a legendary hockey player. The chasm between us grows.

Ava asks me about my schooling. The whole family seems protective of Lily, and who can blame them?

I TAKE a deep breath before I enter Malmö Arena. I have been here many times of course, but not since I quit competitive hockey. What is the point in torturing myself with hypothetical scenarios when my life has taken a different direction? But I realize that avoidance isn't quite the same as being mentally strong. Normally, I would never attend the World Junior tournament. It's not only the hockey people that I'll meet, but the whole atmosphere. I miss playing real, important games. I miss having teammates who are equally committed to hockey. Most of all, I miss the test of the sport: pitting my skill and knowledge against opponents. Using all my senses to read clues, see plays develop, recognize the tells of each shooter. I miss being fully engaged in a moment and having that moment matter.

"C'mon, Gabe." The reason I do so many uncharacteristic things these days tugs on my arm.

We don't even need to have tickets. Being with Jesper Larson means that crowds part and doors open magically until we're in some executive suite high above the ice. But after some small talk, Lily's father decides he wants to get closer to ice level.

"Can't see anything from up there. Especially with everyone jawing at me," he grumbles as we make our way down a back staircase. I like Jesper, he's a very down-to-earth person—like Lily.

We end up in a cordoned-off area. I recognize a few of the men around him but their eyes pass over me. I inflated my self-importance when I avoided hockey. Nobody remembers me. There are empty seats nearby, so we slip into them.

"My dad forgets all about me once his old hockey buddies show up, so it's fantastic that you could come. Otherwise, I'd be totally bored."

"You'd make friends in no time."

She shakes her head. "Swedes don't talk to strangers, remember?"

The current game is between Denmark and Switzerland. The Danes are dominating the play but unable to score. Finally, with only two minutes left in the first period, they break through. The Swiss goalie is technically good, but the defensive structure in front of him is the real key.

Lily jumps up and cheers for Denmark, along with most of the crowd. Many have crossed the Øresund Bridge to attend.

"How do you decide who to cheer for?" I ask.

"Whoever has the cutest players," she teases me. She is so lovely. Her cheeks are rosy in the chilly air, and her face is animated. She is even happier since her father arrived.

"Your family is very accomplished," I say.

"Tell me about it. My younger sister draws, and she's Tumblr-famous. And get this, my little brother is already projected to play in the NHL. He's only twelve years old."

She doesn't sound jealous though, she sounds proud. Once again I am struck by the differences between our lives. Lily's is full of potential, and everyone around her succeeds.

"And then there's me." She laughs. "I'm not famous for anything."

"You are the most loved," I tell her. Because Lily is someone who draws people to her, from poor Jakub to jaded Sally and of course, me. She will have friends and affection wherever she goes.

Lily squeezes my hand. "Gabe, really? That's so sweet."

She leans against me and exhales. "You know, I think I love you too."

The language gap between us is suddenly vast. I meant love in the sense of belovedness. But before I can correct this, Jesper joins us.

"Ah, there you are. Are you enjoying the game?"

Lily nods. "It's good. I prefer an end-to-end game, but this is fine. And there's popcorn." She holds up the half-eaten box she made me get for her.

Jes laughs, then turns to me. "Listen, Gabriel, I've been talking to a few people who know you."

"Ahh?" I clear my throat. Of all the people I want to think well of me, Lily's father is near the top of the list. Has he heard that I'm a quitter? Someone who leaves his team in the lurch?

"Ja. Look, I'm not sure what's going on with you, but if you ever need advice or maybe an opportunity, I can set something up." He hands me a business card. I shove it in my pocket without even looking. I would never take the risk of disappointing him.

He turns to Lily. "I'm going to go out after the games with some old friends. Did you want to come?"

"No, Aunt Karin has something planned. And I want to spend more time with *farmor* before we leave tomorrow."

He nods. "Yes, that's a good idea. I won't be late."

After the Danes win, we decide to leave. Her father is so busy, we don't even bother with a goodbye.

"Are you going to call Dad?" Lily asks me once we're through the crowd and back outside.

I shrug. "I don't have time to play more hockey."

"But you should. You're so good," Lily says.

"Did you ask him to help me?" I ask. Initially I was flattered that he saw me play once and thought I was good enough to be at a higher level. But Lily's involvement makes more sense. He's doing it because she asked him to.

"Not really," she says, but I don't believe her.

"Thank you for whatever you did. But realistically, it's too late for me."

"You're only 22. He wouldn't offer unless he thought you had potential. And he likes to help people. My boyfriend in grade twelve was a good player, but he never got drafted by the Western Hockey League. Once my dad wrote to a few friends in Ontario, he got to play Junior A there and now he's doing really well."

I don't reply. It's too hard to explain how I can love hockey, yet not to want to pursue it.

"He's got contacts here," she continues. "You should get him to hook you up with a new team, one that deserves you."

I look back at the arena and recall the last time I played here. It was a shut out. Then I exhale. "I don't have time," I repeat.

"It's like you want to be miserable," Lily says.

"Let's not argue. You're leaving tomorrow." I want to treasure the last moments of our time together. They are golden jewels that I can take out in the dark moments.

Lily whirls in front of me and takes my hands in hers. "Look, Gabe, there's something I've been thinking about. We really don't have to break up. I know it's a crazy distance, but we can still see each other on Skype or Face-Time. And I get a week off in February, so I can visit. Then in the summer, I'll get a job here and we'll be together for months. Maybe I could even finish my university degree here!"

Her eyes sparkle with a hypnotic energy, the same force that brought me to this moment. For Lily, anything is possible. She knows how to inspire dreams and, for one shining moment, our future together seems possible. It's what I want more than anything. She's all that's bright and warm in my life. But it's wrong to tie her down to something that can never be. To someone like me. Our isolated world was perfect, but now reality is seeping in. Seeing Lily with her family makes me realize how different our futures are.

I shake my head. "It's not possible."

"Gabe, are you even considering what I'm saying?" Lily pleads.

I nod. I can only imagine the richness of Lily's life in Vancouver. She will soon be distracted by something—or someone—new, and we'll break up then. Whereas my life will revert to being what it was. "We're only delaying what is inevitable."

"Why are you so pessimistic? Maybe we will break up, but it doesn't have to be today." She presses her head against my chest and hugs me fiercely. "I don't want it to be today. We still—" Her voice breaks off in a sob.

"Ah, Lily, don't be miserable." I hold her tightly. The way our bodies fit together is the physical manifestation of how well our minds fit. I am wavering. Maybe it would be easier to break up little by little. We'll call each other nightly, then less often, and finally Lily's interest will trail off.

She steps back and takes my face in her hands. The softness of her suede gloves warms my cheeks in the cooling air. Her expression is solemn but determined. A tear has made a shiny path down her cheek, and I brush it away.

"What you said in the arena, you should say it properly now," she commands.

"What did I say?" I ask.

Lily kisses me. Her lips are soft and the pressure is gentle. "I love you, Gabriel Olsson."

My next line is from a movie script, but I've never lied to Lily and I'm not going to start now. "You misunderstood what I said earlier. I meant that you will be beloved, that people are always attracted to you."

Her eyes go wide and her mouth slack. "So, you don't... but how do you feel about me?"

How do I feel about Lily? She is fascinating. When we are together, every moment is new and interesting. When we are apart, I wonder what Lily is doing at that exact moment. I envy the people she is with. I like to think up excursions for us just to experience her pleasure. But all this is natural for people in such a new relationship.

I can't put these complex feelings into words, especially English. "I care a lot about you, Lily."

This is not enough for her, I can tell by her turned-down mouth and wide eyes. Her voice is barely a whisper. "And what about all that watercolour stuff you said the other night? Our spirits mingling. That was so beautiful."

I meant everything I said. I always mean what I say. But it's never enough for Lily—she wants everything, and she wants it immediately.

"Can't this be enough for you?" I ask her.

"What is *this*?" she asks.

"Our time together here." The perfection of all our moments, until now.

"It's because everything is so great that I want to keep things going." Lily puts her arms around my waist. "Gabe, what we have together is incredible. I can totally be myself with you. Even when I'm being a total flake, you have this way of centering me—making me feel I can be a better person."

She squeezes me closer. "It's so special. And I'm sure I make you happier too. Maybe you don't love me yet, but—"

Her confidence and optimism are almost enough. I falter for a moment, but I know the truth. It ends now or it ends in a month or two. But it always ends.

"Lily, we were perfect because our time together is finite. You'll go home and meet someone else. Someone who's better suited to your life."

She steps back from me. "Is that what you think of me? Because I fell for you so quickly, I'm a total ditz who falls in love with any cute guy that crosses her path. Because that is so wrong."

I shake my head. It's more that she's so desirable. Look at Jakub and the others; everyone is attracted to Lily. Besides, I can't be part of her future. It's really about me and my flaws.

Tears are running down her face, but she doesn't seem to notice them. Her expression is fierce and angry. "I thought you got me. But you don't know me at all."

"Lily…" I put my hands on her shoulders and open my mouth, but my mind is full of confused emotion. I'm not sure what I can say that won't make her angrier. And I've never wanted to hurt Lily, but I can't make promises when the future is so uncertain.

She scowls at me. "Why? Why can't we be together longer?"

Now everything I've kept from her makes a simple explanation impossible. If I were actually the person I've presented to Lily, why shouldn't we continue?

"I'm not the right person for you," I explain weakly.

"That's up to me to decide," says Lily. "Even being away from you for two days was so hard. If I leave Sweden now... and I don't know when I'll see you again... I can't..." She begins crying harder, and I pull her to me. I feel the shaking of her shoulders, and her sobs are visible in the cold night air.

I want to soak up her sadness, like felt absorbing sound. I'm used to bearing problems, but Lily is not.

She turns her glistening face to mine. "Don't you think we're worth fighting for? Worth giving it a try anyway?"

I close my eyes. Of course she is right. But she deserves more than I can offer. I shake my head.

Lily pushes my hands off her, breaking the physical bonds we share. "Okay, I'm done here. I'm only embarrassing myself now." Her voice is cold, but there's a tremor in it as she tamps down her emotions.

She looks down at the ground. "It was an exchange thing, right? Sally said I couldn't leave here without fucking a Swede, and I have."

The harshness of her words is so unlike Lily. She's trying to hurt me, and she does.

"There's so much I don't understand here, Gabe," she says. "I can't believe I fell in love with you."

Then she turns and walks rapidly away. I take one step to follow her and then stop. What could I offer her? All she wants is exactly what I want—for the two of us to go on forever. But it can't be.

As I watch her disappear into the transit station, the only sensation I feel is the cold. Everything warm in my life is dissolving.

20

CRASH LANDING

LILY

I LOOK out the window of the plane, sigh, and wipe away my dramatic single tear. Well, is it still a single tear if one falls every 60 seconds? Whatever, it's not full-blown crying in the business class section of KLM. Every minute takes me farther from Sweden—farther from everything I love.

I feel the total emptiness of breaking up with Gabe. Sure, we were scheduled to break up anyway, but the whole event was so messy. From the high of thinking he loved me and that we could stay together to the low of how cold he was when he refused to budge an inch from our original plans.

Luckily all my sighing and sniffling is going unnoticed by my dad, who is wearing an eye mask and power-napping his way through the flight. I manage a nap too, so by the time we land, I can pretend to be normal again. A broken heart isn't visible.

I walk into our house with a pasted-on happy face and go through a hug receiving line. I get squishy hugs from my grandparents, a reluctant hug from my sister Margie, and a painful squeeze from my little brother Alexander. Even our dog Sushi licks my face when I pick him up.

But the wettest greeting comes from my mother, who is crying with relief at my safe return from the dangerous wilds of Sweden.

"Oh, my baby's home," she sobs—even though I'm taller than her. "We missed you so much, Lily." Obviously, my crying genes come from her side of the family and not the stoic Larson side.

All this attention is not the worst thing in the world. I am happy to see my crazy family again, and I'm happy to be back home. Our family dinner is delicious even as I keep nodding off—almost imbedding my face in mashed potatoes.

"The best thing for jet lag is to stay up until your regular bedtime," my mom insists.

"Good thing my bedtime is—" I turn my dad's wrist over to read his watch. "Eight o'clock."

"Lily, you can't go to bed already. I haven't heard enough about your exchange yet."

"Mom, I promise, we can talk more tomorrow. Or the day after. I am home for months now," I say. This makes me sad. I looked forward to the exchange for so long, and now what do I have to look forward to?

Her eyes glisten, and she hugs me again. "Okay. We'll have a day out together. Maybe pedicures and lunch?"

"Yes, Mom." I give her a hug and a kiss. After a million

good nights, I finally make it to my room where I pass out on my bed without even undressing.

I wake up around midnight.

I'm wide, wide awake. There's no way I can go back to sleep. I pull out my phone, and there are many messages. One from Sally, one from Jakub, one from Beatriz, and one from Gabe.

Lily, I'm so sorry. I wish I could express myself better. I hope you are recovered now.

I delete his message—which sounds like something an aging aunt would write. Right now I'm putting everything with Gabe into a box that I'm shoving to the back of my brain. I'll deal with him once I have a little distance and it's not so painful. When I thought he loved me too, I was overjoyed. I really thought that what we had was very special. But he holds back so much of himself and that includes his love.

For now, I want to drift along in nothing world. My wounds are too raw to start poking at them. Maybe in a few days, after a good night's sleep, I can deal.

Ironically Gabe is the one person I most want to talk to. I'm used to unloading all my emotional crap on his broad shoulders. But I can't call Gabe to tell him what an a-hole Gabe has been. To prevent myself from doing something sentimental and stupid, I get up. After all, I'm already dressed even if I could use a shower.

I see a line of light from Margie's bedroom. It's no surprise that she's up, she's a total night owl. I knock softly on her door.

"Is that a burglar?" she asks in a normal voice.

"Yes, little girl. I've come to steal your anime collectables," I hiss into the door. Then I come in.

Margie's sitting at her desk drawing. She's always reading or drawing. She does a Tumblr cartoon that none of us are allowed to read. I suspect I'm a character in it.

Also, she's so quiet that everyone forgets she's even in the room. So when Alexander or I need to know anything, we ask her. If I need to ask permission for something big —like a weekend at my friend's cabin in Whistler, then I'll check with Margie first so I don't go barging in and ask my parents while they're upset or worried. She's the barometer of the house.

I plunk down on her bed. She swivels in her chair and opens up a book, but that's not a sign she wants me to leave. She feels more comfortable holding a book or a sketchpad. They're her armour.

"So, bring me up to speed on what's been going on." I pick up her Totoro stuffy and dance him on my stomach. The amazing thing about my sister is that you don't need to do any small talk or flattery to find out what she knows. She prefers you to come right out and ask. And she'll tell you what you want, as long as she likes you. We get along really well, despite being complete opposites.

"You can never go away again," Margie says. "Having half of Mom's attention almost killed me. She wanted me to go shopping and tell her all about my love life. Those are your jobs."

I laugh. It's crazy that my mother has never noticed how much Margie hates shopping. I'm not sure about the love life part. Margie didn't have a boyfriend when I left, but who knows now.

"She started every day wondering if you were okay. And she tried to read between the lines of the three emails you sent. Why didn't you add her to your Whats-App, so she could stay updated?"

"Seriously?" I'm still pretending I haven't seen my mother's Facebook friend request.

Margie smiles. "Well, I didn't tell her I could see you partying your way through Lund. Who's the old guy with the beard?"

"Gabe's only 22!" Then I realize that Margie is baiting me, and I throw Totoro at her. She throws him back, and I catch him one-handed.

"Were you going out with him?" she asks.

I swallow my sigh along with every other emotion that's welling up. "Yeah. But we broke up when I left." That's going to be my explanation: breaking up is only common sense. Then I can avoid the tsunami of unhappiness that goes along with knowing I wanted to keep going out with Gabe.

Unfortunately, Margie's antennae are highly tuned. "Is that a big deal? You usually don't date guys more than a few months anyway."

While this is true, it's history. I'm older, and I'm different now. What I feel for Gabe dwarfs my previous relationships.

I finally answer her with a deflection. "I don't want to talk about this."

She gives me a look—it's not exactly pity, but it's a mix of sympathy and curiosity. And then—thank you, Universe, for blessing me with a sensitive sister—she changes the subject.

"Not much happened here," Margie says. "Dad closed some big real estate deal. Mom got this wellness coach, and she's making us all drink electron-enhanced water. Alexander has a new therapist."

"Is he okay?" I wonder.

"Honestly? He needs to go to some school where you can get up and wander around every fifteen minutes. Sitting at a desk and listening is not for him. You don't have to medicate someone for having too much energy. He'd probably do well in a human hamster wheel."

"Who's the kid Alexander mentioned at dinner? The hockey player billet who's living with us?" I ask.

Margie's forehead creases. "Seb? He's not a kid."

"Oh yeah? I thought he was a teenager. Doesn't he hang out with Alexander?" I lie back and raise Totoro over my head. He looks back at me in surprise, but that's his normal expression.

"He's nineteen. That's only a year younger than you."

"When you're twenty, that's a lot." I look over at her. "You're not crushing on him, are you?"

"No, of course not. He's a bad boy, and I'm not self-destructive."

"He's a bad boy? What did he do?"

"The reason that Seb is living with us is because he got into trouble living on his own."

"What kind of trouble?"

"I don't know exactly. Mom doesn't even know. But Dad does, and he gave Seb a lecture when he got here. It was in Swedish, so I didn't understand most of it. My theory is that it had to do with sex. It must have been more than regular sex too, because otherwise what's the big deal?"

"Why sex and not drugs or something illegal?" I wonder.

Margie gives me a crooked smile. "He'll be back tomorrow. When you meet him, you can make your own guess."

"What's his full name?" I ask, pulling out my phone.

"Sebastian Söderlund."

I Google his name, but all I find are hockey stats. His personal record has been scrubbed clean.

"I already searched and found nothing," Margie says. Well, if the Internet Mastermind has already done it, there's no point in a mere mortal like me trying.

"He must be good if they're taking all this trouble with him."

"He's one of the leading scorers on the team, and he's going to make the NHL next season," she replies.

"Whoopee."

Margie nods in agreement. We've grown up surrounded by NHL players, so skill is something we take for granted.

"Girls like him," Margie adds. "He is cute, and he scores a lot of goals."

That's pretty much all you need to be popular in Canada. I squint down at the photo on my phone. He doesn't look completely hideous.

"How cute?" I wonder.

"Long blond hair. He's Scandi surfer-cute."

"Hmmm. The real mystery is what he did to get sentenced to live in our house."

"They say it's because he's Swedish and he needs to absorb the 'work ethic of a real NHL player.'" She's making air quotes, so I assume this is something my parents said.

Margie and I exchange significant looks. This guy must

have done something bad to get yanked out of an apartment on his own.

I snort-laugh. "Maybe he's into animals. We better hide Sushi and Mrs. Fluffernutter."

"Gross!" My sister is a huge animal lover. She peeks under the bed, which is our cat's usual hiding place and coos, "Don't listen to her, Mrs. Fluffernutter. She's a sicko."

"If a Swedish teenager comes at you, don't be afraid to use those claws," I call out. "Mawr means no."

My sister laughs. "I missed you, Lily."

We return to speculating about Seb. "How about crossdressing? That's the kind of thing that would drive a General Manager crazy."

"Not Chris though," Margie points out. I'd momentarily forgotten that Chris Luczak is in charge of Vice hockey and nominally Sebastian's boss. Chris is a pretty easy-going guy.

"Well, Chris wouldn't send us someone too horrible. Like a drug dealer. Or someone who's into under-aged blondes," I say.

"I'm not under-aged," Margie points out in a huff. "Besides, Seb would never go out with me. It's against the rules."

"If you mean the rules of common decency, then yes," I agree. Margie might be almost eighteen, but she looks and acts a lot younger. Right now, in her Angry Aggretsuko t-shirt and flamingo-printed pyjama pants, she could pass for fourteen. I've offered to give her make-up tips, but she always turns me down. Lots of people at school were shocked to find out we were even related.

"No, Dad told Seb that his daughters were completely off-limits."

"What? You heard him say that?" A flush of anger rises. "That's so old-fashioned and ridiculous."

"No, I heard him talking to Mom later on. Of course, it isn't really about me, it's about you, but you weren't even home yet."

"He has no right to say who I can and can't date," I say.

"Chill, Lil. It's not you personally; it's about the awkwardness of everything. We're all living like a family. You don't date your family."

I shake my head. I don't want to date this loser. But I'm an adult now, and everyone still treats me like a kid. I couldn't even fly home alone.

Ugh. My complaining is not really about my parents or my supposed level of maturity. It's about wishing I was still back in Lund where everything was so different and interesting. And where Gabe is.

21

STRANGERS IN THE NIGHT

Lily

WE HAVE a goodbye brunch for my grandparents, and then they're off. I'm still so jet-lagged that I defy my mother, crash in the afternoon, and don't wake up until the middle of the night. Having missed dinner, I'm starving.

I tiptoe down to the kitchen to make myself a snack. Our fridge is stuffed with delicious (free) food. Yum, yum, yum. I grab a yogurt tube, an apple, and some peanut butter for a sandwich. Swedish peanut butter tasted weird.

I eat the apple while I make my sandwich because I'm too hungry to wait. I put the sandwich on a plate and add chocolate chip cookies for garnish. Then I get myself a drink. I ignore my mother's bottles of electrified whatever and get a glass of delicious Vancouver tap water.

Click.

The lock in the side door turns. Then the door begins to open with excruciating slowness, like someone is sneaking in. Is this a burglar? A stalker? I duck behind the counter. Damn. I don't even have my phone. And my feet are bare.

Ugh. Why didn't the security alarm go off? One of the weird things about living with a hockey superstar is that while he played, my dad had legit stalkers, both male and female. We have a complex alarm system and locked gate to discourage trespassers. But nobody has tried to contact him in years. These days, if they want to meet him all they have to do is pretend to be interested in buying an office building.

I wait. Even my breathing sounds too loud. I hear the burglar's very light footsteps. At first he's moving away, and then he turns and comes towards me! I hear the click of a plate and realize he's eating my sandwich.

I peek cautiously around the island. I can see two large feet in grey socks with red trim. And skinny jeans. What kind of burglar takes off his shoes to come in? A Swedish burglar.

"Boo," I say.

He shrieks, and the plate hits the floor and smashes. I pop up from my hiding place, and he stares at me with wide blue eyes. He has messy blond hair and pale skin.

"Fuck! Why did you do that?" he asks. "I almost piss myself."

"Because you're eating my sandwich. Now you'll have to clean this up."

"You clean it up. You're the one who scared me." His strong Swedish accent makes me nostalgic for Lund. But it also feels weird, like Sweden has followed me here.

"I can't." I point to my bare feet. "I might cut myself. The broom is in the cupboard."

He grumbles but starts sweeping up.

Luckily, half the sandwich stayed on the countertop. I sit on a bar stool and eat the bitten half while he's working. He's graceful, and his long blond hair falls around his face as he looks down. He's Thor's teen brother.

"So, you must be—" My jet-lagged brain has completely forgotten his name. "Um, the billet guy."

"Ja." He finishes sweeping up and deposits the broken dish in the garbage. Luckily the noise we made hasn't woken anyone up. "You must be the famous Lily."

He comes closer, and I can smell alcohol on him.

"Are you old enough to drink?" I ask. My dad would not be happy that this guy is partying on his watch. Not that I'm going to tell.

"Of course, I'm nineteen. How old are you?" He sits down at the corner of the counter. His eyes are a deep sky blue, a darker blue than mine or Gabe's. He flips his long hair back. His look is Scandi surfer, exactly as Margie described.

"I'm twenty." Far older than you, Hockey Boy.

His hand darts out and steals one of my cookies. I let it go because there are more in the cookie jar.

"Sorry about your sandwich. Sometimes when I miss a meal, your mother leaves snacks out for me."

"That's very un-Swedish of her."

"*Jag vet*, my own mother would not do that. Did you like Sweden?"

"I loved it. I wish I was back there right now."

"Ja. I miss it too." His eyes widen again. "I mean, I

157

love it here, playing hockey and everything. But things are different."

"I know. You think that your world is the way things are. And then you find out things can be completely different somewhere else. It kind of blows your mind."

"Ja, ja, exactly. It's also tough." He looks sadder than a teenaged hockey phenom should. Hockey here must be more challenging than he anticipated.

He steals my remaining cookie.

"I should have brought you back some *kanelbullar*." I'm still going through Swedish cinnamon roll withdrawal. Well, it's really withdrawal from daily *fika* with Gabe, but I'm pretending it's all about the carbs.

"Sweet." His smile is broad and white. He's definitely cute with his round face and wide eyes. Cute in a boyish way, not like Gabe's polished looks. But I enjoy his voice: the up and down inflections of his Swedish accent.

"There are many things I want from home," he says.

"Get your mother to send you a care package," I reply.

"I told you, she's not that kind of mommy. She's a politician back home."

I laugh. "Ask your father then."

"Better idea. So, *kan du tala svenska?*"

"Nej. Well, *lite*." A little is how I describe my Swedish language skills. Otherwise people start talking a mile a minute.

His smile transforms into a smirk. *"Du är jävligt vacker."*

Really? I'm yanked back to earth. Cheesy Swedish pick-up lines are easy to translate because guys worldwide wear the same goofy expression when they use them. The exact face that Hockey Boy has on right now.

"Oh, shut up." Now I understand Margie's cryptic

comment. Whatever sin he committed was sexual because he's a horndog.

I catch him eyeing me and realize I'm in a tissue T and sleep shorts. Welcome to Lilyland where you meet horny adolescents in your own kitchen. Ugh. Now I'll have to get dressed and brush my hair for breakfast.

"You're very different from your sister," he observes. That's true enough. Our hair and colouring are the same, but that's it. Margie is artistic and introverted, and I'm not.

"You hardly know me," I point out. I snip off the top of the yogurt tube and squeeze some into my mouth. My taste buds protest. The yogurt was way better in Sweden.

He watches me sucking on the yogurt tube with a big grin. Honestly, it's like his skull is made of clear plastic and every bro thought is playing out. *You're sucking on something, which makes me imagine you sucking on my cock.* It's really, really too early—or too late—for this crap. I drop the tube. No eating bananas either.

"So, you come here often?" His stupid smirk makes me want to squeeze the rest of the yogurt into his face.

"Just stop. It's a kitchen, not some club. Or wherever you were partying."

"Wouldn't you like to know?" This guy is as mature as my twelve-year-old brother. All the good feelings from hearing his Swedish accent are gone, and I am totally turned off.

There's a noise behind us, and we both turn.

My father is standing there. He crosses his muscular arms. "What's going on here?"

"Uh, nothing," stammers Hockey Boy. He has gone

from fake-suave to frightened little boy in two seconds flat.

"I'm hungry, and I have jet lag," I announce. Obviously my father has jet lag too because he usually sleeps like a dead person. Also, I didn't want to narc on Hockey Boy, who must be sneaking in for a reason.

"Did you just get in, Seb?" he asks. Ah, Seb, that's his name.

"Uh, a little while ago." That lie would work better if he wasn't still wearing his coat.

My father then says something harsh in Swedish. I understand a few words about sleep, hockey, and remembering. Seb's pale complexion turns even whiter. He mumbles good night and disappears downstairs.

My father turns like he's going to lecture me too.

I hold up a hand. "Hey, I came downstairs to get a snack. That's not a crime."

He narrows his eyes and scowls. Maybe his ferocious face worked on pushy opponents back in his playing days, but it has zero effect on me.

"Since Seb is living with us, perhaps you should wear a robe when you come downstairs."

Although I'd already resolved to do exactly that, I resent the lecture.

"You too," I reply. My father is wearing an old Millionaires t-shirt and pyjama pants.

He flushes. "It's not the same thing. A young woman like you—"

"Relax," I interrupt him. "Since you just told him he needs his beauty sleep, I don't think I'll run into him in the middle of the night again."

"You understand Swedish now." My dad smiles for the

first time. I know he's happy that I'm embracing the Swedish part of my background.

"I still can't speak much Swedish, but I understand lots more than before."

"That's great." He's so proud of my puny accomplishments. He sits beside me at the kitchen counter and starts eating an apple. We are so much alike.

"You know, Dad, I was thinking—I might go back there to do a Masters degree."

Originally, I planned to return to be with Gabe again, but I still love Sweden regardless of any emotionally-repressed jerks I may have dated. I could go to Uppsala University next time.

"So, you know what degree you want to pursue now?" he asks.

"Well, not exactly," I hedge. Knowing *where* I want to study is a good start.

"Lily, patience. One step at a time." He shakes his head, but he's smiling.

I hug him. "I love you, Dad."

22

BLEAK HOUSE

GABE

I'M FRYING CHOPPED POTATOES, onions, and sausage when Freja comes home.

"Mmmmmm, *pyttipanna*," she says, sniffing the pan. "Brrr, it's cold out there."

Freja looks in on my mother, who is supposedly watching television, and then returns. Britt-Marie has taken the week off to visit her family while Freja and I are home for the holidays.

"Are you going to spend New Year's Eve in the square tonight?" Freja asks me.

"Not sure. I might stay home." My friends are meeting up at Robin's place first and then going to the fireworks, but I'm not really interested.

"Gabriel, it's a holiday."

"Yes, but it's a holiday for you and *mamma* as well. We

could take her outside at midnight. That's what we did when I was a boy."

"Your mother will be fast asleep by then. Waking her up will be more trouble than celebration. Besides, it's supposed to snow."

Snow now? Lily had wished for a white Christmas, but she only got a few flakes. If only she were here to see the snow. I can imagine her laughing and making snow angels.

"What about you? Would you like to go out?" I ask.

My aunt stands beside me at the counter. "You've been very low since Lily left."

I don't reply to this. I'm not a person to mope or wail, so I think I've been normal. But Freja is very sensitive to moods.

"It must be hard for you," she says.

"Not really. We knew we would part when she went back to Canada."

Of course, the awkwardness of our parting and my clumsy excuses did not help. I imagined that we would continue to write to each other. There are a dozen little things each day that I want to share with Lily.

But how could breaking up with Lily be anything other than dramatic? She lives her life in a high emotional key. Our relationship was like a Hollywood movie—right up to the dramatic split. Of course, we lack the final act: where the hero and heroine reunite through some huge and implausible act.

"*Bättre älskat och förlorat än att aldrig ha älskat,*" Freja says, more to herself than me. She is fond of sentimental quotes, but this one I disagree with. The pain I feel now is not worth the pleasure we had.

"That's crap," I say. Because the worst part of Lily leaving is that my normal life is diminished now. So many places remind me of her. I can't even go for coffee without seeing the exact chair she sat in with her bright presence lighting up the room. And once school begins again, it will be worse.

So really, wouldn't it have been better not to have known the joy of being with her? A man who lives in candlelight and doesn't know the feeling of warm sunlight on his skin is better off than one who has seen the sun turn from him.

I break an egg into a bowl, but I squeeze too hard and the shell cracks into tiny pieces. *Helvete*. I throw the wasted egg and shell pieces into the composting bin. Then I wipe the counter and stare at the slick surface.

I am not aware that Freja is still in the kitchen until she wraps her arms around my waist and hugs me.

"Allow yourself to feel everything. The good and the bad," she says. "And then you can seek the good again."

The coiled emotion that I've held inside for so long loosens. But I don't want to feel the pain of losing Lily. My life has already been defined by loss. Since I try very hard not to look too far into the future, it's difficult to imagine a time when things will be good again.

"Excuse me." I pull away from my aunt. I crack more eggs, properly this time and cook them. I slide the fried eggs and the *pyttipanna* onto plates. The pickled beetroots are already on the table.

I go and get my mother for dinner. Freja chats cheerfully, but it's hard to concentrate on her words. She's urging me to go out tonight. I'm still undecided. It would be better to go, but I'm not in a party mood. Johan is bothering me to visit Vancouver with him next summer, but that is not possible. Besides, he thinks we'll end up seeing Lily and her father.

When my mother and Freja go to the living room, I wash up. Once the dishes are done, I pull out my phone and send a message to Lily: *Happy New Year.* She has not responded to my messages or emails, but I can't help sending them. They are notes in bottles that I keep throwing into the ocean. The ocean is vast and the odds are ridiculously low, but still I try.

After my mother has gone to bed, Freja knocks on the door of my room. She offers me a glass of cider.

"If you're not going out, we can celebrate here."

"*Tack, moster,*" I say.

"I'm no substitute for a beautiful young girl, but I do care about you very much."

"I appreciate that," I tell her. I take my aunt for granted sometimes. She is cheerful and kind, and my life would be much worse without her. But she never tries to be my mother; instead she assumes the role of a big sister.

We toast to the New Year, supposedly a time of new beginnings.

"If you miss Lily, why not visit her?"

"Nej. I have school." Besides, it's impossible. If I can't even contact her, how can I see her?

"Visit after school ends. Having something to look forward to will make you happier now."

"We ended things. It's over."

I cannot explain our whole dramatic ending because it's not something I fully understand myself. Why did Lily become so angry? Was it my inability to declare my love or something deeper? Was it not getting her way?

"Gabriel." She reaches out and takes my hand. "Do you think her feelings were as deep as yours?"

I nod. Lily said she loved me. And that was where I failed her. I kept so much of myself from her that I couldn't respond the right way in that moment. That night, when I had time to consider, I realized I loved her too. It was an emotion I'd locked away for so long that I couldn't even recognize it.

"That isn't going to change in a few days. Or even in a few months. You need to make plans for the future, and Lily can be in those plans. You're so miserable right now, my dear. You have to do something."

"I can't. There's nothing I can do. She won't talk to me."

"It's always been hard for you to accept help. Even when you were young, you insisted on tying your own shoes, going places on your own steam."

I shrug. That's true enough. My mother is the same way.

"And now, you have opportunities. But you're not going to take them."

"What do you mean?"

"Didn't Jesper Larson offer to help you? Wouldn't you like to pursue your hockey?"

"Nej. It's too late."

Hockey is a world I dismissed long ago. I enjoy playing because it's an escape for me. And I still practice because that's an escape as well. But all the guys I used to play with have moved on. The best are in *Svenska hockeyligan* or *HockeyAllsvenskan*, and a few others play elsewhere in Europe. Two went to North America. At least half the team have already quit competitive hockey. Twenty-two is an age where hockey players know exactly where they stand, and I stand on the outside.

Freja smooths her hair with one hand and frowns. It's a gesture that reminds me of my mother, something she did when she was deep in thought.

"If you go there, she will not be able to ignore you," she says.

"Freja, stop. There is no point to this discussion."

"I know you, Gabriel. I never met Lily, but I saw how transformed you were with her. You were more as you used to be, the energetic little nephew I always admired. What a contrast to Eva." My aunt had never liked Eva. "You young people have all these dating apps now, but that doesn't make finding the right person any easier. It only gives the illusion that there are many fish in the sea."

"You're overly sentimental," I tell her. "Lily and I are not meant to be."

"Why not? And why not try?"

All the frustrations of the past week erupt. My anger at myself and my inability to communicate. The feeling of being back in the rink and so close to real hockey. Not being able to talk to Lily. Not being able to touch Lily.

Lily is the window on a world that I can never enter. I'm not going to travel. I'm not going to see things beyond my small part of Sweden. I'm needed here, but these responsibilities have never felt heavier.

"Because I'm not good enough for her."

"That's ridiculous. In what way are you not equals?"

On the surface, all explanations are stupid. Lily's family is rich, Lily's father is famous, even Lily's aunt and grandmother are famous. She's beautiful, confident, and bold—so different from me. But those things are all superficial dust compared to the real reason. I look at the wall to my left—my mother's bedroom lies on the other side. And that is the real reason. Not the care of my mother, but the possibility that I'll be the same some day.

I close my eyes. The darkness envelops me like a vise. Is this what it's like to be trapped in one's own head? It's a prison whose walls are slowly closing in on me with infinitesimal slowness.

A sob escapes me. My voice is a whisper.

"I have no future."

23

IN WITH THE NEW

LILY

"Oh my God, Lily! You're back!"

Instantly I'm in a group hug with my besties: Roxy, Brit, and Taylor. We kiss and jump up and down. Everyone's staring now, but who cares? I'm back with my girls!

Pete's New Year's Eve party is packed and noisy, but we need to chat. We escape to the slightly less noisy living room and take up the corner of a leather sectional.

"How was Sweden?" Brit sits down right next to me. There's a gorgeous streak of blue in her hair, and I stroke it.

"Brit, that looks amazing. I had a great time in Lund. I loved everything—well, the classes were a lot harder than I thought, but other than that."

Taylor clears her throat. "Um, we have some bad news about the apartment." The three of us are planning to live together next semester; it's something we arranged last summer before I left.

"What?" I ask.

"It's Jenny. She's decided not to go on exchange, and she doesn't want to leave. We've tried everything," says Taylor.

"I don't understand. She was so excited about going," I say. This blows. I can live at home, but I'm used to living on my own now. I spent first year in residence, and the last five months in another country. And now I'm stuck back at home?

Brit snorts. "She doesn't want to leave her boyfriend."

"That's a huge mistake," I reply, even though mere days ago I was plotting my return to Sweden to be with Gabe. But since I'm not, I can throw shade.

"Well, I'm happy. Now we can commute together," Roxy says. Her parents are Iranian and very strict. They insist that she live at home while she goes to university.

"That'll be great," I say. "I can probably get the Volvo." I'm supposed to share the car with Margie, but she got to use it the whole time I was away.

"Yesss! I don't mind the morning bus, but there are perverts on the night buses," Roxy says. "And I can get our car whenever my mother doesn't need it."

Brit interrupts, "Lily, you haven't finished telling us about Sweden. Did you meet a ton of hot guys?"

I nod. "So many. Tall, cute, stylish—in a Euro way."

"In my imagination they all look like Alexander Skarsgård," Roxy says. "*True Blood* Alexander Skarsgård. Without a shirt." That's not far off. I remember Gabe's long, slim body and swallow hard.

"So you went out a lot?" Taylor wonders.

"Um, yeah." A smile sneaks across my face

"Who was he?" Brit squeals. "Was it the guy with the beard? He's hot."

Thanks to social media, there are no secrets even across continents. Luckily, I knew these questions were coming, and I'm prepared.

"I met this guy. We went out for a bit."

"Photos!" Taylor's eyes x-ray my purse. I pull out my phone and choose a photo from one of our early lunches outside. Gabe's sitting on the grass in a t-shirt with the breeze blowing back his hair. That was when things were just beginning between us. Now I feel hollow. I regret being so dramatic when I left. He said he really cared for me; maybe that should have been enough. He's snail-slow when it comes to anything emotional. I miss him so much.

"Wakey, wakey," says Taylor. "Spill the details. Name, height, favourite sexual positions."

Roxy squeals and smacks Taylor's arm. "You can't ask that."

I shake off all my regrets and push down my stupid emotions. I'm not going to cry at a big party when I'm wearing false eyelashes.

"That's Gabe. He's about 6' 4". And he likes it all ways."

We start giggling, but I'm fake-laughing. I can't even talk about Gabe and sex without thinking about his warm mouth on my skin, his complete openness about sex, and of course—his insane flexibility.

Brit is studying my phone like it holds the secrets of the universe. "I love his beard. He looks way older. How old is he?"

"Twenty-two. He is way more mature than the guys around here. But Swedish guys are different. They're more respectful and egalitarian." Which is a euphemism for Sally's definition: socially awkward.

"Egalitarian? What do you mean?"

"Um, it means that you can make the first move. That you can sleep with different guys and nobody makes judgements. And you pay for yourself on dates."

Taylor's eyebrows indicate exactly what she thinks of the last idea. She's been known to break up with a guy if his anniversary gifts aren't good enough. "Really, sleeping with different guys is okay?"

"Yeah, they've got this weird reversal. Sexual attraction is important to them, so they have sex first and decide on dating after."

"That sounds like every guy's dream," scoffs Taylor.

"Well, if you see sex as something only guys enjoy. Women like sex too." Oops, I spoke too loudly, and now people are staring.

"Lily? You're back?"

I turn around and see my ex-boyfriend, Jason Hunt. We dated in our last year of high school. We broke up when he went to Ontario to play hockey, and I haven't seen him in ages.

"Hey, Jas."

His smile is as broad and white as ever. Everyone joked about how he played hockey but his teeth already looked fake. His parents are both dentists.

We hug. Jason is not that tall, but he's really jacked. He's a gym rat. He's built like a truck—almost as broad as he is tall. His average height had been a pain when we dated. I'm a smidge taller, so I couldn't wear heels when I went out with him. Frankly, I didn't think it was a big deal, but he's ultra-sensitive about his height since it kept him from getting drafted by any of the good junior teams here. He had to get special permission to play Junior A in Ontario even though the team really wanted him. Getting a letter of recommendation from my dad helped reassure the league that Jason was legit.

"How's hockey going?" I ask.

"It's really great. I'm third in scoring on my team. I've been getting a few looks from U.S. colleges."

"Oh, that's fantastic."

"Yeah, Coach Bradford is great. He's really helped me work on my total game. I mean, there's all this detailed stuff I hadn't really paid attention to. And he's even changed up the way I train." Besides the height thing, the other problem in our relationship was how much Jason talked about hockey. I know a lot about hockey, but that doesn't mean I want to hear about it endlessly. I half-listen as he tells me in detail what tweaks he's made.

"What are you even doing here? Don't you have games?" I ask.

"Yeah. I lucked out because we had a short break in our schedule. I flew home because my mom was going nuts about not seeing me at Christmas."

"Lily? You're back from Sweden?"

It's Rebecca. She's a petite redhead. Well, not petite everywhere as she has a huge rack. Brit used to speculate on whether those boobs were actually real, but I cannot believe that anyone would get implants in high school. Is that even legal? You might still grow.

Rebecca threads her arm through Jason's and kisses him on the cheek.

"I wondered where you'd wandered off to," she coos. In a further show of "he's mine, bitches," she plasters herself against Jason. One plump breast rests on his bicep, something I'm sure he's enjoying. She seems drunk or high.

Rebecca and Jason dated in grade eleven, the year before I went out with him. Apparently they are back together, but whether it's for tonight or for real, I can't tell. But she's put a real damper on our conversation, and we all stand around awkwardly.

"Could you get me another drink, baby?" she asks Jason. He nods and disappears into the kitchen. I turn back towards my girlfriends, but before I can get a word out, someone shoves me in the back.

It's Rebecca, and she's right up in my face.

She pokes a finger at me. "Listen, Lily...."

"Uh, what's up?" I take a sip of my vodka cooler.

"What's up is that Jason and I are back together," she said.

"I noticed. Um, congrats?" She's being a serious bitch here. I only talked to the guy for a couple of minutes, and besides, I'm so not interested.

Her hazel eyes glitter, and her pink mouth twists up in a tight smile. "In fact, we've been back together for a while."

"I'm sorry, is there some reason I should care?" I ask. "Jason and I broke up ages ago. He's free to go out with whoever he wants."

"You're so clueless, Lily. Do you even understand why he went out with you at all?"

"Well, I would assume it was because we liked each other. You know, like normal people." As opposed to whatever rationale Jason has for dating a head-case like Rebecca.

Her little huffs of breath let me know exactly how much I've pissed her off. "The only reason Jason went out with you was to get a letter of recommendation from your father."

"You're delusional," I reply. We dated for four months. Nobody can be that much of a psycho.

"No, *you're* delushionelle!" She's so out of it that she slurs her words. I back up a step and crash into Brit. My girls are all backing me, with arms crossed and total bitch faces as they glare at Rebecca. Her drama llama antics are drawing a crowd.

Rebecca continues. "Jason never liked you. How could he? You're a freaking giant and flat as a board. Fucking you would be like fucking a man."

I don't say a word because I'm in total shock. I've never felt the kind of hate that's radiating from Rebecca.

"Seriously. What the fuck, Rebecca? You need professional help," Taylor interjects.

Rebecca's eyes bore in on me like angry lasers and she continues, "When he fucked you, he had to close his eyes and pretend it was me."

"Rebecca. Shut up." Jason is back. He's scowling. But his eyes can't meet mine, and his expression betrays a glimmer of something. Is it guilt? Jason was always an easy person to read. Something shatters inside me. Can it be that Rebecca *is* telling the truth?

She strikes at him with flailing arms like a human Kermit. I would laugh except that there's this enormous weight on my chest and I can't even take a deep breath.

Roxy takes one look at my face and grabs my arm.

"Let's go." She hustles me towards the door. A sea of shocked faces parts to let us through the kitchen. I've never been into party drama, but I'm getting my fifteen minutes of notoriety. Fuck.

"Lily, wait," I hear Jason behind me. "Don't listen to Rebecca. She's drunk and jealous. That's all bullshit."

"Jason," Rebecca wails. "Why do you even care what she thinks? Her dad is a washed-up ex-NHL player, he's nothing to you anymore."

Damn it, that's it. You can insult me but leave my family out of it. I turn around and face both of them.

"My father accomplished more in one season that you'll do in your whole life," I tell Rebecca. And then I look at Jason. "Or you."

And we leave. Happy fucking New Years.

24

S.O.S

GABE

HAPPY NEW YEAR, Gabe.

Lily has responded to my New Year's greeting! Finally we are communicating. But it must be very late there, around 2:00am.

Good to hear from you, I message.

Immediately, she writes back: *I know. Ugh. I've been an idiot.*

I smile. Lily's messages sound exactly like her. But mostly I'm glad she's talking to me again.

I was an idiot too. I've spent so much time regretting our last moments together. But I still don't see how things can be different.

Have you got time to chat? She asks.

Yes, this will be my chance to apologize. We decide to WhatsApp, but I can hardly see her face. There's only dim light behind her.

"What's going on? You're all dark," I say.

"It's night here. I don't want to wake everyone up." Her voice is a hoarse whisper.

"What's wrong? What happened?" I demand.

"God, Gabe, how did you know something happened?"

"It's your voice. You sound upset."

"Ugh. There's no hiding anything from you." Lily switches on a light, and her eyes are red and swollen. She's been crying, and that triggers a feeling of utter helplessness. She should have stayed here in Lund with me to look out for her.

"Do you want to talk about it?"

She closes her eyes. "I don't know. I just wanted to hear your voice." Then she says nothing for a long time. It's so frustrating to see her like this but not be able to shelter her in my arms.

She opens her eyes. "I saw my old boyfriend at a party."

"Ja?"

"It's not a big deal, I mean, it's not like I care anymore. But..."

There's another long pause.

"There was a ton of drama tonight," she says.

I wait, wondering where Lily's bravery has gone.

A tear rolls down her cheek. "It's a hell of a way to start the New Year."

I reach helplessly towards the phone screen, wishing I could touch Lily.

"I wish I was still in Lund," Lily says, and I agree wholeheartedly.

"Maybe you need new friends," I suggest.

"Yeah, tell me about it. Well, my friends are okay, it's my enemies I need to work on."

Even the idea of that is stunning. Lily is so friendly and optimistic. "How could you have enemies?"

The corners of her mouth turn up. "That's sweet. But everyone has enemies. Sometimes enemies are friends who get turned around."

This idea seems to pain her, and she stops talking for a while. There are a few little sighs, but mainly we're quiet together. Ridiculously, this makes me happy. When we first met, silences made her nervous, but I reassured her that not talking was refreshing too. We would go on walks and stay in our own heads for long periods with random thoughts punctuating the quiet.

"Be honest, okay?" she says.

"Okay."

A tiny smile appears. "I don't even have to ask you that, you're always honest."

Well, that isn't completely true. I am honest when I speak, but dishonest in the things I hide, like my mother's illness or how I feel about Lily.

"As a guy, what do you think of my breasts?" she asks.

How to answer this? I spend far too long thinking about Lily's breasts. They are plump mounds with rosy nipples. I remember how it feels to take them in my hands and tease her points into tight nubs, or to taste her soft flesh and suck until I hear her moan and cry out.

Helvete! Now my cock is rigid and firmly outlined in my pants. And all it took was the word, breasts.

"They are perfect," is what I finally manage to say. My English fails me at the worst times.

Lily lets out another sigh. "But would they be better if they were bigger?"

I shake my head. "Nej. They suit you. They are exactly right."

She's not convinced. "You don't think I'm built too much like a guy?"

Lily's body is strong but lush. I like her height. I like her curving ass and her muscular thighs. Thighs that tense around my head as I lick the folds of her pussy and tease her clit until she comes noisily. I like being inside her, plunging my cock into her hot depths and hearing her groan and scream.

"Gabe?"

Fuck. I'm so busy fantasizing that I'm ignoring the real woman right in front of me.

"Nej. Your whole body is perfect."

But she doesn't believe me. I can tell by her expression.

"Where are these questions coming from?" I ask. "You are usually full of confidence."

Now the words come tumbling out. "Sometimes shit happens that makes me question everything. Sally thinks I have such good judgement, but what if I don't? I thought I had incredible bullshit detectors. But I let someone get close to me, and he was lying all the time."

Her words are too close to my situation. "Lying about what?" I ask.

"Everything. The way he felt about me, why we were together, what he liked about me."

There's a long silence. In the background of her room, I can make out an unmade bed and a framed painting on the wall. Details of her new life.

"No one could spend time with you and not appreciate your kindness, your generosity," I say. "You're a pure spirit."

Finally, she smiles. "That's so sweet, Gabe."

I wonder if it's time for my confessions as well. Perhaps not while she is feeling so fragile.

Lily's voice quavers. "Gabe, I was really upset that you wouldn't at least try to do a long-distance thing. Why was that?"

"Well..." It's time. I've prepared for this many times, but I still can't get the words out. "I'm very sorry about that last day. I'm sorry that I upset you so much."

"You're not answering my question," Lily says.

"I think it was better to end things. I'm not going to be able to visit you."

Lily tilts her head. "What, ever? Is it a money thing?"

"Nej, nej." I take a deep breath in. "My mother's not well. So, I have a responsibility to look after her."

Her eyes open wide. "Oh. That's why you leave at 16:45 each day?"

"Ja. We have a caregiver who must leave."

Lily nods. "I thought it was something like that. Sometimes your friends said things about her, but in Swedish so I wasn't 100% sure. But I knew you didn't want to talk about it."

There's a silence as she takes everything in. Lily peers at the screen. "But why didn't you tell me this? I mean, it's not a bad thing. It's wonderful that you're doing this."

"Anyone would do it." But how to explain all the secrecy? It was something that began in deference to my mother's wishes and then grew. "Perhaps I didn't want you to feel sorry for me."

181

"What's wrong with her?" Lily asks.

"She has early onset Alzheimer's."

"Oh no," Lily leans towards the screen. Her expression is full of sympathy. But her pity is exactly what I don't want. "How long has she had it for?"

"Difficult to say. She was able to mask the symptoms for a long time."

"How long have you been caring for her?"

"Again, it's gradual. But for a while."

"Was that when you gave up hockey?" she asks.

I nod. One clue is all Lily needs to reassemble the jigsaw puzzle that is my life. But she doesn't make the final connection between my mother's illness and my future.

Lily looks solemn. "This must be so hard for you."

"It's not something I question." What is the point of railing against what cannot be changed?

"Sorry. My problems are so ridiculously small compared to yours," Lily says.

This is why I don't tell people. Because they change and try to coddle me by acting like I'm a saint or an object of pity. "Don't do this. Treat me as you did before."

There's a longer silence. Lily shrugs and seems to accept what I'm saying. "Okay, then. Why are you using your mother as an excuse not to be in a long-distance relationship?"

"You should be free to go out with anyone you like."

"That's up to me to decide. If I want to go out with you—long distance—why can't we? I can come back to Lund this summer. What we had was incredibly special. Why don't you see that?"

"We're only delaying what is inevitable," I say. And

maybe that's the truth, I'm not sparing Lily, I'm sparing myself. Lily will find someone else in no time. It's already been wrenching enough since she left. For me to pretend we are still together and then to have to break up all over again is more than I can handle.

"I don't understand you," Lily says. She is crying again, and now it's my fault.

I struggle to confide what's really bothering me, the real reason I don't want her to tie herself down to me. But all I manage is to apologize again. "I'm so sorry."

"Don't. Just don't," says Lily and disconnects our call.

25

DADDY DEAREST

Lily

UNIVERSE: two, Lily Larson: zero.

Now I have ex-boyfriend issues on two continents. Seriously, how many women can claim that? It's a horrible claim to fame, but still.

Ever since New Year's Eve, I've been going through the motions. I'm back at school, my courses are fine, and it's good to see everybody again. I'd like to think that living in Sweden changed me and made me a better person. Unfortunately, my friends chalk up any changes in me to everything that happened with Jason. Which means I haven't changed for the better.

I've spent way too many nights second-guessing myself. How did I go out with Jason for four months and never realize he was a total user? And calling Gabe was an act of desperation. I can't run crying to him whenever something goes wrong in my life. We're not getting back together, and my stupid issues are not his problem anymore.

When I get up for school and go into my bathroom, I have the lovely surprise of knowing I look like crap warmed over too.

"Fuck you very much, Life," I say to the mirror.

My shower helps a little. I get dressed and go downstairs. My mother has her morning conveyer belt going: breakfast, lunches, packed knapsacks. However, Seb is the only one sitting at the kitchen counter. Yippee. Another great start to the day.

"Good morning, darling," my mother says. "Would you like breakfast? Seb is having waffles."

Seb mutters something, which I suspect is a compliment to the waffles but I can't understand him.

"Try swallowing your food first," I suggest.

"Lily!" My mother manages to inject my name with an extra message: *my daughter would never be so rude.*

"Sorry, Mom. You said he was one of the family. I'm treating him just like Alexander." I pour myself a cup of coffee.

"I could make you a cappuccino instead," my mother offers. She has a brand new espresso machine that she loves to use.

"I'm fine." I fix up my cereal. Mercifully, there is no *filmjölk* here, but in every other way I wish I were still in Lund. I woke up happy every goddamn morning. Well, until Gabe broke up with me. Ugh, if bad things come in threes, I'm due for one more.

As I contemplate this horrible prospect, Seb winks at me across the counter. Gross. Can I not find peace in my own house? Maybe his presence in my life is the third bad thing.

I pour more coffee into my travel mug and grab an apple from the fruit bowl. But it's a winter apple, so it's not satisfyingly crisp. Nothing is going to make me happy today.

"I made a lunch for you." My mother presents me with an environmentally-approved Neoprene lunch sack which is probably filled with unnecessary packaging.

"Thank you." I jump up and stuff the lunch into my knapsack. Then I notice that Seb is checking out my ass. I really, really don't have the energy for this. I'm ten minutes early, but I'm leaving anyway, just to get away from Hockey Boy. "Okay, I'm taking the Volvo. I have to pick up Roxy."

When I get in the garage, my father's just leaving. He rolls down his window. "Bye, Lily. Have a good day at school."

"Hey, Dad." I run over and stand beside his car. I haven't really thought this through. I don't usually share all the details of my personal life with my dad, but this involves him.

"Remember Jason? He was at the New Year's Eve party I went to."

My tears are dangerously close, so I blink really hard and try to feel angry instead of sad. At times like this, I hate being so emotional. My dad watches me without a word. We've always been tuned into each other.

"Anyway, he and Rebecca were there, they got back together. Did you know he dated her before me?" I'm having verbal diarrhoea but I can't stop, because if I do, I'll start crying. "She's pretty, you know in that super-feminine way where you wear dresses all the time, and she's got really big, um, anyway, she got really drunk and said all this sh-stuff to me, but the biggest thing was that she said that Jason only dated me to get a recommendation from you."

That blunt fact of my words sits between us like a steaming pile of dog poop.

My dad shakes his head. "That's ridiculous."

"I know. That's what I thought too. But there was this look on Jason's face like it might be true. I don't believe it was the whole reason, but you know, it was a part."

And now the tears come. I hate crying in front of my dad because I can tell how bad it makes him feel. He opens his door, gets out, and hugs me. He's so strong, and there's an oasis of safety in his arms.

He murmurs these little noises to me. I feel like a baby bird. Finally, I'm done crying, and the front of his blue oxford shirt is a damp, wrinkly mess.

"You okay?" he asks, peering down at me.

I nod. After a few moments, I ask, "So, can you call the team?"

Dad tilts his head. "What team?"

"Jason's team. You should call them and tell them what kind of person he really is. I'm sure they wouldn't want someone like that on their team."

My dad expels a breath. It's his frustrated sound. "I can't do that. I gave them an honest evaluation of Jason's hockey skills. I didn't mention how I knew him."

"Yeah, but you wouldn't have done it unless he was my boyfriend, would you?"

"Well, no." My dad frowns. "But I've given recommendations to other players too. I go out and see them play, and then I say what I think. Anyway, what am I supposed to say? That I changed my mind and he's not a good player after all? They know him. He made the team, so obviously they thought he was good enough."

"But you always say that character counts. Obviously, he's a total sleaze."

"Well, yes, but I still don't think it's enough to tell the team. Anyway, if he's that unprincipled, they'll find out eventually."

"How?" I ask.

"Well, if he cons people, he'll lie about something else. You can't hide your real self from your teammates."

This seems completely unfair to me. Jason used me and got on the team he wanted. Next, he's going to go to some big U.S. college and then take the backdoor route to the NHL or something. He and Rebecca will be living this golden life while I'm a stepping-stone that he's squished on the way.

"But it's not fair," I protest.

"Unfortunately, that's life. There's not always justice." My dad frowns. "Besides, Lily, it's not up to us to mete out punishment to everyone. You have a lot of good things happening in your life. Concentrate on those rather than focusing on the negatives."

I swallow. I'm out of tears, but this feeling of helplessness is worse. My life is crap and now he's lecturing me?

"I can't believe that you won't help me."

"I will help you. Your mother and I will support you until you get over this. It's a terrible thing and—if it's true—he's a terrible person."

My father goes to put his arms back around me, but I push him away.

"If it's true? You don't even believe me?"

"Lily, I saw the two of you together. You dated for several months. A person would have to be a psychopath to maintain a falseness like that."

"I know what I saw," I mutter.

"Maybe you should talk to Jason. Clear this up," he suggests. He's trying to be helpful, but he's only making things worse. I'm getting more and more upset. I walk towards the Volvo, but then I turn around.

"Do you know how hard it is to live in your shadow? This would never have happened if I wasn't your daughter."

Then I get in the car and back out the driveway. I never look back at my father because even as I said those words, I knew how much they would hurt him. And right now, feeling vindicated is more important than being nice.

26

FAR

Gabriel

When I get home from school, I hear a deep voice. The sound makes my shoulders tense.

My father is sitting in the front room with my mother and my aunt.

"*Hej*, Gabriel." He rises and extends his hand as you would to a business associate.

I shake his hand but say nothing. What is he even doing here? We don't need him. I pat my mother on the shoulder and kiss her cheek. She smiles at me. But it's her vague smile—she is glad to see me even if she isn't sure who I am. She looks rumpled; her shirt has a small food stain on it, and a strand of hair has escaped its clip. She would hate to have him see her like this.

I smooth her hair and sit beside her. If only today had been a good day, then he might realize how much of a mistake he made when he left.

My aunt pats my mother on the shoulder. "Has this been tiring for you, Milla? Would you like to have a rest?"

"Ja," she agrees. The two of them go to the back bedroom, which leaves me alone with my father. I sit opposite him, and there is a long silence.

"How is school?" he asks me. The timeless question that strangers ask you from when you are five years old until you get a job. After that, I suppose they ask how your job is.

"Fine," I reply. What is the point to go on about subjects he doesn't even know I am studying?

More silence until Freja returns. She sits beside me.

"Did you want some coffee?" she asks me.

"No, thanks." I rise up. "I have homework, so—"

"Wait." My aunt motions for me to sit down again. "I called Magnus and asked him to come here. We need to discuss something."

I sit back down and wait.

"Between us, we have taken good care of your mother for many years now," she begins. "But her condition is worse now."

Still, I say nothing. A sense of unhappy anticipation comes over me.

"I think at this time, she would be better off in a facility."

"No," I reply. "She loves being here. Why should she leave?"

My aunt's voice goes low with emotion. "She's been lost a few times. She is wandering more—sometimes at night. That is dangerous. Anything might happen to her."

"All we need is a better alarm system on the door. We can manage."

"Gabriel, I know how you feel. But she no longer knows who we are much of the time. In an institution, she will have nursing care. They have systems too—the place I've seen, patients can walk as they please. There are monitoring tools. They have stimulating programs: music, art, games, all geared to her level."

I shake my head. "She would hate it."

"She might not like it at first, but she would become accustomed," Freja replies. She reaches over and squeezes my hand.

"I can understand why *he*—" I motion with my head towards my father. "—would think she should be institutionalized. But Freja, how can you suggest it? You know she loves to be here. To see her garden. To be among her books."

"I know that, Gabriel. But these are books she can no longer read. Plants she can no longer attend to." My aunt's voice holds a low tremor of emotion. In the fading afternoon sunlight, her face is lined. She is younger than my mother, but at this moment she looks older. I am on constant guard, not just for my mother, but my aunt as well because they are the closest genetic matches. I stroke the hand that still rests on mine, but she doesn't return her customary smile.

"If you don't want to care for her anymore, I'll do it by myself," I declare. Her face creases in pain, and then I feel terrible.

"That is not possible," my father said. "Gabriel, you're a young man. You've already given up hockey. You can't give up so much of your life to look after your mother. She would not want that to happen."

How would you know? You couldn't even stay with her, I want to say. But I keep quiet and examine the wood floor.

"I know you're angry because I left," he continues. "And in retrospect, I understand that many of our arguments were early signs of her dementia. That is truly sad. But there were other issues too. You couldn't understand."

"How can I understand what I've never been told?"

My eyes meet his. Blue eyes that are exactly like mine. I resemble him in so many ways: our height, our athleticism, our low voices. Seeing him back here only reminds me of how many times I wished he had stayed. When the responsibilities of my life were so enormous that I longed for someone strong to push them onto. But while he is tall and broad-shouldered—inside he's a weak person. All the strength in me comes from my mother. And that is why I can't let them put her away. I have to fight for her the way she would fight for me.

"These things were not your business," he replies. His tone is not angry though. In fact, this whole discussion is remarkably emotion-free for two people who want to sentence my mother to prison. While I might be able to guilt my aunt into putting off this decision longer, my father is immovable. I have no idea how he feels about me now. At first, he tried to maintain contact, but I rejected him. Once he moved in with Sarah and they had a baby, he bothered me less. Our only contact is on my birthday when he sends me a card and transfers money into my bank account. I've never spent that money.

Whatever he's talking about, it's clear that Freja understands. I am 22, and yet everyone still treats me like a child.

"I don't understand why we are discussing this now. What has changed?" I ask.

Again, my father and my aunt exchange looks. He explains, "You are here all the time, Gabriel. But I can see all the changes in her. And Freja knows that it's the right thing to do."

"There's one place I really like," she says eagerly. "It has lovely grounds, and the staff are very caring."

We had toured those places before. The building and staff are fine, but the other patients are frankly terrifying. How could we lock my mother up with those people?

"Gabriel, Freja tells me that you've had an opportunity come up to play hockey again. Through Jesper Larson? That's very impressive."

I shake my head. "It's nothing. He only offered to make some calls for me."

"Still, I'm glad to hear this. It's good that you've kept playing. Anyway, we..." He motions to himself and my aunt. "We think that you should take this offer. Play hockey at a higher level."

"I can't. What about school?"

"Your term is over at the end of January, and you can finish school later. You can only play hockey when you're young." This was another thing that he and my mother used to argue about. My mother believed academics should come first. She only relented because she knew how much I loved hockey.

My aunt says, "Gabriel, you need to do this. You need to do the things that your friends are doing. Maybe travel a little."

Her motivations are crystal clear. She wants me to go to Canada and see Lily.

"He didn't offer me a trial in Canada. He only offered to connect me with people, he meant here in Lund or Malmö. They know me already."

My father remains calm and logical. "Why are we arguing about something hypothetical? Call him and see what he's thinking. Then you can make up your mind. If hockey doesn't work out, perhaps you can go to another school. Get out of Lund."

They were already onto the next stage. Ready to lock my mother away and move on. "She belongs at home," I repeat.

He leans towards me. "You may be right. It might be marginally better for your mother to remain here with you and Freja. But what is the right solution for all of you? You are at a time where you need adventure and experience, not to be trapped in a little apartment in the same town you've spent your whole life. And your aunt has a life too. You cannot make these decisions without thinking about everyone."

Ah, consensus. I lectured Lily on this very topic only a few months ago. And now consensus is determining my life course.

"It's time," he concludes. The matter seems to be settled between them, no matter what I want. He rises and extends his hand again. I shake it, but he reaches out and gives me a quick embrace.

"Take care, son. Sarah and I would love to see you for dinner sometime. And Vivi has grown a lot since she last saw her big brother." He smiles.

I watch at the front window until he climbs into his black Volvo station wagon and drives off. His presence lingers like the stale scent of a cigarette. I open the window to dissipate his aura, and the cold air rushes in. Outside the sky is dark grey. A lone bird perches on a tree. Aunt Freja is right; our community garden looks neglected and barren. What comfort could my mother get from sitting out there? Yet, she still does every day.

Freja puts a hand on my shoulder. "I know you're angry at me for calling Magnus, but it was the only way. He will help take responsibility for her."

"What responsibility? He's not going to visit her each day as we will."

She ignores my question. "The place I went to see, it's very nice. She would have her own room. We can make it homey, we'll bring her books, a few photographs, that rocking chair she loves..." Her voice trails off.

My chin drops onto my chest. "I know she's getting worse. I know she's more trouble now. But the nice moments are still there."

Like that time we laughed over the antics of a squirrel in the yard. She stroked my cheek and called me Gabriel again. The brief moments before the curtain fell. But how long ago had that been? Perhaps four or five months. I'd been busy and distracted by Lily.

"I'm sorry, Freja." I turn around and face my aunt. "I haven't helped you much lately."

She smiles. "It's fine. It made me happy to see you doing all the fun things young people should." She pulls at the button on her shirt cuff. "Gabriel, I'm going to go for a trip."

"A trip? Where?"

"Do you remember Oscar?"

I nod. He's a Danish man that she dated, but he moved away months ago.

Freja blushes, and the pink makes her look younger and prettier. "He lives in Italy now. He's got a research job in Florence. And he's invited me to visit."

"I don't understand. *Mamma* has to go to this place just so you can take a holiday? We could have gotten more aides to come in."

"I'm going to take leave from my job. I'll be staying six months, perhaps longer." Her hands tighten on my shoulder. "And I think you should leave too."

"To where?"

"To Canada."

I swallow. "I told you before, he didn't offer me Canada." A vision of Lily glitters in the back of my mind. How sad she was. How I yearn to hold her again.

My aunt smiles. "But you can ask. When an NHL legend offers you help, you should at least follow up."

Well, Jesper Larson is a legend. But more than that, he is Lily's father. What if I could go to Vancouver? Maybe accomplish something and tell her in person how I feel about her. Just thinking about Lily brightens up this painful evening. If life were a cartoon, red flowers would pop out of the patchy grass in the yard and begin blooming.

But this is impossible. I shake my head. "I can't leave her."

"Listen to me. You know, what your mother has—it could affect us too."

"Ja. I know." I look at her through blurring vision. "I watch you. To see if you have any of the same signs that *mamma* had."

Freja's eyes open wide in shock, and then she laughs.

"Of course you do, Gabriel. You care for others so well. And have you seen them?"

Her voice is joking, but there is a tension beneath. My mother doesn't have the hereditary kind of early-onset Alzheimer's, but the doctors were still unsure why my mother got the disease so young. There could be a genetic component. I try not to calculate the years until I need to watch myself for signs.

I shake my head. "You are as you have always been."

She releases her breath with an audible relief. "That's good to hear. Come sit."

We sit down, and my aunt leans towards me. "When I talked to you about true love, I realized I have been a hypocrite. So I contacted Oscar again. I was glad to stay with Milla as long as it made a difference to her. And I wanted to be with you, too."

I manage a smile. "Freja, I would not be who I am without you."

"But now, can you honestly tell me that we're making a difference to Milla?"

Freja waits while I ponder the question. Is my mother's greeting to me the same as the smile she has for Britt-Marie? My mother's temper has been worse lately. And twice I caught her trying to go outside without a coat or shoes. She could have frozen if I hadn't stopped her. Are her issues becoming more than the three of us can handle? Could my mother be better off in a facility?

"I'll have to see the place first," I say slowly.

"Of course. If you don't like it, we will search until we find someplace you approve of. And I would not leave until she's settled into the new place."

I've spent so many years protecting my mother and our

life here. What would it be like to make decisions that are purely selfish? That total freedom is terrifying.

Freja pats my head as she did when I was a small boy.

"As your favourite aunt, I tell you it's time. Time to have adventures. It's what Milla would want for both of us."

The same words sound better coming from my aunt than my father. I feel guilty for even considering deserting my mother. But does the guilt hold me back from living my own life? I can't deny a growing sensation of excitement. Of having adventures and not knowing what will come next.

And perhaps I was wrong. There may be a future for Lily and me—if she still wants one.

27

SWIPE RIGHT

LILY

"TONIGHT WE'RE GOING to exorcise Jason," says Brit. She is as solemn as the head priestess at a religious ceremony, but instead of ceremonial robes she's wearing yoga pants and a pink sweatshirt with a llama on it.

My parents are out at some fundraising dinner, so I'm hosting my own intervention. It's actually turned into an intervention/girls night because my mood has improved. I ordered pizza, Roxy made a salad, and Brit bought a cake with *Jason Sucks* iced on it. I got to make the first cut, right through his name. If cakes are voodoo dolls, Jason's now lying eviscerated on a dressing room floor. Hopefully!

Now we're up in my room doing these Korean facial masks that Roxy swears will change our lives. She has gorgeous skin, so I'm willing to believe her. We all have pale sheets stuck to our faces, and we look like we're auditioning for *Friday the Thirteenth, Part One*

Million. The villain in that movie was also named Jason. I make a mental note never to date guys who have the same name as a serial killer, even a fictional one.

"I'm not upset anymore," I say. I'm lying, but I'm pretty good at it.

Taylor lifts a skeptical eyebrow but doesn't challenge me. It's weird, but she's been nicer to me lately. We're not BFFs again, but she's not so distant anymore. I suspect that the whole deal with Jason made her sympathetic. "Well, why don't you start dating again? That'll show Rebecca and Jason how little you care."

"I haven't met anyone that I want to go out with yet. I've only been back two weeks." Honestly, it's going to be ages before I feel like dating again.

Brit pauses from filing her nails. "Too bad your Swedish boyfriend wasn't at that party. That would have shown Jason that you're over him and onto someone else."

"Literally," snickers Taylor. "What was his name again? He's way hotter than Jason."

"Gabriel," I say. Even saying his name makes me feel sad. Currently I'm not replying to his messages because avoidance is my coping method of choice. I keep reading them though, and trying to decode whether *hej* is short for "Darling Lily, I miss you more than *fika*."

"You should ask him to visit," suggests Taylor. "We'll parade him everywhere."

"He can't visit, he's got school. Besides, we've broken up." People, read my lips: We. Broke. Up. How many times do I have to repeat this?

"Well, if not him, ask someone else out. Make the first

move," Roxy suggests. "Guys find you daunting, you know."

"Me?" And why is this the advice I'm getting on both sides of the planet?

"Yeah, you're very confident and opinionated. And you're so tall, blonde, and pretty."

"Not that pretty." Taylor snickers.

I stick my tongue out at her, then frown. "Well, I'm not that confident anymore."

"Lily! You don't believe all that crap Rebecca said, do you? We saw you and Jason together, you guys were totally legit," says Brit.

"Yeah," agrees Roxy. "He was really into you."

"My brain knows you're right..." I begin. There was no way that Jason dated me *just* because he needed a recommendation from my dad. Even if it was only a tiny percent of why he asked me out, that still sucks. I want people to like me for who I am, not who my family is. But that's impossible.

"But your heart says no?" Taylor finishes my sentence because I'm lost in why-things-suck-land.

"It's more my body. All the stuff she said was so personal. And Jason's not that tall, maybe he is more attracted to petite women."

"Only you could call a guy who's just under six feet short," says tiny Roxy. But he was short for hockey. If Jason had been a bigger body, he would have had a better shot at getting into the WHL. And he wouldn't have needed any help.

"Try a dating app," Taylor says.

I groan and pull out my phone. "Which one? I hate them all equally."

"Tinder. Or Bumble, Bumble's good," says Brit.

"Tinder's better for hook-ups," Taylor suggests. "Which do you want?"

What I really want is to be back in Lund with Gabe, but everyone is bored of hearing me whine about Sweden. But when I think about sex, all I can picture is Gabe's endless torso and his large gentle hands on me. I shake my head. *Lily, get a grip*. It's over.

I scrunch up my nose. "I don't know. Maybe a hook-up." It's completely embarrassing, but I want someone to find me sexy.

"When's the last time you even looked at your Tinder account?" Brit asks.

"I looked in Sweden. The guys were hot, but I couldn't understand the slang they used. Words that weren't in my Swedish-English translation app." One night Sally, Gabe, Robin, and I sat around her room, and the guys translated what was being said to her in Tinder messages. Disappointingly, it was exactly the same come-ons as here. I travelled halfway around the world so guys could ask me in Swedish if I was DTF.

Taylor grabs my phone and opens my Tinder app. "You should change your password more often than every ten years," she suggests helpfully.

"What's the point of looking at Tinder while I'm home? Euw, maybe I'll get Mr. Elliot." Our divorced neighbour is one of those yucky middle-aged guys who asks way too many questions about school so he can look down your top. He's on Tinder and thinks that women in their twenties would be a good match. He appeared in Taylor's feed once, and we nearly threw up.

"Okay, look when we're at school then," says Roxy.

"But you have to do something. You need a confidence boost!"

"Wait! This guy is hot, and he's less than a kilometre away. How can that even be?" Taylor's voice rises. "Oh my God. His shirtless photo is blazing fiyah!"

We crowd around my phone. The guy has a broad muscular chest, well-defined abs and his jeans ride low enough to see a golden trail of hair leading down to a distinct bulge in the denim.

Then I look up at his face. "Fuck me. That's Seb. Quick, swipe left."

I reach for my phone, but Taylor pulls it away from me. "I'm not done here. This guy has more than a six-pack. Is there a name for it if you can count eight of those ab muscles?"

"Octodominals? The Great Eight?" suggests Roxy. We pitch popcorn at her.

"Who's Seb?" asks Brit.

"He's our hockey billet. He's from Sweden."

"Wait. This guy lives here? In this house?" Brit asks. "How come we didn't see him?"

I check the time. "I guess he came home after his game. He lives downstairs in the nanny suite."

We all look down at the floor as if it could open and reveal Seb lying half-naked on his bed. It's tough to imagine him any other way since all his Tinder photos are shirtless.

"Well, it's pretty clear he just wants to hook up," Taylor says. "Sounds like the perfect solution to your problem."

"I can't hook up with Seb!" Not only for all the normal reasons like *euw, he's not my type*, but also Gabe's voice saying that I find any Swedish guy good looking. That's not true. Maybe I'm a fan of all things Swedish, but that doesn't include potential hook-ups.

"Why not?" Roxy asks. To my surprise, all my girl-friends are nodding.

"He's too young."

"He's only a year younger than us," Taylor says. "That's not a big deal."

"Plus he's physically mature," Brit is gazing at my phone. "Rawr. He says he has a lot of stamina."

I roll my eyes. "That's Seb. He's ridiculous."

Taylor leans towards me. "Wait. You mean he's already been coming on to you?"

I snort. "Only every chance he gets. At least when my father's not around." He invited me to the Vice's New Year's Eve party, and in retrospect, I should have gone.

"Lily, you are seriously the luckiest girl on the planet," Brit says. "You don't even need Tinder because you have guys falling from the sky like rain. And not just any guys, Sebastian is an extremely hot professional athlete."

"He's going to be an amazing fuck," Taylor says, like it's a done deal.

I hold up both hands. "No, stop. We're supposed to be his family here in Canada. I'm like his big sister or some-thing. I should be looking out for him and not going all Jesse's Mom on his ass."

"His large, muscular ass," adds Taylor, holding up a photo where Seb is looking over his shoulder so we can see the rippling muscles on his back and yes, a big, taut hockey butt. Seriously, his profile pics are so obvious. But they must work because he's already been in enough trouble to get busted down to our house.

"How can I sit at the dinner table every night with a guy I've slept with?" I demand.

"You said that sex is no big deal to Swedes, right?" asks Brit. "It's cool. For him, it'll be like flossing his teeth."

"Thank you. I hope that sex with me is more memorable than dental hygiene." It's hard to believe that someone who was voted most-likely-to-do-something-crazy-and-impulsive four years in a row is suddenly the voice of reason.

"I just mean that it won't be awkward afterwards. He won't be standing outside your window with a boom box and an engagement ring." Brit seems to be confusing several teen movies of the eighties.

"Why would he stand outside when he could just walk into her bedroom?" Taylor asks.

That's a horrifying possibility. But if he saw me right now with this ridiculous mask, it would be an erection killer. "See, that's another reason not to do this. What if he wants to keep hooking up?"

"How long is he here for?" Roxy asks.

I close one eye. "Until hockey season is over. I'm not sure if they're making the playoffs, so April at the earliest."

Brit nods. "That's not too long. Look, you need to be absolutely clear upfront. Say it's going to be a one-time only thing. That'll probably spur him on to really perform."

"No, no, no. And no," I reply. There's no way. "Can we change the subject?"

Roxy shakes her head. "Lily, do you find this guy attractive?"

I hesitate. Of course, Seb is attractive. Physically, the guy is a ten on any scale. But he's so immature and corny. I've graduated to men, so Seb would be a step backwards. The only way I could have sex with him would be if he promised not to say anything. And that's the equivalent of asking someone to wear a paper bag on his head.

"Ah ha! You do," says Taylor.

Roxy's phone pings, reminding us it's time to take off our masks. We squeeze into my bathroom and peel them off.

"Do we wash our faces now?" Brit asks.

"No. Now you gently pat your face with your finger-tips," Roxy instructs us. We obediently tap away, looking like a bizarre shiatsu class.

I peer into the mirror, but I don't see any big changes yet. My skin's actually pretty good, but I have these pores by my nose that Roxy assures me will diminish.

When we get back to the bedroom, I hope we've forgotten about Seb. Brit is seeing a new guy so we discuss him. And the latest news is that Jenny broke up with Nathan and is now regretting that she didn't go on exchange. I have zero sympathy for her.

Taylor yawns. "I guess we better head home. Too bad this isn't a sleepover."

"You're the one who insisted we had to go home. Don't you have an early practice tomorrow?" Brit asks. Taylor plays varsity soccer.

"That was before I found out that Hottie McHockey-pants lives here. Does he go shirtless at breakfast?"

I groan. "Yes. No pants either. Makes for exciting times when he spills his coffee."

We all go downstairs. Unfortunately for Taylor, Seb

doesn't show up even when she makes a series of loud and inappropriate comments about my sex life ending in: "Lily, that lingerie you're wearing is really hot."

"They're sweatpants," I reply.

"You're no fun," Taylor says. "And we are coming back here when you-know-who is around."

"Bye, crazy ladies." I watch them walk down the driveway giggling and then close the front door.

And I turn and walk right into Seb.

28

THE ONE YOU'RE WITH

LILY

"*HEJ*," says Seb. His greeting is as casual as if we were passing on the street instead of being so close that I can feel his breath on my cheek. Unlike his Tinder pics, he's wearing a shirt. It's a navy T, but his rippling pec muscles and eight-pack abs are already burned into my memory banks.

"Oh my God. You scared me," I stammer. Was he right here all the time? What did we say about him? Ugh, whatever it was, it was inappropriate.

Seb holds up his phone. "I got your message."

My eyes narrow. "Wrong number, Hockey Boy. I didn't send you any message."

I try to walk by him, but he sidesteps to block me. He turns the phone to face me, and to my horror I see that Taylor has sent him a message on my Tinder account. It's only a *"hey babe"* but naturally Seb went nuclear on that and now here we are.

"I'm sorry, but I didn't send that. It was my friend, Taylor. She's the one who's interested, so I can hook you guys up." So there, Taylor. The girl you just threw under the bus has gotten up and driven the bus over you.

Seb smiles at me. He has the dirtiest smile of anyone I know. I need a shower whenever he looks at me.

"I knew you liked me. So, your place or mine?" he asks.

"Hello? Are you ignoring everything I said? That wasn't me. I'm not interested in you."

"Ah? We both know that's not true. Besides, your friend is right—it's not healthy for you not having the sex. Let's fix that."

My newly-cleansed cheeks are now bright red. "You heard that?"

He nods. He runs a finger along my collarbone, and I shiver.

"Okay, maybe there is something, a tiny vibe, between us. But seriously, Seb, we can't do anything." I pull his hand from my neck despite how good it feels.

"Lily." He says my name with that up and down Swedish cadence which melts more of my resolve. "You live in Sweden, you know that sex is just a way to talk, like communicate with each other."

Now he puts both hands on my shoulders, and his touch is surprisingly light and gentle. My dad said that Seb has soft hands, but this isn't what he meant.

"Seriously, we can't. My dad would kill you."

His hands freeze and fall away from me. He scowls. "Ja, I know."

For some reason, this reluctance makes him more attractive. Finally a guy who isn't sleeping with me because of my dad. In fact, it's the opposite: he's afraid to sleep with me because of my dad.

"But my parents aren't going to be home for hours." As soon as the words leave my mouth, I want to cram them back in. *Lily, shut up, you're going to get into serious trouble here.*

Seb perks up like a meerkat on guard duty. He moves closer, close enough that I can smell his body wash. It's Axe, which is yet another strike against him. But there's a musky, masculine scent underneath the artificial one that's unnervingly attractive.

"Would you like a drink?" he asks.

"I'm home. If I want a drink, I'll go to the fridge and get one."

"But I have schnapps," he says. "I know you like Swedish things."

And for a moment, everything with Gabe rushes back to me. Me drinking too much and him taking care of me. How he slept sitting up all night, just in case I needed him. His beautiful smile. A sweet card he slipped under my door early one morning. How easy it was to be together.

Seb interrupts my reverie by caressing my cheek, his fingers landing on my mouth and tracing the outline of my lips. Seb's eyes are a much darker blue than Gabe's blue-grey colour. But comparisons will only make me sadder.

"C'mon, Lily. Loosen up," he urges me. "I know you want me."

"Please, you are so not my type. And before you

mention Tinder again, I told you—that was my friend. I had zero to do with that. Seriously, I would never swipe on a guy who only posted shirtless photos. That's so lame."

Seb's confident grin finally fades. "What kind of guys do you like, then?"

"Well, I like guys who are smart, interesting and—" I search for something Seb would never do. "—read poetry." Gosh, subconscious mind, I wonder where that came from?

"I'm smart and interesting," said Seb. "And I'm a top hockey prospect. I'm the leading scorer on my team."

"Then how come you didn't go straight into the NHL?" You can't impress the daughter of a true NHL superstar.

Seb finally gets pissed and starts spouting facts about the new NHL and player development. He concludes, "What is your problem? Any chick would wanna get with me."

"That's my problem. You treat me like I'm any random chick who should be honoured to experience your golden penis. Grow up."

Of course the word penis makes him smile.

"So you have been thinking about my cock. Because I've been thinking about your—"

Before he can finish whatever delightful compliment comes next, I interrupt. "Tell me one real thing you like about me."

"Uh, you're hot." When I roll my eyes, he continues, "And you're..." He searches for the right word. "—chill."

He's so generic. I can't believe he gets any women at all.

In desperation, he blurts, "I like that you don't really like me."

Now he's got my attention. "What? The fact I don't like you is appealing?"

"Ja. There's a lot of girls out there, they see me play and they want to fool around with me. At first, it's great. Who's not gonna wanna fuck? But they tell everyone, and then Coach gets mad. I'm like, fuck, what is happening?"

"Which is how you ended up here?"

He nods. Now that his bravado shields are down, he's more human. Seb continues, "I don't wanna be someone's trophy. That feels like shit."

Then we hear a sound upstairs. It's late, but Margie is always up late. It's not Alexander, because he's at a sleepover.

"Maybe we should go down to my room," he suggests. Despite a warning voice in my head that sounds exactly like my sister, I follow him downstairs.

Seb's room is a mess, but that doesn't bother me. Mine is too. We have a housekeeper, but she's gone back home for a month so things have slacked off. Because there are clothes and crap on every chair, we sit on the edge of his bed. Maybe that's his strategy, although I'm pretty sure he's never had a girl in our house. Margie would have known.

Encouraged by the fact that I'm actually in his room, Seb sidles closer to me. "Hey, if you don't like me, we could hate-fuck."

I laugh. I can't help it. He has such a one-track mind.

"But I don't hate you," I say. Between missing Gabe and the whole deal with Jason-the-Jerk, I haven't given a ton of thought to Seb. He's been an irritating part of the background. He'd be insulted to know that though.

"That's good. I don't hate you either," he replies. He's looking at me like I'm something delicious to eat, and his admiration is softening my resolve. Normal Lily would have no problem rejecting Seb, but Sad Lily is not as strong. Maybe Gabe was right—I fall too fast and too easily.

"You're a sweet kid," I reach out and put my hand on his. This spurs him to grab my hand, turn it over and kiss the palm. His lips are soft and warm; they open, and his tongue draws a wet circle on me. It's alarmingly hot.

"Ummm," I stutter.

Seb moves even more fluidly than he does on the ice. He turns my body towards his, and then leans closer. That Axe scent is gone now, overpowered by Seb's own pheromones. When his mouth meets mine, his kiss is gentle and tentative. Is Seb more talk than walk? But the moment our tongues touch, he's galvanized into action. He holds me tight to him and pulls us onto the rumpled bed. His kiss turns hot and demanding—all open mouths, hot breath, and tangled tongues. His body against mine is harder than human flesh should be.

"Ah, Lily," he breathes between kisses. "You get me. You get what I'm going through."

Maybe. But then what am I doing here? This is not good for me or Seb. Is this some ego thing where I'm sleeping with him because I've had my feelings hurt?

Lily, sex is not a big deal here. The words of everyone in Sweden come back to me now. Maybe sex can be casual, and maybe it will fill the hollowness inside me.

"Seb, wait." I put my hands on his chest.

"Ja?" He blinks at me.

"It's not a big deal between us, right? Just this one time."

He looks confused but nods. "Sure, ja. Whatever you like." He uses the break to pull off his t-shirt and jeans.

Seb's body is ripped. He's a human Ken-doll: all smooth, muscled, and hairless. But Ken never had such a prominent bulge in his bizarrely colourful boxer briefs. I run my hands down his biceps, and he flexes the muscle beneath my touch, which makes me smile. When you're built like Seb, you don't need to show off. He's any girl's wet dream, and yet I can't break through my detachment. *Get into this, Lily.* Obviously, some part of me wants this, I've come to his room, we're making out, and yet something's missing.

I move my hands onto his flat stomach. I hear Taylor cooing over his eight-pack as let my forefinger bump up and down the washboard. He groans as I get closer to his briefs. The waistband is patterned with repeated *Björn Borgs*. Sally said that this was the underwear of choice in Lund.

Ordinarily, I'd be pulling off my clothes now too, but I can't get over this weird shyness. I close my eyes. Seb undoes the ties of my very sexy sweatpants, pulling them down and pulling up my t-shirt in swift succession.

"You look hot," Seb says.

I open my eyes. I'm wearing a strappy lace bra and panty set in a bright pink and orange that Seb clearly approves of. But this only makes me feel more insecure. What if he doesn't like my body once I'm naked? Ugh.

Seb has zero hesitation. He undoes my bra with ease and figures out the many straps on my panties too. I lie there completely exposed. I watch him seeing me for the first time, his eyes darting between my breasts, my stomach, and the tiny patch of hair between my thighs. I can't breathe.

"Fuck yeah," he murmurs. He's stereotypically bro, but for some reason that's exactly what I need to hear right now: that my body is attractive.

I close my eyes and lay my head on the pillow. I can feel his mouth fasten onto my nipple. The suction feels good, and then he begins tweaking the other nipple with his hand. "Oh, yes," I moan softly, even though it's impossible for Margie to hear us.

He lifts his head and kisses me with lips wet and warm. "I like your tits," he tells me before he begins sucking the other nipple.

And that stupid, infantile compliment breaks me. Tears run down my cheeks, silently at first, but then I sniffle and choke back a sob.

Seb stops. His eyes widen when he sees my face. "Fuck. Lily, am I hurting you?"

"No, no. I'm sorry—" And that's all I can say before the tears really start to flow. Seb scoots up the bed and cradles me in his arms. My wet face is plastered against the muscular chest I was admiring moments ago. This is so humiliating, but I can't stop the tears that have been simmering since New Year's.

He holds me until my crying stops. I feel the flexion of his chest as he moves. Then he offers me a bunch of tissues. I clean the tears off my face, then blow my nose. Now I'm super-attractive, I'm sure.

Seb caresses my cheek. "We don't have to do this, *okej*? Are you a virgin or something?"

"Nej," I answer in Swedish. I struggle to explain without sounding like a total loser. "Um, I had this boyfriend. And he made me feel bad."

"About the sex?" asks Seb. He's completely mystified, but he keeps his arms around me. I can see through his tight briefs that his erection has already gone down. Not surprisingly, hysterical crying kills the mood.

"No, about my body." My words hang in the silence. I can hear Seb breathing.

Finally, he speaks. "*This* body?" His tone is incredulous, like I'm a Barbie doll and someone must have switched heads on Jason because the body before him is so great. I feel a rush of warmth towards Seb. Maybe he's driven by hormones, but he's also sincere.

"Thank you." I smile at Seb. He's a sweet kid.

We lie there a bit longer—not speaking or touching. I'm struck by how wrong it feels to be with him. I sit up, find my t-shirt and pull it back on.

"Wait," Seb pleads. "If you're okay now, we could still —" Apparently snotty crying isn't a complete turn-off after all.

I yank my sweatpants on and stuff my underwear in the pocket. The crying signalled to me that I'm in a really bad emotional place right now. Maybe it's about Jason, but more likely it's because I'm still in love with Gabe. I've never been a hook-up person, so why did I think that would work now?

Besides, maybe I'm trying to prove Gabe wrong. I'm not going to fall for the first cute guy that crosses my path; I'm going to hold out for someone real. I'm a better person than he thinks I am.

Poor Seb watches me as he lies on his side. *What the*

fuck happened is written across his face. Even his half-mast penis looks sad through his boxer briefs.

"I'm sorry. I know I'm being a total head case here. I feel really bad, and I didn't mean to lead you on, but it's not going to work between us."

"I don't understand," says Seb.

"Join the club," I reply, but he's clueless to what I mean. I lean over to kiss him on the cheek, but he tries to go lips and our noses bump painfully instead. Awkward and totally symbolic of our whole evening.

"You're a sweet guy, and super-hot too. It's all my problem," I say as I back out of the room. After I close the door, I hear a big sigh and then the rhythmic creak of his mattress. Poor Seb is going to be taking things into his own hands tonight.

29

FRIENDS

LILY

I GOT A SURPRISE 4 U.

I'm in my bedroom doing some readings when I get this text from Seb. I check my phone, and it's almost midnight. He must have just gotten home from his game.

What is it? I message back.

Come & see.

I tell him I'm busy, but he replies with various excited emojis and the word PLZZZZ, if it is even a word. Am I back in grade four?

OK, I type. I brush my teeth and hair. The fact that I'm fixing myself up to go downstairs in my own house is pathetic and weird. I don't even know why I'm agreeing to visit Seb, except I do feel guilty about the other night. Maybe we can talk and make things less awkward.

Unfortunately, I run into Margie in the hallway.

"Just getting a snack," I say and realize my mistake

immediately. Normally, I would never volunteer what I'm doing, especially something as mundane as eating.

Veronica Mars is on the case. Margie folds her arms and blocks my path. "Are you fooling around with Seb? That is such a bad idea."

I shake my head. While technically, I may have fooled around with Seb a little, I don't plan to do it again. But I'm not going to ignore him completely either.

Margie's not done. Not only is she smarter than me, my younger sister is also more mature. "Lily, if you're doing this to get back at Dad, it's totally going to blow up in your face. And he's going to kill Seb."

"Nobody's going to find out anything," I say. "Er, not that there's anything to find out. And talking in the hallway won't help, we're going to wake up Mom and Dad."

She moves to let me by. "It's like you go around with a death wish."

Yeah, impulsive is my middle name. But I like me that way. I'm feeling better these days.

I snag a couple bottles of the electron water my mom's been pushing from the fridge. I tap softly on the downstairs door and then walk in. Seb is sitting on the couch, but instead of gaming he's reading a book.

"Impressive," I say.

He flashes me a crooked grin. "Ja, I listen to you. You like guys who read."

I sit beside him and push up the book so I can see the cover. *The Night They Stole the Stanley Cup*. He's reading one of Alexander's old Screech Owl books.

"Oh, come on. This is not a real book, it's your first chapter book."

"I read them when I was a kid. I really like them."

"Not impressed after all." I twist off the cap of my water, and he does the same.

"Could you read a child's book in *Swedish*?"

I laugh. "Okay, good point. My Swedish reading level would be a picture book. So, what's the surprise?"

He gets up and rummages in the cupboard.

"Woila!"

It's a cinnamon bun. A gigantic one lathered with cream cheese icing and blueberries.

"Whoa, where did you get this?"

"Someplace near the rink. Devo said they are the best."

I hold the plastic clamshell and pull off a chunk. It's super sweet and gooey.

"Iss goo," I say. My mouth is kind of glued together, and I have to lick the icing off my lips.

Seb squints at me. "You're hot when you eat."

Yeah, no. I tear off another piece and offer it to him.

"You feeding me? Fuck. That's sexy as—" I cram it into his mouth so I don't have to hear any more. Then I drink some water. The bun is delicious and a nice gesture, but I'm not really hungry.

"Seb, seriously. Drop the sex crap. I think we could be friends. I bet you don't have a ton of girl-friends."

He nods. "Well, not here. I do back home. I have two sisters too." He's mentioned his sisters a few times, so I know he's close to them.

"How old are your sisters?"

"Katrin is two years more than me, and Clara is one year less."

"You miss them a lot?"

He nods. "We look out for each other."

"Sometimes I wish that we lived in this global village, so I could have all my friends from Vancouver and all my friends from Sweden together." Sally's pragmatic sarcasm would be welcome these days.

Seb considers this. "Would it be here or in Sweden?"

"In Sweden," I say without hesitation.

"Ja, me too. I miss it."

"Everything is different, right? Like this cinnamon bun. I mean, it's delicious but it's a hundred times more sugar-loaded than the ones in Sweden."

"Also, it tastes soft," Seb points out.

"That's right, Swedish ones are kind of crunchy."

This is the first conversation we've had that's not sex-related, as in my reluctance to have sex and his insistence that we do. I like it.

"I have a recipe for the Swedish kind." The one Gabe gave me.

"Will you make it for me?" Seb asks.

"I'll give it to my mother, who can actually bake."

"Ja, that works too."

There's a short silence. Seb moves closer to me, so our thighs are touching. So much for platonic conversation.

"If you feel better now, maybe we could have the sex," he coos.

I shake my head.

He puts his hand on my thigh and rubs it. "It was hot between us."

"Really? My crying like colicky baby is a big turn-on for you?"

He chuckles. "You're funny. And you have a very sexy body."

While I do enjoy his compliments about how hot I am,

we're not in sync in some very elemental way. And while Seb keeps offering up that he's ready, willing, and able, I suspect that he'd be like that with any available woman in the vicinity.

I'm changing the subject. "What else do you miss about Sweden?"

"So, talk now and have sex later?" If he's this relentless on the ice, he *will* make the NHL.

"No," I reply. "Let's talk now, and I'll go back to my room later."

Seb makes a big pouty face.

So I begin. "I miss *fika*. I know I can go to Starbucks or wherever and have a coffee and a pastry, but it's not the same. I loved the fact that everyone goes for *fika*, and that you can stay in a café and chat for hours and nobody ever tells you that they need your seat for paying customers."

His eyes widen. Well, his blue eyes are already wide and round, but they get even bigger. "They do that here?"

I nod. "Makes it hard to relax."

"I miss *fredagsmys*," says Seb.

"That's when you stay in with your family, right?"

"Ja, it means cozy Friday. When I was a kid, we all eat tacos and watch a movie together. Sometimes we play a game, but usually a movie."

"It's not Donald Duck movies, is it?"

"Donald Duck?" Seb asks.

"Yes, like *Kalle Anka*." On Christmas Eve, Aunt Karin had interrupted the party to turn on the TV for these old cartoons and everyone—even my dad and *farmor* —watched and laughed.

He laughs. "Nej, nej. That is just Christmas."

"We could do that here," I say. "Have tacos and watch a movie with my family."

"Ja. Sure. But the tacos are different here."

Poor guy, he doesn't really want a cozy night in, he wants a cozy night in with his own family. Not my insane one.

"Look, if you're struggling with anything, you can always ask me. Think of me as your big sister."

We both make a face when we realize how inappropriate that sentence is.

"Your father," he begins. My shoulders tense up. "I don't think he likes me. Even though he lets me live here."

"Well, I don't know the whole background between you guys, but I know he hates when a player's work rate doesn't match his talent."

Seb releases a breath. "But I work really hard on the ice. Isn't that what matters?"

I consider this. My dad is a serious guy, and he takes hockey very seriously. So, he doesn't understand someone like Seb who fools around when he's off the ice. My dad never had to let off steam. *Farmor* says he was born old.

"Well, first off, he's supposed to make sure you got off to a good start, so he's probably a lot stricter with you than normal. And second, he doesn't get to see everything you do on the ice. Maybe you can go over your off-ice routine with him. Show him what you're doing every week and ask him what else you should be doing. He'll like you being proactive."

Seb has been nodding, but now he frowns. "What is proactive? Isn't that for your skin?"

I giggle. "No, it means getting out in front of something. Like telling your parents you've done something before they can nag you."

"Ja, okay. I'm gonna try it."

We smile at each other. Seb has an open face that's easy to read.

"You are a nice person, Lily."

Seb reaches out and holds my hand. This time it's not about sex, it's about being lonely and longing for human connection. I felt the same way in Lund. You miss the safety net of your family and friends. You're unmoored without the familiar details of your life.

I close my eyes and remember holding hands with Gabe. Ever since I came home, Seb has reminded me of Gabe. Beyond their colouring, they look nothing alike. Their personalities are nearly opposite. And holding Seb's hand doesn't light me up inside the way Gabe's would.

I took a marketing class in first year, and I know that nostalgia can be used to sell things. You buy a perfume because it invokes your trip to Paris. Or a food product brings back something your mom cooked for you as a child. And maybe Seb does remind me of Sweden, how happy I was there and all the things I miss. But nostalgia isn't the same as the real deal. And Seb is not Gabe.

30

PRACTICE MAKES PERFECT

GABRIEL

IF I DO GET my chance, I must be ready. I call Holger. He's the assistant coach from my last competitive team. He played goal and he's also a kind man, so I decide to try him first.

"Gabriel, it's been a long time."

"Yes, how's the hockey season going?"

"Good."

I'm not quite sure what team he is coaching now, so I jump right into my request. "I would like to polish up my goaltending skills. Could I work with you or do you know someone good?"

"Ach. Let me think." There's a long pause. "May I ask why now? Last I heard you were playing only for your university."

"Ja, I'm hoping to get a tryout with a competitive

team." I don't mention Canada because that's not for sure.

"Really? It's a funny time of the year."

"Yes. It's an odd opportunity." I can tell that he's not convinced of my commitment. After all, I was the one who left his team mid-season. So I deal my trump card. "I met Jesper Larson over Christmas, and he has some connections."

"Ahhh, Jesper Larson. I heard he was at the World Juniors. And he's taken an interest in you, that's good."

I hear some scrambling at Holger's end of the line. "Okay, we have a practice tonight at 20:00. Can you come after that?"

"Ja." My classes are winding up, and soon I will have no responsibilities at home. I will have too much time.

We arrange to meet at the arena, and I thank him.

It feels odd to be back. I get changed and then wait at the side of the rink. The familiar shouts of the coaches and the scrape of blades on the ice comfort me. The rink is my second home. After one long whistle, the players head off. Holger and Daniel, the head coach, both confer for a few moments. Daniel turns to look at me. I nod, but he returns no greeting. Holger motions me onto the ice.

"Get warmed up," he tells me. I skate a few laps, and then stretch. Holger sets up some pucks in front of the net.

I skate into the crease and shake out my arms.

"Are you ready?"

"Ja. Ready."

"We have only half an hour of ice. So, I'll start by seeing where you're at now," Holger says. He takes shots at me but stops frequently to make corrections.

"You're sloppy," he tells me. "Playing against bad players will do that to you. Good teams get rebounds, and you're too far out of position on every save. Don't show off."

I must focus. I have to regain my form. I concentrate on economy of movement.

In almost no time, our practice is over. I notice Daniel at the end of the rink watching us, but he's scowling. He leaves as soon as he sees that we're done. We move the nets so the ice can be scraped.

"Daniel doesn't approve of your coaching me?" I ask.

"Well, you're not insured because you're not on the team. But Daniel has other reasons."

I left his team five years ago, but he's still upset. We leave the ice and go into the change room. Holger sits across from me and makes notes on his clipboard while I get changed. He's writing out exercises for me.

"It's always tough to evaluate you because you're better in games than practices. I remember the first time I saw you in practice, I was shocked. 'That's our new backup goalie?' I asked, and Daniel assured me he had seen you play and you were excellent." Holger laughs. "And you were the starter in no time."

"Thanks to you," I say. Holger was the first one who really talked to me about the technical aspects of goal-tending. Before then, it was read and react.

"Nej. You were always good. And you kept improving. I'm not sure if it was technique or the way you read the play and the players." He shakes his head. "That's why Daniel Wallin is still pissed off. He thought he could win a championship with you. Then you quit!"

"That's not quite true. I was cut from the team," I say.

"Oh come on, Gabriel. You stopped coming to practice. You missed several games. How could we keep you on when you set such a bad example?"

"I understand that. I was only correcting your statement."

Holger throws back his head and laughs loudly. "Yes, this is the true Gabriel Olsson, getting the details perfect. You should have told us your mother was ill though. We could have worked something out."

But at that time, we didn't know exactly what was wrong. There were so many tests and doctor appointments. I had to be there because my mother couldn't seem to remember what the doctors were telling her. And she had so much pride. It was easier for me to say nothing than to admit that she was failing. It was what she wanted.

"Now that I have you here, there's one thing I have to know." Holger leans towards me. "Even when you were missing practice, you kept getting better. Were you practicing somewhere else?"

I shake my head. "Nej. It was visualization."

He waits for me to explain.

"I had a lot of time to wait, in medical clinics and on the train. So, I would work out scenarios in my head, players coming in from one side, shots up high, cross-crease passes. I would imagine and react to them." At first, I reacted physically: moving my hands and feet or shifting my body. I must have looked a fool. But eventually I learned how to react mentally. I could sit motionless on a hard plastic chair in the midst of a noisy clinic and transport myself to the net in a cold and quiet hockey rink. Perhaps that was my happy place.

"Were you upset when we cut you?" Holger asks. His voice is unusually gentle.

I shrug. I had been upset, but it wasn't about leaving the team. It was more that so many things were changing in my life at once, and hockey was a touchstone. But I couldn't keep travelling with the team, and my dismissal freed me up. At a time when my mother needed endless patience, I had more time. Freja is right; these days our attention to my mother means less and less. So it's good that I was there when it did matter.

"I understood why it happened," I say.

"Okay, so now you want to get back in game shape?"

I nod.

"How much free time do you have?"

"A lot." I hadn't yet called Jesper. Then I would know what was next for me.

"Well, I'll get you a lot of ice time then. We never have enough crazy men to play goal."

THE NEXT DAY, we move my mother to her new home. The past week has been difficult because she is sensitive to all the tension in the house.

Freja planned everything. The care facility she found is one we toured before, but it's been renovated since then and, according to her, there is new management. It's a nice place, for an institution. My mother's room is at the end of one of the wings, and there's a good-sized window facing out. There is a bare garden and trees that they assure us are beautiful in the summer.

We drive in Freja's ancient Saab. My mother is agitated because we seldom drive anywhere other than to see a doctor. We park in front of a low building with a large, fenced yard. There are a few people sitting outside on the porch even though it's a rainy day.

"Welcome, Milla." Two women have come out to greet us. One is a dark-haired woman in a suit and the other is a tiny woman in casual clothes. My mother squints at both of them. Then she shakes her head.

"Nej, nej. What is this place?" She doesn't want to go inside the institution, but we cajole her along. When we finally get to her room, she looks around in puzzlement. Freja and I came earlier. We arranged the room with her books, her favourite paintings, and even her wooden rocking chair. My mother recognizes the familiar objects, but not the place. She sits down in the chair and rocks, but a suspicious look remains on her face.

The woman in the suit is Ursula, the director. She gives us all a welcoming speech and some brochures, then leaves. The tiny woman stays.

"I'm Camille. I'll be looking after your mother in the daytime. There are several of us who work on shifts. But we try to ensure that she gets the same people for the first three months as she adjusts." Then Camille pulls out a clipboard and begins asking us a lot of questions about preferences and interests. She seems kind and smart, which reassures me that my mother will be well cared for.

"Would you like to come to lunch with her today?" Camille asks. "You'll be able to see that our food is quite good."

"Milla has a good appetite," my aunt says. She rises to go for lunch, but I shake my head.

"I'll stay here. There are still some things to put away."

231

I motion to the closet where there's a suitcase and packing box.

The three of them leave. I begin to hang up her clothes. The truth is that I don't like the dining room. It's not the food, which looks fine, but all the old people. In time I will learn their names and personalities, but they are so much older than my mother. Once again I'm struck by the unfairness. My mother should still be out in the field, doing research. She shouldn't be in a home with the elderly. Freja tells me there are other younger people here, but I haven't seen them yet. Besides, it doesn't matter. My mother is past making friends. She will exist here—doing appropriate activities, going for walks, getting visitors. It's not a life.

But is her life at home a life? I've been pondering ever since the decision to send her here. If a life consists of the same activities over and over, then my life is hardly better than hers. But maybe that will change soon. I pull Jesper Larson's card out of my wallet. Freja urged me to call him right away, but I wanted to wait until my mother had moved. Some part of me was unable to even reach for a new life until the old one was over. I turn the card over and over. It's become a talisman to me.

I am finished with the extra books and clothes by the time my mother gets back to the room.

"That was a lovely lunch, wasn't it, Milla?" my aunt says. "You must be hungry, Gabe. I brought you back a sandwich."

"Thank you," I say. I put the wrapped sandwich in my coat pocket. I have no appetite right now.

Freja clears her throat. "Well, I guess we should be going now."

I nod. I go over and hug my mother. "Bye, *mamma*. I'll see you tomorrow."

When Freja does the same, my mother's eyes dart around the room. "Nej. Don't go."

She rises to follow us. Freja coaxes her to sit back down. "Would you like to watch television?"

I switch on the remote and by luck there's a nature show on, which is the sort of thing my mother enjoys. But she's too upset to watch anything.

Camille strides into the room. "Milla, will you show me your photo album?" She settles my mother onto the couch and takes a family photo album off the shelf. "Tell me who all these people are."

This diversion seems to work. My mother looks down and points. "My little Gabriel."

Freja tugs at my sleeve so we can get away while my mother is distracted. My aunt has to pull me along the hallway. My feet stumble as if they're torn between coming and going.

When we get inside the car, my eyes are drawn to the window of her room. What will she do when she notices we are gone? How will she feel? She asked us not to leave.

"Will she be okay?" I ask. It's a ridiculous question since Freja knows no more than I do.

She pats my hand. "Don't worry. They warned me that things will be bad for the first week or two. But once Milla becomes settled, she'll be fine."

I barely listen. *My little Gabriel.* The tenderness in my mother's voice pulls at me. As I buckle my seat belt, a tear rolls down my cheek and falls invisibly onto my black jeans.

31

A CHANCE

GABRIEL

I'VE REHEARSED this a dozen times, but I'm no less nervous. I call Jesper Larson at his office.

"Hello." His voice is deep yet reminds of Lily's in some indefinable way.

"*Hej*, Jesper. It's Gabriel Olsson. From Lund?" I'm not sure whether to speak Swedish or English, but I decide that English will be better for my purposes.

It takes a few beats for him to even remember who I am, and I fear that this whole scheme is pointless.

"Ah yes, Lily's friend."

"You had offered to help me play a higher level of hockey..." I begin.

"Right." He snaps to attention. I can hear in his voice that the hockey part appeals to him. "Do you want me to contact Gunnar Lundström? He's scouting in your area, and he knows all the teams. It's pretty late in the season, but you can get in the door and then next season, you'll be set. I have other friends in Malmö too."

"Actually, is there any place I could play in Canada?"

"In Canada?"

"Ja. Anywhere really. Any level. I'm looking for a new experience."

There's a long silence. When he speaks again, his voice is cold. "Does this have to do with Lily? No team is going to pay your way here so you can have a holiday. Besides, she has school. Don't you?"

"My term is over now," I explain. "I am going to take the next term off."

"Look, Gabriel, you should do this the right way. Start playing for a team in Malmö and then—if you're good enough—you can come to training camp here next September. I'll talk to Gunnar about that. Or if you want to see Lily, talk to her and make arrangements. Maybe in the summer."

But it might be too late by then. This is my opportunity to see Lily and tell her exactly how I feel. It's our chance to be together again.

"I understand that. It's not about money. I can pay my own way there and make my own accommodations. And if the hockey doesn't work, I will visit Lily for a short time and return."

"Why all the urgency?" he asks.

I take a deep breath. It's time to be as open as Lily. "For a long time, my mother has not been well. I gave up hockey to look after her. But now, things have changed. I hope to play again."

How can I explain to him what Lily awakened in me? I've lived my routine life for so long, but now I dream again. My dreams are about becoming someone more than average—someone who deserves a person like Lily. While I could play in Sweden, I want more.

"So your mother is better now?" he asks. His voice is gentle now, the tones he uses with Lily.

"Nej. She is worse. She moved to a care facility this week." Since my mother has made this sacrifice, I want to do something worthwhile. I want to journey far away and take chances. If I were to play hockey in Lund, she could still be with me. I will leave, then Freja will leave, and our lives will shift.

"I'm finally free to pursue something new," I explain. To test myself against the world.

"Okay," Jesper says. "I understand you more. However it's not up to me. It's definitely not the right time, but teams are dealing with injuries now."

I wait in hope.

He sighs. "Gabriel, I'm going to have to get back to you about this."

"Thank you. I will appreciate anything you can do." I make one final plea. "I'll be better than what you saw. I've been practicing hard."

"No promises," he says. But the coldness is gone from his voice.

LILY

THERE'S a knock on my door. These days, knocks cause panic because Seb is taking way too many chances. He's going to get into deep trouble if my dad catches him in my room. He seems to have accepted the whole friends thing, but he's an opportunist. If I have another bad night, he's ready, willing, and horny. But I'm not going to have another bad night.

"Come in," I say.

My dad walks in. Well, this is awkward. Things have been tense between us. Initially, I was pissed that he wouldn't do anything about Jason. Now that I've cooled down, I realize that I may have been a little unreasonable. But I'm not willing to apologize either.

I'm half-lying on the bed, but I sit up.

"What do you want?" I ask. My tone is sharper than I intended, and he flinches slightly.

"I got a call from your friend in Lund. Gabriel Olsson."

"Gabe called you?" I'm so shocked that I almost fall off the bed. "Why?"

"He wants to come to Canada. To play hockey."

What the what? Gabe is coming here? I feel a flush of happiness. Is Gabe coming to Vancouver to see me? But why hasn't he talked to me about this? Guiltily, I remember I haven't been answering Gabe's messages. It's like I've been deliberately cutting myself off from the people I care about the most. Lily Larson, idiot.

"Can he even play here?" I ask.

"Honestly, I don't know. He's too old to play junior hockey, and I'm not sure if he's good enough to play pro."

"So, what did you tell him?"

"Well, I told him I'd ask around. Then I called Chris. Apparently, the Vice have been going through a lot of goalies lately. They sent one guy up to the Millionaires and called up someone from the ECHL. So they might be interested in an ECHL goalie."

"That's one step below the Vice, right?" I ask, and he nods.

"Yeah, there's also a league below that, but I don't think he'd want to play there. He'd be better off staying in Europe." My dad runs a hand through his short hair. "The thing is, we don't know how good he is. He looked great when I saw him, but the quality of opponent was very low. According to Gunnar, he used to be quite talented. But who knows what he's like now."

"Gabe is really smart. You always say the best players are smart." I'm still numb at the news. "It would be nice for him to get a chance."

"I wanted to check with you before I do anything," my dad says.

"Why?"

"Because..." He leans towards me. "This isn't going to turn into another Jason situation, is it?"

For one shattering moment, I wonder if it is. Did Gabe go out with me just to get a chance to play hockey in Canada? No, that's ridiculous. I shake my head. "Gabe didn't even know you were my dad when we became friends. In fact, I'm really surprised that he called you. He said he didn't want to play hockey in any serious way."

"Frankly I could care less about what he wants. I care about you. Would you like Gabe to come here for a tryout?"

A whoosh of air goes out of me. Gabe—my rock—here in Vancouver. That would be amazing. I nod.

"I'm just so surprised. Last time I spoke to him, he said he couldn't travel anywhere."

"Because of his mother?" my dad asks.

"Yeah. Did he tell you about her?" Now I'm ready to fall off the other side of the bed. Gabe never spoke about his mom the whole time I was in Sweden, and now he's blabbing to everyone.

"Yes, apparently she's in a care facility now, that's why he can come. It's admirable that he quit hockey to take care of her." Another thing my dad likes in a hockey player is character. And Gabe has a ton of character.

"Why don't we invite him to stay here while he tries out?" I suggest. "I don't know how much money he has."

My dad shakes his head. "Well, let's check with your mom first. It's getting to be a crowded place with Seb here."

Oh Seb, I forgot all about him. I'm sure it will be okay with my mom, who loves to entertain. But I'll volunteer to do laundry and even cook if it means I'll be under the same roof as Gabe.

32

DOSTADNING

Gabriel

THE EMAIL RESPONSE from Jesper Larson is amazing. I can come to Vancouver for an evaluation. Their AHL team, the Vancouver Vice, needs a new goalie in the system, at the ECHL level. What an opportunity!

But will this be okay with Lily?

My hand is shaking as I message her.

Your father has invited me to Vancouver for a tryout.

I wait. After a few minutes, I get a response.

I know. He told me.

Of course he did. They are so close. It's only in my family that we do major things without consultation. My father has no idea that I'm going to Canada. I intend to tell him, but I am waiting until I have concrete news.

Another message comes up: *Why are you doing this now? I thought hockey was over for you.*

I take a deep breath. It's a good question. If I'm going to be more honest with Lily, now is the time to start.

I want to come to Vancouver so I can see you.

There's another long wait. Am I being an idiot? Is she still angry with me?

Then my phone buzzes. It's Lily on Facetime.

"*Hej, hej,*" I say. Seeing her beautiful face inspires me. Perhaps all this sacrifice will be worthwhile.

"*Hej* yourself." Her expression is guarded, but not angry. And hearing her voice makes me feel better. "So, you're going to all the trouble of a hockey tryout just to visit little old me?"

She is neither little or old, but I'm sure she knows that. "Of course I am taking the hockey portion seriously. I have been practicing. But yes, you are the main reason."

"Hmmm. But last time we talked, you were all, 'Oh, Lily, we can never see each other.'"

I will have to work my way back into Lily's good graces. "My situation has changed."

Her voice drops to a serious tone. "What's happening with your mother?"

"She's had to move into a care facility," I explain.

"And how do you feel about that?" Ugh, with Lily it is always about exploring your feelings. I hate this. Probably because I still feel guilty—like I shouldn't have done it. Despite the promises, my mother does not appear happy there. The last time I visited, she cried. I believe she wants me to take her home, but Camille tells us that she is content when we are not there.

"I feel like shit."

"Oh Gabe." Now Lily's expression is wide-eyed and sympathetic.

I rush on. "She is upset being there. She is surrounded by persons much older and more infirm."

It is the finality of the move that bothers me most. While I knew that my mother would never get better, now she can only get worse. The remaining stages of her life are illustrated in the other patients.

We don't speak for a few moments, then Lily adds, "I'm sure your mother wants you to live your life though."

That is a platitude I keep hearing, but I can never know if it's the truth. But I agreed with Freja and my father that this would be the better and safer place for my mother, so constantly questioning that consensus decision is not helpful. Intellectually, I understand this is the right move for her, but I feel lost and bereft. I miss her presence each day.

I won't keep dwelling on this. I'll focus on the trip. "I have never flown this far before."

"I'm really looking forward to seeing you again. And I get to show you Vancouver."

"Ja. That will be nice." Nice seems inadequate for everything I want to express to Lily. "I have a lot to tell you. You know, to share with you."

Lily giggles. "You had a lot of trouble with the word 'share.'"

"I'm Swedish. We're not good at this."

"That's not true," she replies. "Lots of people I met in Lund were good at sharing."

"Okay, then it's only me. I'm not good at this. But I'll try."

She lowers her voice. "Do or not do. There is no try."

I laugh. It's the first time I've laughed in a week. Lily is a tonic for me. "Okay, Ms. Yoda. I will share. Once I get there."

"When are you getting here?"

"I'll get my ticket and let you know."

"You can stay with us," she offers.

"No, that would be too much trouble. I'll find a hostel or something."

"That takes hockey bags? Look, it's no trouble. It'll be easier because my dad will want to be on top of what you're doing."

"Okay. Thank you very much."

"Great. Send me your flight details, and I'll pick you up at the airport," she says.

"*Tack*, Lily," I say. Thank you is inadequate for everything I feel right now. Only a few words with Lily, and her energy warms me again. And soon, we'll see each other in person.

I'm almost overwhelmed by everything that must be done. Jesper's email asks me to come as soon as possible. Luckily, this is exactly the kind of task that Freja excels at. She's the one who arranges for my open-ended flight ticket, makes a packing list for me, and helps fill out the forms the team has sent. And she's delighted to do it all.

The other good thing is that my mother is finally settling into her new home. At first, she'd regressed a lot. She was disoriented and miserable. I wanted to bring my mother back home, but Freja insisted it would only be a transition period. And she turned out to be right.

My aunt is happier too. She is ready to begin the next phase of our lives.

"Gabriel, this is exactly what you deserve. An adventure! You need to embrace life with two hands."

Since we are both leaving—me now, and Freja later—we must clean out the apartment and put the excess in storage.

Going through my room is simple. There are a few poetry books I want to keep, but most other things I can give away. I've never been one for memorabilia anyway, so my room is already spare.

Then we proceed to my mother's remaining things.

"I think she went through her belongings when she knew she was sick," Freja says. "There are no letters or journals. I know she kept journals."

"She did a cleaning when my father left."

She was fuelled by anger then, an anger we didn't realize was part of her illness. I assumed it was a rage against him, which I gladly took on. All reminders of him were thrown out.

"Ahh, look here." Freja has found a few boxes at the back of the closet. They are shoebox-sized and bound tightly with string. Tucked under the string is a note.

My mother's bold black handwriting jolts me. She was fond of note writing. I would come home from school to notes instructing me on dinner or activities, or explaining where my parents would be. When I was younger she would slip good luck notes into my hockey skates.

Freja unfolds the first message carefully. She must be feeling the same shock that I am. It's like opening a time capsule.

"To be burned," she reads. She peeks into the box. "Ahh, these are her journals I think. It seems a shame to burn them, she was such a good writer."

Freja is wavering. Her nature is curious, and she longs

to leaf through the journals. "I wonder if she anticipated that we might read them?" she posits.

"She may have, but I don't think we should. Johan's family has a fireplace, I'll take the box there and burn it."

I gently remove the box from her hands and put it behind me.

Freja laughs. "You are very like Milla. If the tables were turned, she wouldn't read my journals."

Then she unfolds the next note. "Oh! This is for me." She fumbles with the string and finally opens the box. There are letters, photos, and a few mementoes.

"Aha. I had all forgotten about this." She holds up a tiny scrap of red and yellow fabric. "Our mother made us blouses from this fabric, and we hated it. So garish, like clown costumes. So your mother arranged for an 'accident' and our tops were ink-stained beyond repair. Of course we got in trouble, and we had to wear old blouses that spring. But it was worth it." Freja caresses the tiny swatch and laughs. "I can't believe she kept this scrap all these years. Milla was so bold. I always wanted to be more like her."

For years my mother has been a shadow of her former self. But examining old objects is bringing back so many memories of her. Her strength. Her quick wit. Her protectiveness.

My aunt continues to sort through her treasure box, and I pick up the last shoe box. Even as I unfold the paper, I know what it will say.

For Gabriel.

I feel uneasy as I open the box. I don't want mementoes of my childhood like Freja's, because I don't want to live in the past. What I want most is some explanation of how she feels now, of whether sending her to an institution is the right thing or merely for my own convenience. But how can she answer a question that never arose before? Once we knew she was ill, her grasp on the present became so tenuous that the future was unthinkable.

I pull off the lid. My box is not stuffed with memorabilia. There are only two envelopes: one fat and one thin.

I open the thin one first.

My dear Gabriel, it is a great challenge to write to you without knowing if I can communicate my meaning. Each day I feel diminished, as if I am losing parts of myself. I apologize for my strange behaviours. I am aware, yet cannot stop myself.

The hardest ordeal for me is not to see you become an adult. But I am comforted by knowing what a good person you are already—moral, strong, and kind. Your future will be bright.

Someday you too will know the great joy that comes from being a parent. And perhaps I'll see my grandchildren, but who knows? I would like them to know me in some way though, so I am passing on some small remembrances.

Gabriel, my love always. I am proud of the man you are already.

Mamma

My vision is blurred as I open the second envelope. Inside tissue wrappings, I find a silver baby spoon. It has a curved handle and feels solid in my large hand. *Bebis Olsson* has been engraved into the handle. She arranged this with her last energies, not knowing what the future would be, but wanting to be part of it. To feed a grandchild she may never touch.

There are two more tiny packages. The first contains a silver chain with a charm that's shaped like a soaring bird.

This must be for my daughter. I open the last one and find a pair of thick silver cufflinks. They must be for my future son, but I'm going to wear them now. I will pass them on to him. And I can tell him stories about the woman who gave him this gift.

I curl my fingers around the cufflinks. They feel oddly warm. I can never know how my mother feels now, but she saw a bright future for me, and I'm going to grasp it.

33

ROUGH LANDING

Lily

"Miriam is coming back next week."

My mother is assigning chores from her to-do list *while* we help with dinner. It's like pouring water into a glass that's already full. Actually, Margie and I are helping with dinner, Seb is fooling around on his phone, and Alexander disappeared into the bathroom ten minutes ago. I complain loudly and am answered by an echoing yell of "I'm pooping!" The Larson family at its classiest.

"So, everyone needs to clean up their rooms," Mom adds. "Even you, Seb."

"Ja, no problem," he answers. Due to his mother and sisters, Seb has a healthy respect for female authority. Miriam is our full-time nanny turned housekeeper. She still looks after Alexander, but also does the million things that keep our large home running smoothly. Although we've had Molly Maids in every week, my mother's been a little harried during the month Miriam's been away. Mom loves cooking, but hates cleaning.

"Also, Lily, don't forget you're picking up Gabriel at the airport tomorrow afternoon."

"Right. What time was that again?" I ask.

She checks her planner. "Um, 15:30... which is 3:30."

"Shoot." Ironically, while I have been nervously anticipating Gabe's arrival and everything that I'm hoping will happen, I somehow got it into my head that he was arriving at 5:30pm. Stupid 24-hour clocks.

"Is there a problem?" my mother asks.

"Nooo, um, yeah. I've got an in-class test then. Well, it's not a big deal. I'll message Gabe and ask him to wait at the airport until I can get there. It'll only be a couple of hours."

"Lily! That's so inconsiderate." She consults the holy planner further. "Let's see, maybe I can... oh no, Alexander has power-skating after school, so I'm already... well, perhaps Margie can get him."

"I have school then," says Margie. And if she didn't, she would sign up for an after school club. Nothing would make Margie more uncomfortable than having to drive a total stranger anywhere, especially a young guy.

"I'll ask your dad then," says Mom. Maybe she could put more disapproval in her voice.

"I can do it. I have no game or practices," offers Seb.

"Oh really, Seb? That would be wonderful," says my mom.

"Yeah, happy to greet a fellow Swede." That's true, it will be nice for Seb to have Gabe here to speak Swedish with and to marvel at the weird ways of Canadians. Now that he's stopped hitting on me at every chance, I like Seb a lot more.

"Thanks. I'll connect you guys so you can meet up," I say.

"Why don't you show Seb a photo of Gabriel," suggests my mom, who is dying to see a photo herself.

I do an internal eye-roll but search through my phone. Most of them are goofy selfies of us in front of various attractions in Lund. I linger on one where he's kissing my cheek and I'm laughing. Finally, I find a photo that's him alone and show Seb. My mother peeks over his shoulder.

"Oh, he's a very nice-looking boy," she says before resuming her kitchen command post, no doubt scheduling all my free time for the next six months.

"Here, Seb. Give me your phone, and I'll put his number in. That way if you miss him, you can message each other."

Seb nods, and we trade phones. I add the name and number and when I look up, Seb is scrolling through my photos.

"Hey! That's private." I snatch my phone back and return his.

"Who is this guy again?" he asks.

"He's a friend. From Lund."

Chatty Seb doesn't say another word. Then Alexander finally emerges and gets assigned to take out the compost and recycling. I set the table and imagine tomorrow night's dinner when Gabe will be here in person. I can't wait.

———

Gabriel

I AM 10,000 metres above the Arctic Ocean. Flights mean adventure and something new. Even before my mother got sick, we never took adventurous holidays. We had a summer cabin in the north. I've been to Stockholm and, of course, Copenhagen many times, but hardly any place else.

On my way to the airport, I visited my mother one last time. I told her I was going to Canada, but not when I'll be back. While Freja keeps reassuring me that my mother is happier now, I still feel guilty. These exciting new experiences I'm having are at her expense.

My father has kept his word and visits as well. My mother is always happy to see him. He promised to keep me updated. Of course, it is part of a scheme to stay in touch with me, but I can accept that for her sake. He was excited about my playing competitive hockey again, but I warned him to keep his expectations low. Jesper Larson couldn't make any promises. I understand that. He saw me excel in an unimportant game, but it will be up to me to earn my own opportunities.

The Vancouver airport is very beautiful. There is an indoor waterfall and Native Canadian art. The customs line-up is long, but the people are friendly. I finally get through and go to find my bags. I offered to get to their house on my own, but Lily said she would pick me up.

I find my baggage carousel and wait. My suitcase arrives, and I'm directed somewhere else to get my hockey bag.

"*Hej*. Gabriel Olsson?"

I turn, and there's another Swede there. He's stocky with long, blond hair and about my age. He speaks in Swedish, explaining that's he's here to pick me up. He's smiling, but it's not a sincere smile.

"Seb Söderlund." He holds out his hand, and we shake.

I still don't know why *he's* here though, so I ask, "Who are you?"

"The Larsons are my billet family." Seb says.

He's inserted an English word I'm not familiar with, so I ask about it. "What does 'billet' mean?"

"Well, it's the family you live with, you know, while you play hockey."

"How old are you?"

"Nineteen," he replies.

"Why aren't you living on your own?" I'm not even sure why I've taken a dislike to Seb. Maybe it's my disappointment at Lily not being here.

Seb ducks his head. "I was. But the team thought it would be better for me to have, you know, support."

"Who do you play hockey for?" I ask.

"The Vancouver Vice." The AHL team. A level above what I'm being considered for.

I don't say anything to that and he continues, "I'll be in the NHL next year though. I almost made it in training camp this year."

We walk outside. The weather is grey and rainy. But a bit warmer than Lund, where it was snowing when I left.

"I hear you're trying out for our ECHL team."

"Ja. Do you know them?"

"Sure, a few guys on my team have been called up from there." He opens the trunk of a metallic blue Ford Mustang, and I put my luggage in. We climb into the low-

slung seats. It's exactly the car I would imagine him driving. Seb reminds me of teammates who were convinced they were going to be NHL stars. They would fantasize about the way they'd live once they'd made it—cars, homes, women. This car is the fantasy of a fourteen year old.

"The call-ups are pretty happy to get here," Seb adds.

"Well, naturally," I reply. "To make a better league."

"Ja, but more to live in Vancouver." He motions outside the car, but right now all I can see are airport buildings.

"Where is the ECHL team?" I ask. This is something I should have researched, but everything came together so quickly that I didn't have time.

"Uh, it's in Flint." Seb says.

"Flint? Is that near here?" There's only one Flint I've heard of, and it's famous for having water problems.

"Nej. It's in Michigan."

Michigan? In the fucking United States? That's across the continent from here. I've come all the way to Vancouver to see Lily, and if I succeed I'll be flying across the country again. I run a hand through my hair.

Seb is smiling now. "Ah, you didn't know? Gotta do your homework if you want to play pro hockey."

Having this teenaged asshole lecture me isn't making things better. I realize that the reason I didn't like him was because I sensed he didn't like me. He's happy that I'm upset.

"So, how do you know Lily?" Seb asked.

"We met in Lund," I reply.

"Unh." He accelerates past a truck. "She's amazing, right?"

"Ja." I don't like where this conversation is going.

"I'm sure a lucky guy." Seb glances over at me with a smile on his face. "To get to be with her."

Finding out where the ECHL team is located is nothing compared to this blow.

He continues, "Some jerk hurt her badly. So she needs someone she can depend on."

Was that me? I was a complete jerk when I broke up with her that last day. I should have told her the truth. And that's why I'm even here—to get a chance to explain. She seemed happy to have me come and visit. Her messages since have been full of her usual positivity. Yet this is exactly the situation I foretold. Lily is an amazing person. She could have a new boyfriend in a moment. Maybe she's rebounding with this guy, who's clearly not her equal in any way. But neither am I. I hurt her, and this is what I deserve.

"So you live together and date? That's very convenient." Also surprising. My impression of Jesper is that he'd prefer not to be involved in his daughter's love life. My invitation to stay with them was Lily's initiative.

"Well, we have to keep things a secret right now." Seb concentrates on the road. "So, we can't go out that much."

Wait. Could it be that this guy is bullshitting me? But why would he do that when it's so easy for me to ask Lily if it's true?

He continues, "Nobody in her family knows. We're waiting for the right time to tell them."

I have to ask. "What kind of relationship do you actually have?"

His mouth twists up in that smile I'm beginning to hate. "The usual. We hang out. We have sex."

34

NHL CRIBS

GABRIEL

WE TURN off the highway onto a winding road. It's evening, so all I can see are dark hedges and glimpses of houses beyond. The neighbourhood looks pretty nice.

Seb slows in front of a pebbled driveway with a metal gate. He pulls out a remote, and the gate slowly began to slide open. Do they live in one of those gated communities I've read about? He manoeuvres up a steep driveway and parks in front of a four-car garage. In the twilight gloom, sparkling lights highlight a wide two-storey house the size of a small hotel.

"We're here," says Seb. "Pretty nice, right?"

Helvete.

I grab my suitcase and hockey bag from the trunk and follow him up the front steps. Okay, I know that Lily's father is a former NHL superstar. And I know how much money NHL superstars make. But I've never understood how rich her family is. They live in a mansion. I should have guessed from how casually she'd suggested I could stay with them. They could host an entire team of Swedish hockey players. My home could fit in their garage.

The front door swings open.

"Gabe!"

Lily flies out and hugs me. The press of her body, the tickle of her hair on my cheek, and that familiar hum of energy—all of it elevates me. I wrap my arms around her.

"Lily. So good to see you again," I murmur into her ear.

I never want to let her go, but Seb clears his throat loudly beside us.

"Lily is getting wet," he points out, as if I'm deliberately trying to expose her to pneumonia.

She smiles at him. "Thanks so much for picking up Gabe, Seb."

I watch them carefully but I can't detect anything special in the way she speaks to him. There's an intimacy, but it doesn't seem to be a secret relationship.

"Gabe's here," Lily declares as we enter the house. A medium-sized brown dog is the only one who responds to her call, and he begins sniffing me. I remove my shoes and wonder what to do next. It feels sacrilegious to even drop my crappy bags on the polished marble floors. As I hold them, a woman comes down the stairs to greet me. She is tall and slim with blonde hair curling around her face. She wears jeans, a white shirt, and some gold bracelets. She looks twenty years younger than my mother—and much more glamorous.

"Welcome, Gabriel. I'm Dori." She pulls me into a perfumed hug. "How was your flight?"

"Fine. Good," I say.

"Are you tired? We're going to have dinner in about an hour, but you could rest until then."

"He's not an old man, Mom," Lily says. "Nobody our age would have a nap."

"Hockey players nap before games," her mother points out. On the surface, Lily and her mother look alike, but Lily resembles her father in the direct way she speaks and acts. Her mother is softer and more polite. She smiles at me. "Jes tells me you're an excellent goalie."

"Well, perhaps. I hope so." I motion to my bags. "Where should I put my things?"

"We've got you upstairs in the guest room," Dori says. "Lily, can you please show Gabriel his room. I have to pop out and pick up Alexander."

"Sure. Follow me." She skips up the wide staircase, and I hoist my bags. Seb follows too.

Lily has already disappeared down a hallway by the time we get upstairs. She pokes her head out. "In here, slowpoke."

"I'm carrying heavy bags," I point out.

"Yes, I guess a good hostess would have volunteered to carry something, but they look way too big."

Or Seb could have helped, but his main aim seems to be preventing me from being alone with Lily. Should I have even have brought my hockey bag upstairs? My mother always banished it to the shed because of the smell. This house smells fresh and citrusy, and I don't want to destroy that.

Not surprisingly, my room is huge with a king bed

with many, many pillows decorating it. Lily points out all the features like a woman on a game show. "Closet here, the dresser's empty so feel free to use it, your bathroom is there, and—" She fans herself, "It's kind of hot, the room thermostat is here."

"Why is he up here near you?" asks Seb.

"Because you already have the guest suite," she answers.

"Lily, your home is so nice," I say.

Then I forget all about her home as I take a really good look at Lily. She's as lovely as ever in black jeans and a ruffled blouse that makes her look like a sexy pirate queen. My entire body yearns to be close to her, but I resist the temptation. If there is a possibility that she and Seb are dating, that changes everything.

"Did you want to unpack, shower, or have a tour of the house?"

Only one of those options means being with Lily. Besides, if I don't have a tour, I'll probably get lost. "I'll take the tour, please."

Then I remember something. I unzip my backpack and take out a little cardboard box.

"It's for you, from Lund."

She opens it up. "*Kanelbulle*! Oh my God, thank you." She hugs me again. And then she begins to eat it right away. "Soooo good. This is the flavour I've been missing."

"I should have got you to bring me some Kalles," Seb says. Ja, except why would I bring fish paste for someone I didn't even know existed? Lily never mentioned him at all.

Lily continues the tour, motioning towards rooms with a half-eaten *kanelbulle*. Crumbs fly across the polished wood floors, but she's oblivious.

"I'm across the hall from you." She swings open the door on a bedroom that is strewn with clothes, papers, and general crap. Underneath the decor is very girlish. Not what I would have expected from Lily.

"It's very, uh, pink," I say.

Lily punches me in the arm. "Are you teasing me? My mother decorated it. I was going to redecorate, but then I was leaving for university anyway."

"What happened? I thought you were living with your friends when you got back."

"I was supposed to. But Jenny—one of the roomies in our house—backed out of her exchange. There wasn't room for me. I didn't want to move in with a bunch of strangers, so I'm going to wait until next fall. I'll have a lot more options then." She points to a closed door and speaks loudly. "That's Margie's room. She's always doing weird stuff in there."

"I can hear you," a soft voice declares from behind a door decorated with a wooden letter "M" painted with cats.

"I know you can, Squirt. Come out and meet Gabe."

The door opens, and a young blonde girl appears. Her face is broader than Lily's, and her hair slightly darker. She smiles awkwardly at me.

"Nicetomeetcha," she says and then the door closes again.

"And that will be the extent of your conversation with my little sister," Lily says. "She's not real big on talking to strangers."

"Somebody has to listen," I point out. So far, I've only met Jesper, Dori, and Lily, and all are extroverted.

Lily widens her eyes in mock outrage. "Was that

shade? You haven't even met my brother yet, and he's the chatterbox of the family." She swings open another door. "This is his room."

This bedroom is also untidy, but blue underneath. Somehow it makes me feel more comfortable that the bedrooms are untidy. The house looks like a furniture showroom downstairs, but real people live upstairs.

"That's my parents' bedroom." I catch a glimpse of a vast master bedroom through the doorway. It has its own sitting room.

The three of us go back downstairs and pass quickly through the living room with its oversized furniture and view of the twinkling downtown. A dining room with a table that could seat an entire hockey team. Two home offices. I'm shaking my head, and Seb nods in agreement. "It's unbelievable, right?" he says in Swedish.

And then we get to the kitchen. It's huge and gleaming. There is another table in here, which appears to be where normal eating takes place. It's already set for dinner.

"If you want a snack or anything, help yourself." She opens various cupboards to reveal unfamiliar packaging. The final cupboard she opens turns out to be a giant refrigerator neatly stuffed with food.

"Okay, let's go downstairs." Lily leads the way.

"There's another floor?" I say.

Lily makes a face. "I know. It's too much, right?"

"Nej. But this is the biggest house I've ever seen in real life."

"You probably won't believe this, but I miss my little room back in Lund so much."

"I miss it too," I say, remembering our intimate times

there. I am certain that Seb is trying to murder me with his glare, but I don't care. I've seen nothing to indicate that Lily likes him at all.

I follow her downstairs. There is a vast media room featuring an immense television and leather couches.

"This is my room," says Seb. It's a large suite consisting of a bedroom, sitting room, and small kitchen. Well, small by the standards of this house. It is only slightly smaller than our kitchen at home. It doesn't look like Seb is doing any cooking here. The kitchen is pristine, while the rest of the place is untidy.

Lily leads me through a game room with a ping-pong table, a foosball table, and a poker table. Then she opens the door on a home gym.

"You can work out here, but put things back where you found them. My father has a routine that he doesn't want anyone messing with." She rolls her eyes.

I am distracted by an adjacent room with Plexiglas panels around it. It's dark, but looks very familiar.

"Is that...?"

Lily laughs. "Yup. It sure is!" She opens a wide door, flips on a switch, and lights up an indoor rink. Instead of ice, the floors are smooth laminate, but there are boards, painted lines, face-off circles, and goalie nets at each end.

"You have your own rink?" I am having trouble closing my mouth because my jaw is so slack.

"Yeah. It's crazy, right?"

"Did your dad practice here?"

"Nah, it's just for fun. We used to play as a family. Mostly in shoes, but Alexander likes to wear in-line skates too."

"I can't believe you have a rink in your house," I repeat like a parrot.

"Well, I'm sure you'll get to try it out. Nobody ever wants to play goal, so having a real goalie will be the best. Do not let Alexander suck you into playing hockey when you don't feel like it."

I haven't played as much hockey as I wanted since I was a small boy. But now, what can stop me? I have no school and no responsibilities other than the goalie tryout. I feel as light as a dandelion blossom.

I grin. "It's like living at Disneyland or something."

Lily snorts dismissively. "The happiest place on earth? Hardly."

"I am very happy here," Seb announces. He moves behind Lily, and his stance is protective. Lily looks over her shoulder and frowns.

Dori appears in the doorway. "Lily, can you give me a hand with dinner?"

Lily makes a face but nods. She leans towards me. "We still need to get caught up."

"Ja, for sure. Can I help you, Dori?" I ask.

"No, no, you just relax," Lily's mom replies. "I know you had a long flight. You and Seb can game or whatever. Dinner will be ready soon."

Once Lily and Dori have gone upstairs, Seb sprawls on the couch. He's clearly trying to assert his territorial dominance. He flips on the TV and scrolls through games. I sit down as well.

"I told you to leave Lily alone," he tells me in Swedish.

"What happens between me and Lily is up to her," I reply.

"I know guys like you. My sister dated one. He had to cut her down to make himself feel big."

I shake my head. I have never insulted Lily in any way. Even our break-up was because I believed that she was too good for me. "You know nothing about me."

"You hurt her. You messed her up big time," Seb says.

Yes, but Lily told me she wasn't mad anymore. "If Lily forgives me, why is it your business? Because I don't believe that you're having any kind of relationship with Lily—except in your imagination."

He turns to face me, and once again that stupid fucking smile is on his face. "Here's what I do know: Lily likes to be kissed on that mole she has—right here."

And he points to the exact place on his upper thigh where Lily has a prominent mole.

35

CROSS PURPOSES

LILY

SOMETHING'S WRONG WITH GABE. I didn't think he was going to walk in, sweep me off my feet, and declare his undying love, but I was hoping for some signal of affection. But he's giving me zip. Now at the dinner table, he's practically comatose. I want him to make a good impression on my family, but Gabe's acting like he's undead.

Seb begins the hockey inquisition. "If you were playing in the highest league when you were sixteen, why did you drop out? Did you get cut?"

"No, I had family reasons."

My Dad knows what's going on, but my mom looks mystified. I catch Gabe's eye and send a telepathic message: *Please make an effort.*

He clears his throat. "My parents split up, and I had more responsibilities."

My mom tilts her head sympathetically. Well, if she can't be impressed by his personality, pity will have to do.

"It's gonna be great to have a goalie around to shoot at," Alexander says. "Uh, Lily, pass me the potatoes."

Gabe's not even eating that much. I wish we had been able to talk alone, but Seb insisted on tagging along for the whole house tour. He must be so happy to have another Swede here.

"Did we ever play each other in Sweden?" Seb asks Gabe.

"I doubt it. You're three years younger."

"I played up though," Seb says.

My father gets back to Gabe's tryout. "So we'll have to figure out when we can get you out on the ice. Lucky— Chris Luczak—really wants to see you. They need to shore up their goaltending, and he hasn't been satisfied with any of the prospects he's seen."

"Ya, that's true," Seb says. "Makey is good, but there's a big gap between him and our backup."

"It's tough to tell because Mark Pillsbury hasn't played that much," Dad says. "Goats has been riding Mäkinen." When my dad starts talking hockey, it's like another language.

"That's because Coach wants to win. Whenever Doughy starts, we lose," Seb points out.

"So that's the goaltender's fault?" Gabe asks. He looks pissed off. Seb shovels more salmon into his mouth instead of replying.

My dad clears his throat. "Well, we're going to find out how good Pillsbury is now that Mäkinen's been called up. And they called up the starter from the ECHL team. If your workout looks good, that's where you could end up, Gabriel. It's quite a few levels above your last team."

Gabe only nods. He doesn't even look that excited.

"Where is the ECHL team?" I ask.

"It's in Flint," my dad says. "Michigan."

What? I was hoping that Gabe would end up playing here. "Why is it so far away?" I ask.

"It's not ideal, but their last ECHL franchise went under, so they had to make a deal with a new team. Michigan's a good state to play in, lots of hockey fans there." says Dad. Ever since his best friend started running the team, my father has gotten extremely interested in the Vancouver Vice. He and Chris must discuss the team during their day-long bike rides on the weekend.

"They have the best name," my brother says. "The Flint Flying Squirrels." Gabe looks unimpressed at becoming a flying squirrel. I'm not that excited either.

"So, when would you like to come in for your tryout? Do you want to rest up for a day or two?" my father asks. I realize that he wants Gabe to succeed. I'm not sure if this is to prove his scouting abilities or because he actually likes Gabe. Dad and I still don't talk like we used to, and I feel pretty guilty about that.

"Tomorrow is fine," Gabe replies flatly. I want to shake him and make him show some excitement. Look at all the things he's done so far: travelled around the world, taken a term off school, made a financial commitment. None of this shows.

"I'm happy to come if you need a shooter," Seb offers.

I smile at Seb. That's the kind of energy my dad likes to see, and sure enough he's nodding. "Good idea, Sebastian. I'll call Chris tonight and see if what works for them.

weeks, so it's a good time to have a look at you."

"Maybe you can finally come to a game, Lily," Seb suggests.

"Sure, I'd love to."

Now Gabe is scowling at me. What is his problem?

WHAT TO WEAR to bed tonight? On one hand, I have school tomorrow, so I have to sleep. But on the other, Gabe might come and see me. Sexy lingerie means I'm expecting him. So I go with cute pyjamas. I wash my face, but leave my eye makeup on. Without mascara I look like an albino bunny.

And then I wait. I lie in bed and try to read, but I'm too excited. Gabe came 7,000 kilometres in my direction, so perhaps I should walk the seven steps to his room. But his coldness at dinner makes me hesitate.

It's not my family, is it? We're a little crazy, but not abnormally so. Maybe it's our house. Our house is pretty insane if you're not accustomed to this neighbourhood. But Gabe's not a material person.

Tap, tap.

Finally! I try to sound casual and surprised. *Why my stars, who can that be?* "Um, come in."

The door opens, and my mother walks in. Disappointment plus.

"Hi, darling." She perches on the bed beside me.

"Hey, mom. What's up?"

She lowers her voice, as if anyone in the house without electronic spying equipment could even hear us. "He's very nice."

She's based her impression on the dozen words he said at dinner. Or maybe it was his offer to help with dinner.

"Oh great. I'm glad you like him."

"Did the two of you go out in Lund?" she asks.

"Well, yeah," I admit. It's not top secret, but I don't want to discuss this until I figure out what's happening with Gabe right now.

"And now he's come all the way here to see you," she says. My mother loves this kind of thing. She's even sappier than me.

"He came here for a hockey tryout."

She gives me a secret society smile, like "We know that's not the real reason." He did say he was coming to talk to me. Maybe he's outside right now, waiting for my mom to leave so he can come in.

"Was there something you wanted?" I ask.

"Oh yes, I was going to offer to take Gabe sightseeing tomorrow. If he doesn't have his tryout. Maybe we could go to the Anthropology Museum at U.B.C. and then meet you for lunch."

"Well, I'll check with Gabe first. He may have his own plans. But thank you." He may be the museum type, I have no clue. But if I have to spend another meal with Gabe, but not be alone with Gabe, I will go crazy.

My mom pats my arm. "Okay, dear. We can decide tomorrow. He may want to rest up after the jet lag." This is an option she never gave me.

"Thanks, Mom. Thanks for letting him stay here too."

"No problem." Then she squints at me. "Lily, if you don't remove your makeup properly, your eyelashes will break off and you'll develop milia."

Thank you for that disgusting image, Doctor Mom. "Okay, I will. Good night."

Then she leaves. I stay awake for another hour of hope and expectation, but my door remains un-knocked. I remove my make-up and go to sleep feeling frustrated and mystified.

36

TRIAL AND ERROR

GABRIEL

"ARE YOU READY?" Jesper asks me as we drive to the rink. Mercifully, Seb took his own car, so I don't have to put up with his boasting any more.

"Ja," I say. I'm tired, my head aches, and my soul hurts. But I'm ready to try out for goal. What does it matter now if I play in Michigan or back in Sweden? I lost my chance with Lily when I told her I didn't care and I didn't want a long distance relationship. How can five minutes of my life have screwed up so much?

Of course, the fact that she's dating Seb only confirms what I thought would happen: that Lily would find someone new, someone better. And Seb's bragging is true; I looked him up online, and by next season, he may play in the NHL. He'll have money and fame—just like Jesper Larson. Seb Söderlund is exactly the kind of guy Lily deserves. Well, except that he's an asshole and a braggart.

And I hurt her badly. Seb told me so. I hurt someone who has only been sweet and generous to me.

It's my own fault for allowing my expectations to rise so high. I should have known better. But Freja, my father, and especially my mother have made so many sacrifices for me to even be here. I will have to try my hardest today, even if my heart is no longer in this.

Jesper is quiet on the drive. I come out of myself long enough to notice that he is not quite right either. When I met him at Christmas, he was more joyous in spirit. Now he seems preoccupied and worried. No matter how perfect your lifestyle, there are always troubles. It's silly to imagine that money and success can make a person happy.

There is also a strange dynamic in the relationship between Jesper and Seb. Jesper lectures and advises him like a son. Clearly Seb is already a member of the family while I am the outsider.

Jesper pulls into the arena parking lot.

"Are you nervous?" he asks me.

"A little." I have a routine before games, but this is not a game. I have no idea what to expect.

"It's just an evaluation. Play your regular game, and you'll be fine." Jesper is a man of few words, but those words comfort me. It wouldn't take a therapist to figure out that I crave a father figure in my life, having rejected my own. And I prefer men whose actions speak for them. Men like Jesper.

We meet Seb in the tunnel, and he guides me to the dressing room while Jesper goes off in the opposite direction. The arena is old, but the player rooms are newly renovated.

"Here's where the goalies dress," Seb tells me in

Swedish. "I'm going to find my gear, and I'll be right back."

I lay out my pads and began the familiar ritual of getting ready. I'm not nervous now. The resignation I've been feeling all morning has calmed me. Whatever happens, happens.

Seb and I dress in silence. Having established his superiority, he no longer needs to say more.

"Hey, guys." A man pokes his head in the room. "Gabriel, I'm Luke Howard. I'm the goalie coach for the Millionaires, and I'll be running you through your paces today."

"I'm almost ready."

"Okay. See you out there." He nods at Seb.

Wow. An NHL goalie coach is going to be working with me?

"Is he the goalie coach for the Vice too?" I ask Seb.

"I think so. We don't have a full-time goalie coach, but I've heard them saying they want one. You should see the difference between this place and the Millionaires dressing room. Everything is so nice up there."

I stretch my neck. All this time I worried whether I was good enough to come here, and now I'm going to find out. If I don't make it, I'll spend the next week sightseeing in Vancouver and then perhaps look up a friend in Calgary before going home. I may move to a hostel as well. I don't want to see Lily and Seb together.

We skate out onto the ice, where Luke has already set up the net and pucks. I go through a short warm up: skating and stretching. It's odd to be the focus of an ice session. But in some ways, goalies are always alone. It's a team game, but while everyone else's mistakes are gone in a blink of an eye, mine remain forever.

I don't mind that though. I like being responsible. To me, stopping pucks is an intellectual battle. Figuring out what is going to happen next, which players will always shoot first, and more dangerously, which will pass. If an opposing team is made up of individualists or team cogs. A true team is the most dangerous, players who sacrifice their own glory for that of the team. But at the levels I've played at, there are very few real teams. Guys are always trying to be noticed so they'll make it to the next level.

Ironically, I'd given up on all my hockey dreams years ago, and now here I am—far beyond any level I'd imagined.

Luke blows his whistle, and I come back to earth. Time to play.

For the first ten minutes, the goalie coach tells Seb where to shoot on me, and he does exactly that. Seb is very good. Not that I'd expect anything less from an NHL prospect. It's a chance for me to channel the anger I feel about him. After his first two shots whizz by me into the net, I'm determined to stop him. After all, Luke is calling the shots, so I don't even have to guess. I can commit easily.

Then the coach changes things up. He gets Seb to skate in from the half boards and call his own shots. I'm still making saves, but more are getting by me.

Tweeeet.

Luke comes over and talks to me. He has some suggestions about my positioning.

"You need to come out of the net more and challenge

the shooter. Your reflexes are good, but I can see you haven't had a ton of technical coaching."

He shows me exactly where my feet should be, demonstrating where I should be relative to the net depending on the player's approach.

"Got it?" he asks.

"Yeah." I've had good coaches before, but his advice is on a different level. Over the years, I've gotten sloppy and relied on my natural reactions. But at a higher level, technique will be the key.

I try to incorporate everything Luke tells me. It feels awkward though. I concentrate on establishing muscle memories which I can visualize later.

We work out for about half an hour and then Luke tells us to take a break. Seb and I skate over the bench. I take off my helmet and drink some Gatorade.

"Too bad you have to face me," Seb says. "You might be doing better against a lesser shooter."

It's hard to believe he's Swedish because he's such a braggart. Apparently, the Law of Jante does not apply to him. "My hard luck," I reply.

Up in the stands, Jesper sits with two other men. The three of them are deep in conversation.

"Who are they?" I ask.

"The guy in black is Chris Luczak. He's the head of hockey operations for the Vice. And other is Coach Gauthier."

I nod. I've heard of Lucky Luczak, of course; he was an NHL superstar who retired a couple of seasons ago.

"What's the coach like?" I ask.

Seb makes a face. "Scary. Intense. Smart."

Oh, that kind of coach. The kind who believes that fear

is a good motivator. But I won't have to play for him anyway; the choice for me is the ECHL or nothing.

Luke skates over to the other side and talks to Coach Gauthier. Probably figuring out what else they want to see from me.

I feel surprisingly calm now. When everything fell apart last night, it wasn't a total surprise. Lily was the best thing to happen to me in years. It's crazy to think that she would wait around. But if life knocks you down, you get up. What alternative do I have?

The rest of the tryout speeds by. I like the familiar feelings of being out on the ice, even in a new country.

Seb and I shower and change in silence. It doesn't bother me, but he's the talkative kind so it's a strain on him. That's fine.

Jesper and Chris Luczak walk into the room together.

Chris introduces himself. He looks over at Seb. "Sods, you're giving Gabriel a ride home, right? Is it okay if he meets you in the lobby?"

"Sure thing." Seb leaves. I'm getting a bad feeling now.

Chris sits down beside me. "Well, Gabriel, thank you very much for coming in. I know you came a long way on your own dime. You've definitely got some skills." He looks over at Jesper, as if to acknowledge his good scouting. "Anyway, it's a tricky time in the season. We've had some injuries and call-ups but we need guys who are familiar with the North American game and ready to go. Unfortunately, we can't fit you in right now. If you're still interested, I'd welcome you to try out for our ECHL team next season. You'd definitely have a chance."

"Okay, thank you for the trial." We shake hands. After last night, today's disappointment is nothing.

Perhaps this outcome is what I deserve for leaving my mother.

Chris leaves, and Jesper takes his place on the bench.

"You knew it was a long shot, right?" he asks.

I nod. I sense he's disappointed. He takes pride in his hockey acumen. "Thank you for everything. When I was working out with my old goalie coach, he reminded me that I look much better in games than in practices. So, perhaps that influenced you."

Jesper smiles. "Too bad there's no video of you actually playing. Look, I think that at this point, the best thing would be for you to play at a higher level in Sweden."

"I haven't thought beyond this trip," I reply.

"I'm going to make a few calls when you go back," he tells me. "Meanwhile, at least you get to enjoy Vancouver. You've never been here before, have you?"

"No. It's a beautiful city."

"Well, I'm sure Lily has plans to show you around." Another thing that bothers me is the whole secrecy of Lily and Sebastian's relationship. Why would they not let her family know? In the brief time I've seen Lily and her father together, they aren't as close as they were back in Sweden.

Jesper checks his watch. "Well, I better get into work. I'll see you at home."

I grab my gear and walk out to the lobby where Sebastian is slouched in a chair on his phone.

"You ready?" he asks.

"Ja."

"Didn't look like good news," he says.

"No. I'm not going to be playing for the ECHL team," I reply. No point in hiding something he'll find out anyway.

He smiles. "You're out of your league. Besides, Lily deserves someone who's going to the NHL. Not a nobody."

I'm not a nobody. I'm someone who loves Lily and appreciates her more than Seb, who seems to view her as a possession. But if he is her choice, I must respect it.

37

THE UNDERCARD

Lily

ROXY IS CHATTING AWAY on our drive home from
school, but all I can think about is Gabe. How did his
hockey tryout go? Why is he acting so distant? And most
of all, where's the big talk he promised me on the phone?
Tonight I'm going to take Gabe out for dinner—alone—
and ask him all these questions. I will fight anyone who
tries to stop us. I barely slow down to let poor Roxy out
before I'm speeding home.

When I rush into the kitchen, nobody is around but
my mom and Miriam.

"Hey, Miriam, welcome back." I give her a big hug.
When Miriam started working here, I was too old for a
nanny, but she still acts like my second mom. "Did you
have a good time at home?"

"Yes, lovely. I can see that you all missed me. This
place looks like a bomb hit it." Miriam replies.

"I had a cleaning service in," my mother protests.

"Those services are no good. They only clean the surfaces. It's going to take me all week to get things back up to my standards," says Miriam.

"Where's Gabe?" I ask my mother.

"Oh, he's downstairs playing hockey with Alexander and Seb."

"Okay." I grab an apple and head downstairs.

The boys are all playing in the rink room. They have half of their equipment on. Seb is wearing gloves, Alexander is wearing a helmet and gloves, and Gabe is wearing a helmet, a catching glove, a blocker and a chest protector. The chest protector seems like overkill until I notice how hard they're going at it.

Seb's shots are hard and high, and even in the two minutes I'm there, he hits Gabe in the mask twice. It's like he's trying to kill Gabe instead of score. They're using a road hockey puck. Those things hurt when they hit you.

Then when Alexander brings the puck in, Seb not only screens the goalie but backs right into him, knocking Gabe over.

If I were a ref, I'd be calling goaltender interference, but instead I watch Gabe pull himself up and crosscheck Seb. Next thing I know, both of them have dropped their sticks and are shoving each other.

I yank open the door, stick two fingers in my mouth and let out a screeching whistle. Yeah, there's no end to my lady-like talents.

All three stop and stare at me.

"Holy crap! What is wrong?" I demand. "Are you actually fighting?"

Gabe mutters something in Swedish that I know to be x-rated.

"It's his fault," says Seb. "He's a fucking fuckwad."

My brother is already bug-eyed at the fighting, and if my mother heard the language in this room, she'd flip. No Swede here is winning a Nobel Peace Prize.

"Alexander, go upstairs and get ready for dinner," I tell him.

"Awwww, it's way too early. Besides, things are getting good here," he says. Seb and Gabe are eyeing each other like cobras ready to strike.

"Go," I say. Alexander finally leaves, grumbling all the way.

I stand between Gabe and Seb with my arms extended. Lily the linesman. "Okay, what is going on here?"

"Your boyfriend is an idiot. Being a hot shit hockey player doesn't make you a decent human being," says Gabe.

Seb snarls back, "At least I'm good enough to play hockey here. Not a fucking loser. What kind of human being makes his girlfriend feel like shit? Lily was crying because you made her feel bad about her body. She's beautiful, but you can only criticize. My sister dated a fuckwad like you. Breaking up with him was the best thing she ever did."

What in the ever-loving heck is going on here?

"Can we back this truck up?" I say.

I point at Gabe. "First, I'm not dating Seb. Why did you think I was?"

He scowls. "Because he said you were. And he did seem to know... some things."

Oh crap. My face is so red now. Pretty sure this is the

universe's way of telling me not to attempt random hookups. Yeah, plus guilt and that whole hysterical crying jag. Teensy clues that I should not have fooled around with Seb.

"Er, I can explain that. Later." I turn to Seb. "The second thing is that Gabe is not the ex-boyfriend who made me feel lousy. That was Jason."

Seb's round eyes widen. "Really? You have a lot of ex-boyfriends."

Their glares have flipped to embarrassed frowns.

Seb apologizes, "Uh, sorry. I thought you were someone else. Why didn't you tell me you'd never hurt Lily?"

Gabe looks at the floor. "Because I did hurt Lily, and I felt bad about that."

I shake my head. "Yes, hurting Lily is apparently the new international pastime, but I'm hoping that fad is over. Anyway, Gabe, what you did was nothing compared to the whole thing with Jason. And then with my dad..." I realize that neither of them understands what I'm talking about. "Never mind. Anyway, shake. You guys should be friends."

They shake hands with muttered *sorrys*.

I turn to Seb. I'm pissed that he's the reason that Gabe's been acting so weird. "I get that you were trying to protect me, but you can't do that by lying about us. You should have talked to me instead."

Seb doesn't meet my eyes. "Sometimes girls don't do the right thing, and they need help."

I'm torn between hitting him and hugging him. "Whatever."

"Are we still friends?" he asks.

"Yeah, of course." Now I hug him.

His eyes dart between Gabe and me. "Okay, I'm going to take a shower now." He disappears into his suite and shuts the door.

Finally, we're alone. But I feel nervous. There's so much I have to explain.

We sit down on the couch in the games room. Gabe sits back, but I perch on the edge of the sofa so I can watch his expressions.

"What happened with your tryout?" I ask.

Gabe shakes his head. "I'm not going to Flint. Not this season anyway."

"Oh, that's too bad. Are you upset?"

"It was always a small chance." His face is unreadable.

"Okay, before we start on what you want to say, I should tell you, Seb and I are only friends. But one night, we did—"

Gabe puts his hand on my arm. A tiny tremor goes through me. It's the difference between being touched by someone you really care about. We still have this intense physical connection. Or at least I do.

"It doesn't matter what happened between you and Sebastian." Gabe's blue eyes lock into mine. His sincerity is what I missed so much.

"Okay, but nothing really happened. We fooled around a little, but we didn't actually—"

"Stop. We were not going out. You were free to do as you wished." Gabe's words are neutral, but his forehead is creased. Having to imagine me with Seb clearly pains him.

"I'm so, so sorry if this whole thing—which, you know, wasn't anything—hurt you. Something really horrible happened on New Year's, and then I was in a really bad place and I did a bunch of stupid things. But I'm working

282

hard on being more mature, which is why I didn't..." I can tell my words are still bothering Gabe so I finally shut up, which I should have done two minutes ago.

"New Year's was when you called me and you were crying," Gabe says.

"Yeah, I ran into Jason, this guy I dated in high school. And Rebecca, his girlfriend." This time I tell him everything. Because Gabe is the one person I've wanted to confide in since that night. As I talk, I look down at the carpet. I feel ashamed—not only about Jason, but all the foolishness I did as a result of Rebecca's words. This is what Gabe does for me: he allows me to vent in a judgement-free zone.

Gabe puts a hand on my shoulder that feels like an invitation. I snuggle into his side, and the words pour out. I've rehashed that night so many times, but this will be the last time. Whatever Gabe says I'm going to trust as the final word. I finish and wait to hear his response.

"It's not possible," Gabe says.

"What's not possible?" I ask.

"It's not possible for any guy to spend so much time with you and not care. Unless he's an actual psychopath." Gabe's tone is completely matter of fact. It's almost exactly what my father said as well, but this time I believe it.

"You're right." Jason is the past. My mistakes are the past. I'm learning and moving on.

We sit in silence for a few minutes. Gabe rubs my arm in a very comforting way. Comforting, yet hot. It's everything about him: his size, his scent, his quietness, all of it turns me on.

"Okay, your turn," I say.

Gabe turns me around to face him. His hands rest lightly on my arms, and he looks like he wants me to read his mind. But I can't. I'm not going to keep pushing our relationship. I need to know what he wants.

It's only a few seconds of silence, but it seems excruciatingly long.

Then Seb pops out in only a towel.

"Oh, sorry. Forgot my phone." He darts out, grabs his phone from the table, and disappears.

Gabe shakes his head. "Before anyone else interrupts, I must say this."

I hold my breath.

"I love you, Lily. Do you still love me?"

Wow. This guy doesn't fool around. All Gabe does is tell the plain, unvarnished truth. The beautiful truth.

The room spins around me. Can emotion alone make me dizzy?

I raise my face to his. "I do. I love you."

And then he kisses me. I feel the softness of his lips, the tickle of his beard, and the intensity of my need for him. Our kiss is sweetly familiar and yet uniquely beautiful. As I inhale his scent—a mix of fresh air, rainy days, coffee, and cardamom—I realize that Gabe and Sweden are one for me. I said I missed Sweden, but I really missed Gabe. I love Sweden, but I love Gabe more. I relax into the bliss of his mouth hard against mine, letting the warring senses of security and desire build up inside me. A crashing wave sweeps me up and pulls me under. I'm drowning in happiness.

38

SUNSHINE AND RAIN

GABE

LILY TELLS me to put my rain gear on and then we get into her car. We drive a short distance and end up in an ocean-side park. There's a small food stand where we buy two boxes of fish and chips. We sit down at a rain-soaked picnic table and eat. I can't seem to let go of Lily's hand, even when it's awkward to eat this way. Perhaps I'm afraid I'll awaken and find it's not my reality.

Lily shakes her head, but she understands me. "Could you at least let me cut up my fish? I'm not going anywhere."

I release her hand, but take it back as soon as the fish is dissected.

"You're being a goof." She laughs at me.

But Lily too feels the intensity of this moment. We are back together after all we've been through while apart.

She hardly speaks. But it's a good silence. She still loves me, and that's all I need to know.

After dinner, Lily takes me by the hand and leads me towards the ocean.

"Oh great, the tide's out," she says. We walk along a rocky outcrop to a tiny stump of an island. Although it's ruggedly beautiful, the drizzling rain means few people are here. Once we get on the island, we can look out onto the ocean, or back to the trees and shoreline. The air smells salty and fresh.

"Happy now?" she asks.

I nod. Of course I am happy. In the past hour, I learned that Seb is not her boyfriend and she still loves me. And I saw Lily's face when I said I loved her. First there was surprise at the suddenness of my words, and then a beautiful glow that spread across her face. I felt the great joy of making Lily happy with a few simple words. Simple, but heartfelt.

The only shadow is that I still don't know what will happen for us now.

"It's a beautiful, wild place." I motion to the whitecaps in the churning Pacific Ocean. "I like it very much."

"I know how much you like being outside," Lily says.

"You did this for me?" I ask.

"Duh."

Her generosity strikes me. Lily is so giving, and she asks for so little in return.

I step up beside her. "I want to apologize. For not telling you the truth back in Lund."

Lily's eyes narrow. "What's the truth?"

"The truth about why I thought we should break up."

"Oh. You mean your mother? The only insulting part

of that is that you didn't think I'd understand. But whatever." She turns her head away, and I reach out and touch her arm. I feel the warmth of her muscular arm through her jacket, and the body memory of our time together is vivid.

"No. It was more than my mother." Still, I can't bring myself to confess my biggest fear.

"Isn't our love enough? To overcome your doubts?"

Her question is so simplistic. Love is never enough. If love could cure, my mother would be well.

"Lily, do you realize—" I hesitate. It's so hard for me to discuss this. I look out at the ocean. The wild beauty of it reminds me of northern Sweden, and the nature calms me. I concentrate on the roiling ocean and force out the words. "What my mother has—I could get it too."

Lily is silent as she takes in the full meaning of my words. "Is it hereditary?"

"Nej. There is a hereditary type of Alzheimer's, but it's not what she has. But they don't know exactly why she got it so early, and there may be a genetic component."

She motions to me to sit down on a rocky outcrop. Then she sits across from me and takes my hands in hers. Her jacket hood is up and frames her bright eyes and her solemn beautiful face.

"When did your mother get sick? Like what age?"

"In her forties. The exact date we cannot determine."

"And you don't want to date me now because you're worried about getting sick in twenty years?"

When she states it in those terms, my fears seem foolish. But it's one thing to date Lily when I know she is leaving and another to be together when the future is unlimited. With Lily, I feel so much.

"Maybe I'm being ridiculous. But don't you feel the potential of what we have?"

She nods eagerly and smiles. "I do. And that's why we should go for it." She squeezes my hands tighter. "Tons of things can happen. We can't predict the future. But I'm sure your mom doesn't regret living her life and having you. Would she have changed a thing if she knew?"

"I can't know that," I reply.

"No, but you can try to imagine. Look, Gabe, maybe you'll get this or maybe you won't. But in either case, you need to live your life to the fullest. Have fun, play hockey, travel. What do *you* want to do?"

I consider this question, which has occupied my mind for the past month. Perhaps I can imagine how my mother felt. Her last note to me showed how much having a child meant to her. She would have not changed that.

"I'd like to have children," I say.

Lily recoils with a giggle. "Whoa. It's waaaay too early in this relationship to say something like that. Right now I'm busier trying *not* to get pregnant."

I shake my head. "I do not mean now, of course. But you asked what I want."

"Take it down a notch. You're going to scare away women if that's your opening line."

"Do I scare you?" I ask.

"Well, no. But I know you. You say whatever is on your mind."

Maybe I am crazy. But the dreams Lily has inspired in me include a dream of the two of us together for real—I don't know in what country, what we're doing, or even when it happens, but I see us together. Lily is right though. It's too early for this; first we must get our current relationship on track.

"We are going out again now?" I ask her.

"Yes, please," says Lily. She leans forward and kisses me. The air around us is cool, but her lips are warm. Being together so intimately again is a thrill. After we kiss, she leans her forehead against mine.

"I'm glad you're not going to Michigan anyway. How long can you stay here?"

"My visa is for six months. But I won't stay that long." I need more purpose in life than being a tourist and waiting for Lily's free time. A long visit, and then I'll return to Lund, get a job, and a new place to live. Perhaps Lily will come back for the summer. Then in the autumn, school or hockey. All these interesting options make me feel free and alive.

"Gabe, can I ask you—" Lily's voice quavers. "Why did you like me?"

Ah, this is the uncertainty I've seen in her these past two days. Because her old boyfriend betrayed her trust, she seeks reassurance. I swallow. This feels like the most important thing I'm ever going to say.

"I like so many things about you. Your confidence. Your optimism. Your intelligence. Your generosity. Your humour." I sense that she needs more so I keep going. "I like how tall you are. And that you're strong. Beautiful. I like your smile. Your eyes. The way you walk. Your teeth."

Lily laughs. "You can thank my orthodontist for that."

I take her hand in mine and feel her squeeze me back. She smiles, and her smile goes right to her eyes. I hope I've said enough to make her feel comforted. But I've only begun to list all the reasons I like Lily.

"I wasn't honest though. I never told you about my family," she says.

"We like each other for who we are. You didn't feel sorry for me because my mother's not well."

"And you don't care who my father is. Or my aunt. Or even my *farmor*."

"I think that means we like each other for the right reasons."

Lily nods. She edges closer and wraps her arms around me, laying her head against my neck.

"I missed you, Gabe."

The feeling of Lily against me, her strong body yielding to mine, is exhilarating. Warmth and energy surge through me. Only a few weeks ago, I believed I would never find this happiness again. But now, everything seems possible.

Lily turns her face towards mine for a kiss. Her mouth is first pliant and then demanding, opening and thrusting her soft tongue into my mouth. I kiss her back, and it feels beautifully familiar and yet achingly new as well.

Finally, she pulls away. "I hate to leave, but this place is tricky. If the tide comes in, the path is gone."

"Okay. We can go back." She takes my hand in hers, and we head back down.

"Once we were apart, everything seemed to go wrong," says Lily. I nod. But perhaps that makes us appreciate what we have more. "I fought with my dad about Jason. I wanted him to contact Jason's team. Do you think I was wrong?"

I squeeze her hands. "No. I understand how upset you were. But your father's hockey reputation is important to him. He was nervous that I do well in my tryout."

"I wondered if you were using me too," Lily admits. "But only for about five seconds."

"Seeing as you never told me who your father was, that seems unlikely. It must have been something else that attracted me to you." I reach out and squeeze her firm ass. Lily squeals, but doesn't move out of my reach. Instead she kisses me on the cheek.

"Now we can go out on a real date."

"What makes it a real date?" I ask.

"You have to pay," Lily says. "Canadian rules."

She laughs and pulls me by the hand to her car. When she unlocks it, she looks over her shoulder at me. Her expression is full of mischief.

"Did you know that the Volvo C30 has a very roomy back seat? You should try it out."

What is she talking about? She pulls open the back door, and motions for me to get in. When I do, she follows me and closes the door. I watch her in puzzlement.

"I've really missed you," Lily says. She leans over and starts kissing me. While the kissing is good, I'm distracted by her hand, which is rubbing against my now-rigid cock through my jeans.

"Lily—"

"Shhh," she says. She undoes my belt and begins unzipping my jeans.

I reach down to stop her. "What are you doing? We're in a public park."

Lily's smile is more of a smirk. "We're in a car. It's raining and nobody is around. Besides, this is your new life philosophy: we're carpe-ing the diem." She uses both hands to pull out my erection, and I groan. Her cool hands encircle my cock and pump it until coherent thought isn't possible.

"I'll bet you've never had sex in a car before," she coos.

"Nej," I groan. The only car I've driven is Freja's ancient Saab. Having sex in that would probably break the suspension.

"See, it's a totally North American thing to do. Like in the movies." As she speaks, she removes her own jeans. She's wearing a tiny black thong that she whisks to the side. She reaches down for her purse and pulls out a tiny flowered pouch. "My sex kit," she explains and waves a condom packet. I can't help but smile. Sex with Lily is incredible, but she always adds something unexpected. I open the packet and ease the condom on. Then she produces another foil packet.

"What now?" I ask.

"Lube," she says. "It's good for quickies. Here, put it on me."

I squirt the gel onto my fingers and then apply it to her warm folds until they're nice and juicy. I pay special attention to her tiny clit and am rewarded by Lily's low moans of pleasure.

"Hurry up down there," she grunts. She reaches down to help, and the sight of her inserting a finger into herself is almost enough to make me come on the spot.

She shudders as I also insert two lubricated fingers inside her. I plunge them in and out a few times, but as good as this feels, I'm still tense about having sex so publicly. Luckily, the windows are now steamed up enough that nobody could look inside.

Lily pushes me half-down onto the seat. It's cramped,

but she manages to mount me and lower her welcoming heat onto my erection.

"Ugh. I missed feeling you inside me," she mutters. Then she begins bumping up and down on my rigid cock. I keep my eyes open because I want to see all of this. All of Lily.

Her familiar puffs of breath begin. She exhales every time her pelvis grinds against mine. I pull her towards me and kiss her, but at the same time, my hand goes between us so I can play with her clit. I know her strong body so well.

Her body tenses, and I finger her frantically. I'm going to come in an embarrassingly short time, and I need to make her come too. Her body jerks responsively to my touch, and she makes the ragged inhalations that mean she's close to climaxing.

"Ja, Lily, come for me," I mutter through gritted teeth.

"God, Gabe."

Our voices cross as we both achieve release. I stretch out my body, and Lily slumps onto me.

"Älskar dig," I whisper.

Lily lifts her head. "Does that mean what I think it does?"

I nod.

"I love you too." She collapses back on me, but her face is close enough to kiss. I feel the weight of my contentment pulling me to unconsciousness. Perhaps it's jet lag, but I could fall asleep right now with Lily as my blanket and my lips on hers.

I feel an odd vibration between us, and Lily pulls away.

"Damn phone." She switches it off, without even looking. "Now where were we?"

"We were right here." I nip her lower lip, and then pull it into my mouth.

Then my phone buzzes as well, which is odd since the only person here who might call is right in front of me. When I stop kissing her, Lily growls her disapproval.

"Sorry. This might be my aunt." I pull out my phone and look. It's from Seb.

Huge fuckup. Lily must come home.

39

DOES YOUR MOTHER KNOW?

LILY

I'M SITTING in my father's home office, which means I'm in big trouble. There are different levels of parental discussion in this house. Kitchen discussions are minor and public. If Mom or Dad comes to my bedroom, it's for an intimate little talk about rules or expectations. On one horrifying occasion, my mother explained the facts of life to me, even though I was only five. They use long car rides to get information out of me. But my dad's office is the equivalent of principal's office: huge offences. And getting tag-teamed by my parents is the worst. They discuss things first and back each other up.

I'm waiting for my dad to begin, but instead he looks at my mom. Because my father is a big, tough ex-NHL defenceman, everyone thinks that he's the family disciplinarian. But he was away so much that it's actually my mother who lays down the law. It's been years since I've been in trouble. I'm usually the good one. And I have zero clue about what I've done now.

My mother reaches into the pocket of her dress pants and pulls out a tiny pink and orange scrap of fabric and lays it on the desk.

"Are these yours, Lily?"

I look more closely. It's a lace thong, and yes, it's mine. It matches one of my bras. But did we have to play lingerie lost and found in front of my father? My cheeks flame up, but they're not as red as my father's face.

"They're your brand," my mother adds, in case I'm going to deny ownership.

I remove the offending item from the smooth oak surface and stuff it into my jeans.

My mother continues, "Miriam found these when she was cleaning Seb's bedroom. Do you have an explanation?"

Oh, shit. Too bad I'm not a Victoria's Secret girl like everyone else. I wonder if I can get away with pinning a lingerie fetish on Seb. It's probably true. It takes me all of 30 seconds to search for an exit door to this crisis and come up empty.

So I exhale loudly and tell the truth, "We fooled around a bit."

Nobody says a word for what seems like an hour. I can actually feel beads of sweat forming in my armpits. And it's hard to take the high moral ground when I just had semi-public car sex with Gabe.

"But you went out with Gabriel tonight," my mother says. "So, you're not actually dating Sebastian."

I shake my head. "Look, it's not a big deal. Seb was

lonely, and I felt bad after everything with Jason—so we... made out a bit. We didn't actually you know, do it."

It's hard to know who's more embarrassed about this confession: me having to say it or my dad having to hear it. But if a huge chasm would open up in the floor and swallow me right now, that would be peachy. All hail Her Highness of Humiliation, Lily Larson.

"Seb and I are just friends. I'm helping him adjust to life here."

This is met with an eyeball roll from my mother. And she's right, Seb needs zero adjustment in the area of sex.

"We're both adults," I add, but it sounds hollow and silly. This is not my best moment.

My dad rubs his forehead. "Yes, you're both adults. But the reason that Seb is living with us is that he's immature. He needs guidance and discipline if he's going to succeed in hockey. As his billet family, we're supposed to be his role models."

My mother leans forward. "Lily, imagine if this situation was reversed. If we sent you to live with a family in Sweden, and then discovered their son was fooling around with you, we'd be furious. We'd demand that they be banned from ever hosting kids again. Because it's about trust and protection."

I feel hot tears coming to my eyes, but I blink them back. What happened between Seb and I wasn't really wrong, but it wasn't right either. Margie warned me and spelled out Seb's issues. He wasn't supposed to get involved with me, and it doesn't matter who started what. Deep down, I was upset and this was my lame idea of rebelling or making myself feel better—by doing something stupid. Even if I did stop myself before I did something stupendously stupid.

Would it have been any better if Seb and I actually dated? At least if we had gone out first, it would have given my parents a chance to get used to the idea or even veto it. But I did exactly what I wanted, and now I'm going to face the consequences.

"Are you going to tell Seb's parents?" I feel terrible about the fact that Seb will get into trouble.

"We'll discuss that with Sebastian," my father replies. "While I don't want to give up on him, he can't continue to live here. He's not listening to me anyway."

Now a few tears do leak out. Poor Seb.

"Lily, we're very disappointed in your behaviour," my mother says. "Let's be clear about one thing, we're not shaming you because you have a sex life. However, you need to use common sense in choosing your partners. Having sex to bolster your hurt feelings is not healthy. And you can see that this has consequences for Seb as well."

My father's voice is flat. "You have a lot of advantages in your life. Yet you don't think first. You act like a spoiled child."

This is his ultimate insult. Dad has always tried to instill his personal values of hard work, thrift, and planning for the future. Swedish values. And now I've basically kicked all those values in the teeth after claiming how much I love Sweden. I am a complete hypocrite. All my resentments whoosh out of my body, and I feel empty and sad.

"I'm so sorry," I say. "It was a terrible decision. And I

disrespected both of you, as well as what you were trying to do for Seb."

My father nods. "That's a start. But there will be consequences for your actions."

No, no, no, no, no. Gabe and I just found each other again. Please, don't.

"You're grounded for a month," says my father.

"But I'm twenty." My voice is a whisper.

My mother leans back in her chair. "Lily, we're well aware that you're legally an adult. And if you want to sneak out or skip classes to meet whoever your current boyfriend is, we can do very little to prevent that. But we expect you to respect our request that you not go out for a month. You've lost your car privileges, and you'll stay home at night. Also, we're going to pay for a hotel for the rest of Gabriel's stay in Vancouver, since it's no longer appropriate that he stays in our home."

I automatically glance at my dad, who is more lenient. But he looks back at me with such coldness that I feel I'm shattering inside. What an idiot I was to take my connection with my dad for granted.

"If you want to be treated like an adult, you must act like one," my father says.

Well, I'm going to start by not arguing about this. Even though they're kicking him out, Gabe's my best example of how a responsible adult acts. I nod and leave the room. Seb is sitting upright on a chair in the hall, not even looking at his phone. Our eyes meet and then we drop our gazes, like we're denying any connection between us.

My mother comes out of the office. "Sebastian, Jesper wants to talk to you now."

She walks past me without a word. Her step is slow, and her shoulders slumped. The woman who loves to hear about my life looks like she'd rather I wasn't even in the house.

Although I'm longing to run to Gabe and tell him everything, I'm not sure if I should. It's pretty hard to ground someone when the only person she really wants to see is in her own house. But I don't want to disobey my parent's wishes right off the bat. When I get to my room, I notice that Gabe's bedroom door is open and he's not there.

Where is he? What should I do now? I pace around my room, full of pent-up energy. I spot a framed family photo on the shelf. My mother makes us do a photo shoot with a professional photographer every summer, so she can send it out with her Christmas cards. When we were little, she would colour-coordinate our outfits, but once I was thirteen I put my foot down. No more red sweaters or blouses in the hot sun. I pull down the latest photo and examine it. We're a happy family on the surface—all blond hair and orthodontically-perfect smiles. But if you look closer, the reality is different. Alexander's manic grin is the only sign of his medicated hyperactivity. Margie's scowl is her protective armour from all the kids who had been bullying her at her school last year. I'm supposed to be the golden girl, the one with no problems. Ha.

But we are lucky—lucky to have great parents, lots of money, and opportunities. Maybe I have been taking that for granted, but I won't any more. Knowing what Gabe has been through makes me want to be a better person. It's so frustrating that I can't go and find Gabe. I want him to hug me and make things better.

I decide to FaceTime him. Just seeing his face makes me feel a bit better.

"Why do you call if we are at most a few metres from each other?" Gabe's expression is solemn and puzzled.

"Ugh. I don't know what to do. I'm grounded, so I'm not sure if I'm supposed to see you or not."

"What does it mean to be grounded?" he asks.

"Well, for me, it means that I'm not supposed to drive the car or date. I'm supposed to stay home for a month."

"How can we avoid each other if we're in the same house?"

I blow out a breath. "That's the other thing. My parents are going to arrange a hotel for the rest of your time here."

"That's not necessary," he replies. "I can look after my own accommodations."

"Let them do it. They have the money." It occurs to me that I have no idea what Gabe's financial situation is. He could be rich or poor. He's the type of person who would wear exactly what he wants, regardless of branding. And he would live a simple life. I know that without even seeing his home.

Gabe shakes his head. He's so self-sufficient. Adult. Everything I'm not. He peers at me. "Why are you in trouble?"

There's a short silence. "It's because of what happened with Seb. Before."

"Ah."

Of course, it's not just Seb; I'm being punished for being immature and thoughtless, but I don't want to tell Gabe in case he hasn't noticed all my flaws.

"Don't cry, Lily," he says tenderly.

I feel the moisture on my cheek and realize that I cry so much, I'm not even aware of it.

"I don't know what's wrong with me. It was totally out of character for me to do this, and now I've wrecked our time together, which I was all I wanted in the first place." I grab some tissue and swab my face.

Gabe waits for me to finish my stupid emotional fit.

"Better now?" he asks.

"Yeah, kind of." I smile at him.

"You are a good person, Lily. But in the future, I think you should address your anger to the correct person."

"Who?"

"Jason, of course."

I sigh loudly. "Yeah, you're right. Next time, I'll handle things differently. But what about us? We can't see each other for a month."

Gabe shakes his head. "Tonight, when you said you still loved me, that is all I need. One month doesn't matter. We'll make plans for later."

I can't help but smile. "Are you going to teach me patience? Because a lot of people have failed at that task."

"*Den som väntar på något got, väntar aldrig för länge,*" says my beautiful poet-boyfriend.

"Translation, please."

"You cannot wait too long for something good."

40

MAN TO MAN

GABRIEL

I AM SITTING in the living room with a book. There are so many rooms to choose from here, but this room has a beautiful view of Vancouver. I can see the sparkling lights of the bridge, large ships, and the towers of downtown. It looks like a postcard planet.

It's frustrating to see Lily so upset and not be able to help—even though I'm right here. North American parents are much more involved. I cannot imagine Freja grounding me for any reason. But Lily's moods change quickly, and she will feel better tomorrow. The main thing is that we've straightened things out between the two of us. The hockey part of my trip was a failure, but the Lily part is more important.

Perhaps I'll go to Calgary now and visit my old school friend. When I return to Vancouver, things will have calmed down.

Jesper walks in the room without seeing me and switches off the overhead lights. He sits down in the large armchair and looks out the window. I clear my throat to let him know I am here.

He turns. In the faint light, there are deep lines around his mouth. He looks tired and unhappy. "Ah, you surprised me."

"Would you like me to leave?" I ask.

"No," he replies. He straightens his shoulders. "I'm going to have to ask you to stay at a hotel for your visit. Dori will make arrangements."

"Lily told me. On the phone," I add, since I'm still not sure exactly how grounding works. "I've already booked an Airbnb room, so I'll leave tomorrow."

He runs a hand through his cropped hair. "Damn. It's too bad you arrived in the middle of all this."

It is surreal to be talking to the legendary Jesper Larson in such a familiar way. Someone we all admired as a hockey god turns out to be so human and vulnerable.

"No, I appreciate everything you've done for me. I'm only sorry that my goaltending wasn't good enough."

A long silence follows this. The only sound in the room is the clinking of ice cubes in his drink as he takes a sip.

"Perhaps I'm not as good at hockey evaluation as I thought. Did Lily tell you what happened with Jason?"

"Ja."

Although I can hardly see him, I can hear him swallow. "Do you think I should have done something about him? Afterwards, I mean. That's what Lily believes, that I should have told the team what his character was really like and gotten him off the team."

How can I answer that? I understand Lily's side, her father had given a character reference and then Jason had proven himself to be false. But I also understand Jesper's side; it would be pointless for him to intervene after Jason was accepted. The team wouldn't cut a player because someone's daughter was upset.

Finally I say, "I believe, truly, that character will be revealed in time."

This is a lesson I need to absorb myself. My own father has come through. He visits my mother regularly and manages her care. It's time to accept that although he had many reasons to do this, the biggest one is that he wanted me to have a chance. A chance to succeed or to have an adventure. He did it out of love for me. I've lost a parent, but gained one too.

Jesper cracks his knuckles. He looks exhausted and much older than his forties. "I never told Lily, but I made a few calls about Jason. Scouts told me not to worry. Teams never use only one recommendation, they have multiple sources, and mine was only one opinion. It wasn't satisfactory, but I asked."

"It's all you can do." Like me, I wanted to cure my mother, but none of my sacrifices could do that. Freja and Lily were right. I had my own life to live now.

"Unfortunately, Jason is doing quite well. There's talk of college scholarships."

And that was the way things could be. A boy who hurt Lily terribly and harmed her relationship with her father could still succeed.

"Life is unfair," I conclude.

We both consider that blunt truth. How a successful man who lives in a mansion with a beautiful wife and family could be unhappy. How an easy-going young Swede turns into a worried old man because of a genetic flaw.

He smiles slightly at me. "I can see why Lily trusts you. You are easy to talk to."

It's easy to talk to him as well. I want to confide in him how much I care about Lily, and how I would never hurt her. But it's not the time.

"It's because I know unhappiness. I expect it," I say.

He nods. "How is your mother doing?"

"Not well today." This morning, I spoke to Freja and my mother on the phone. *Mamma* was very withdrawn. Freja assured me it was only a bad day, but seeing her so sullen was painful. And since I am not there, I can no longer distinguish a temporary mood from a permanent state.

"I'm sorry," Jesper says.

I miss her daily. In truth, I miss her essence. Now the outer shell of my mother is all I have. Maybe she doesn't recognize me anymore, but I certainly know exactly who she is. And I truly believe that deep down inside, she's still there, trapped inside a mind that betrays her in every way. Those beautiful moments when she returns and makes a matter-of-fact comment or asks a question have become so rare. They are like a gold ring that once turned up when she made me dig her garden as a boy. The glint of sunlight among the mounds of dirt. But the only way to capture those moments is to be there all the time. I'll never find that treasure while I'm here.

"*Det svenska vemodet,*" Jesper says. The Swedish melancholy. It is a phrase I haven't heard for a long time, but perhaps it describes me well. He continues, "My wife complains that I'm too negative, but people here are

306

constantly measuring happiness. Life is not always about happiness."

Could it be that we enjoyed unhappiness? Not unhappiness exactly, but more the idea that things were going badly so they could not get worse.

"When I first saw you and Lily together, I envied your relationship. You are so close and so familiar." It must be difficult for Jesper to be the disciplinarian.

"Not right now," he says.

"But you will be again. Lily has a generous soul. I know that she hates being on the outs with you."

His face lightens a little. "I know she's a good person. But she's young—younger than her age."

I nod. Lily has hurt me too. By refusing to speak to me and then not telling me everything, she kept me outside when I could have helped her. And she could have helped me work through everything with my mother if I hadn't kept so much from her. We will have to be more honest in the future. But at least we have a future—together.

This thought warms me, and I smile. For Lily, our separation feels like the end of the world. But for me, I know we are only beginning.

41

BREAKFAST OF CHAMPIONS

LILY

THIS IS by far the most awkward meal I've ever experienced. And that includes the time that the NHL Commissioner came to dinner here and Sushi barfed on his Fendi dress shoes.

It's breakfast time. Around the table are me, Gabe, Seb, my mom, Margie, and Alexander. My father claimed an early breakfast meeting and disappeared. Everyone knows about the sex scandal that hit this house last night, except my little brother.

"I don't understand why Seb has to leave," Alexander whines.

"Seb needs his independence," my mother replies. This is the cover story we're going with, although whether my dad is currently eating an overpriced omelette and telling Chris Luczak the truth is anyone's guess. They are best friends, but saying "Lily and Seb fooled around" may be too much information.

Right now, I'm less upset about the hit to my reputation than the consequences: my parents being so upset and my not being allowed to see Gabe.

"Well, why does Gabe have to go too?" Alexander asks. "He's not even here that long."

"I have found a room downtown," Gabe replies. "It will be convenient to see Vancouver."

This is partly true too. Gabe was shocked to find out there's not much public transit in our neighbourhood. But I feel worse about Gabe leaving than my brother does. He's going to be here in Canada, and I can't even see him. I'm not asking for the exact rules of grounding until my parents have cooled off.

"More bacon, Gabe?" my mother asks. It's killing her to have to rescind her hospitality for Gabe, who is only a concerned bystander to the bus crash that is my life.

"When are you leaving?" I try to keep the misery out of my voice, but fail.

"Today," he replies. Gabe had already made his arrangements before I'd finished crying off my mascara last night.

"Maybe Gabe can leave his hockey bag here when he goes," I suggest. At least he'll have to come back then. And when I miss him, I can become a literal jock sniffer.

"Nobody wants to share a house with a hockey bag," my sister points out to help me. I'm lucky that she's not the type to say "I told you so," but she has been giving me significant eyebrows all morning.

"Of course, leave it in the garage," says my mom. "And I'll be happy to drive you to the new place today."

Damn. My only chance to be alone with Gabe has been foiled. Well, that and the fact I'm not allowed to drive.

"Hey, Gabriel, if you like you can stay with me in my new place. No charge," offers Seb. The only good thing to come out of last night is that Seb and Gabe are becoming friends. Which only makes sense, given that Seb is homesick for Sweden.

"*Tack*. We'll see once you get a place," answers Gabe. "I haven't really seen Vancouver yet, so I'm looking forward to staying downtown. And I may visit a friend in Calgary too."

My spirits perk up. Maybe Gabe will stick around until after my mandatory confinement is over. And if he can stay for free with Seb, he could be here indefinitely.

"Morning," Roxy calls out as she walks in the side door. Then she stops short at the sight of Gabe and Seb. She nervously smooths her hair, because who expects to see two hot guys before 9:00 am?

"I'm almost ready to go," I say. As I get my lunch, I watch Gabe. His hair is perfectly styled, his posture is relaxed, and his face looks content. Again, it's because he's the mature one who takes the long view of life.

I want to kiss him goodbye. Heck, I want to skip school and hang out with Gabe all day, but I'll suck it up. As I leave, I cast one longing glance back at him, and he winks at me. Gah. Quit being so freaking adorable when I can't touch you.

After school, I take the bus home, back to a house that's now minus Gabe. Even with the transit delays and annoying weirdos, I'm still home in time to do one very important thing. I messaged Jason earlier, and he got back to me *tout suite*. We arranged to FaceTime. I fix myself up because looking good at a time like this gives me extra confidence. As I groom my eyebrows, I plot my strategy. I have to make him confess and apologize. Suffering will be a bonus.

His face appears on my laptop, and he looks all sincere. Fake sincere. How did I ever find someone that slick attractive? He's the handsome guy in the teen movie who turns out to be the villain.

"Lily, thanks so much for calling."

Jason leans into the screen, his brown eyes wide and no smile. This is his earnest look, a signal that he's completely trustworthy.

Last time I saw that face, he was telling me that he wouldn't be drinking on the guys trip to Vegas because he was underage. Yeah, and having an older brother whose ID he could borrow never occurred to him. He was shocked when I told him he could do whatever he wanted as long as he didn't bring back any STDs. Jason spent the first month we went out apologizing for a bunch of things I really didn't care about, which gave me a good idea of what his previous relationships had been like. And then he kept telling me how "refreshing" I was. So yeah, I was surprised to see him back with Rebecca. But the penis is mightier than the brain.

"I needed time to cool off," I explain. But I'm sure he knows that already. I get moods, but they pass. Also, I can be a conflict-avoider.

"So, Rebecca's full of shit, okay? Like she's always been jealous of you, and I'm not even back with her. Yeah we hooked up over Christmas, but I had no idea that she was going to be such a psycho when—"

"Stop. Stop it." I hold a hand up.

Jason looks sulky. "I'm trying to explain here."

"No, you're not. You're trying to blame Rebecca. But I wasn't upset by what she said." Much.

"Sure you were. Why else haven't you been taking my calls? And your friends have been dissing me too. Man, have you looked at my Insta lately? That Brit left these comments about—"

Again, I interrupt him. I don't have time for all his crap. I have a grounding sentence to wheedle down.

"Okay, Jason, I'll tell you what bothered me. You looked guilty when she was saying all that stuff. I know you, and I know your expressions. That's how I knew she was telling the truth. Otherwise, I wouldn't have believed a word."

I liked Jason. We had a good time together. We were never going to be serious, because he's not the kind of guy I could see being with for real. But he was fun.

And I trusted him. He knew that one of my issues was around my father and all the people who've manipulated me. That's why I was so upset.

His face is so easy to read. I can actually see him churning through options as his carefully-planned explanation goes up in flames. But he's got more, I can tell by the fake-sincerity of his furrowed forehead.

He opens his mouth, and I stop him again.

"Before you feed me one more bullshit excuse, why not try the truth?" I say. "Otherwise this call is over."

Jason sighs. "What I hated most about dating you was that you were too smart. You never let me get away with shit."

"That's not true," I say. "You pulled the biggest con of all on me, just to get onto a hockey team."

He shakes his head. "It wasn't like that. Really."

He scowls, and now the truth is coming. He's upset because what he's going to say will not make him look good. "Okay, when I first started hanging with you, I had this dumb idea that maybe your dad could help me. But you're fun. We were having a good time, and I rolled with it. What happened between us wasn't bullshit. Jesus, you know me, Lily. I'm not smart enough to pull a long con."

I can't help but smile at that. Jason notices and is encouraged to go on.

"Like, if you remember, you were the one who offered to get your dad to help me. Because you're nice. I wasn't going to suggest it because I knew that stuff bothered you."

Then he takes a deep breath, and I hold mine, knowing the worst is coming. "So, what I felt shitty about, was that when I started hooking up with Rebecca again, she couldn't shut up about you. She's really jealous. Anyway, to keep her happy, I told her that I'd only gone out with you for hockey shit. I didn't know she'd say all that back to you. And she added her own shit too. I never said a thing about your tits or how tall you are."

He leans towards the screen. "Seriously, Lily. I broke up with Rebecca that night. I told her she was a bitch and I didn't want all her bullshit in my life anymore. You probably think I'm apologizing because I think you'll get your dad to do something, but I'm not. I'm apologizing because you're a nice person, and I feel like shit that you got hurt. And it was all my fault."

Finally hearing the truth eases the tension in me. I was right in that Jason used me as a connection, but I was wrong in that our relationship wasn't fake.

"Okay," is all I say.

"Okay what?" he asks. "Are we good now?"

"No. I'm going to need time to process all this," I say. Because I'm finally learning not to say the first thing that comes to mind. I'll probably forgive Jason eventually, but he's still kind of a dickhead. "But if you're worried that I'm going to try to sabotage your hockey career, I won't."

When he exhales, he motorboats his lips, and I can't help smiling. He's a goof. He grins back at me.

"Bye, Jason," I say and click off the screen.

Then I go downstairs and look for my dad. He's not home yet, but my mother says he'll be here any minute. I go to the garage and sit on Gabe's hockey bag. Sure enough, a few minutes later the garage opens up, and my father's Mercedes pulls in.

He doesn't see me and remains inside listening to the radio. I slip in on the passenger side.

"Hey," he says, his expression neutral. Does he remember how badly things went last time we talked in this garage?

"Hey, Dad." I smile at him. "I wanted to tell you, I talked to Jason today."

"Ah?" My father looks wary now.

"Yeah, we had it out, and I got an explanation from him about everything that happened on New Year's."

I reach out and touch my father's arm in his smooth wool coat. "I should have done this in the first place. I mean, Jason has an explanation, it's not a great explanation, but I believe him and I feel better."

My father nods. Then he reaches out and covers my hand with his large one.

I blink back tears. I have stuff to get out without

crying. "I'm so sorry I took out everything on you, Dad. I know I'm way too emotional, but I'm trying hard to be better."

"You can do it," he reassures me.

"And what I said wasn't true." I look straight at him. "I love being your daughter. I loved it when I got to go to games and see you play so well. I love it now. I appreciate all the fun things I've gotten to do because of you."

He's not smiling, but his forehead is smoothing out and his expression lightens.

"When I saw you at the arena in Lund, I was so happy. There were so many people in Sweden who reminded me of you—their height, the way they walked, or just the shape of their heads. But when it was really you, that was the most amazing moment."

I eke out a pathetic grimace/smile. My dad smiles back at me and holds out his arms. I dive in for a hug and feel the last of the tension knot in my tummy dissolving. My dad strokes my hair.

"I love you, Dad. So much."

"I love you too, Lily. Don't worry, you're maturing. You'll be fine."

The soft cashmere of his coat feels good against my cheek, but not as good as the feeling that everything is back to normal. Gabe is right: once the important stuff is settled, the rest doesn't matter.

42

EBUG TO THE RESCUE

GABRIEL

MY PHONE RINGS. It's startling since I seldom get calls. I don't recognize the number.

"Ja, hello?"

"Gabriel, it's Jesper. Where are you now?"

I sit up straighter, even though he cannot see me. "I am having *fika*. On Robson Street." I have been sight-seeing in downtown Vancouver. My new Airbnb is only a bedroom but very convenient.

"Well, I'm not in a position to ask you a favour, but I will. The backup goalie for the Vice tweaked his groin at the morning skate. Turns out it's serious."

"Ah, that's unfortunate." I reply.

"Pillsbury is the starter. But they need a backup. And Flint is too far away to fly someone in for tonight."

I wait. I'm not sure what I have to do with this.

"Chris called me, and he was wondering if you could do it."

I have never experienced a cold sweat before, but now my whole body is drenched in something clammy. I hope it's not piss. "Me? I can't be the goalie for an AHL team. I wasn't good enough to make the ECHL team," I remind him.

Jesper laughs. "You don't have to play. All you do is get dressed and sit on the bench. It's a regulation that the team must have two goalies. If it's not you, they'll have to find someone from the university team."

I exhale. "Ja, sure, I can sit on the bench."

"Besides, it will be good for you. They'll get to know who you are—for next season."

"Thank you, Jesper." It will be an adventure to tell my friends about when I get home.

"Oh, you're welcome. Lucky will be grateful when I let him know. So, your gear is all at our house, right?"

"Yes. Dori put my hockey bag in the garage."

"Do you usually nap before a game?"

"Not really." It's been so long since I played a real game that I have no routine.

He clears his throat. "Okay, how about if you come to our house for a pre-game meal? Sebastian can take you to the arena with all your gear."

"Are you certain this is okay?" I ask.

"Yes. Since you're backing up, we'll all go to the game. Lily too."

I'm not sure if this means she's not grounded anymore, but I sense some sort of apology in his voice. I'm glad to do a favour for Jesper since he's been very kind

317

to me. I thank him again, and we arrange to meet to later this afternoon.

"IT'S LIKE OLD TIMES." Dori laughs. "I'm making pre-game meals for everyone."

She adds a platter of roasted, skinless chicken breasts on a table already laden with food. There is a brown rice casserole, steamed vegetables, and some kind of grainy salad.

"This is great! It's all the things we're supposed to eat," declares Sods before he digs in. Since we are to be teammates, he told me to call him by his hockey nickname —it's short for Söderlund. I doubt that I will get a nickname for one game.

"I was trained by the best," Dori says. She plants a kiss on the top of Jesper's head as she walks behind him. They are such a loving couple.

"We're all going to the game tonight," Alexander declares. "Since both of you are playing."

I laugh. "I will not be playing. I'll be cheering the Vice on—like you guys."

He scowls. "Are you getting paid at least?"

I look over at Jesper, who shrugs. "I don't know either. I guess you'll sign a PTO or something. If you do get paid, it's not going to be much."

"It's not about the money," I say. "It will be a cool experience." I've already messaged a few friends back in Lund. After a bit of hesitation, I let my father know too. Nobody will be paying attention anyway, since the game starts at 4:00 in the morning there.

Lily beams at me across the table. We haven't had a

moment alone, but it's nice just to look at her. She's beautiful in her pale purple sweater and jeans. "It will be amazing. But how are you going to feel if you have to play?"

"If I have to play, don't look too closely at the back of my goalie pants."

Lily, Sods, and Jesper snicker. Even Margie smiles. It takes Alexander a few beats, but once he figures this out, he goes into hysterics. Milk shoots out of his nose.

Dori gives me a look, and I apologize. "Sorry. Not proper dinner conversation."

Sods speaks through a mouth full of chicken. "Don't worry, it's only Bakersfield. They're not that good. Even you can stop their shots."

"Don't ever underestimate the opposition," warns Jesper. "You let your guard down, and that's when they strike."

"Just trying to make Olly feel better," Sods says. He's in high spirits despite everything that's happened in the last 24 hours. Olly must be my Canadian hockey nickname; Chris used it as well.

"The best way to overcome nervousness is to mentally prepare for the worst," Jesper suggests. "Think about how you would feel if you had to play. Try to relax and imagine yourself in your normal game. You were excellent when I saw you play."

Sods laughs. "Yeah, but wasn't that some university game? That's like the difference between facing shots from your sister and shots from a grown man."

"That's sexist," replies Lily. "Besides, you said your older sister used to play against you, and she was good."

He laughs. "Yeah, but my older sister plays for the Swedish national team."

"Then she'd probably boot your butt if she heard you saying that," Dori suggests.

"Older sisters are scary," Alexander agrees and then ducks the cloth napkin Lily tosses at him.

After dinner, I go up to my old room to change into the only suit I brought. As I'm doing up my shirt, there's a tap on the door.

"Come in."

Lily pokes her head in. "Hey, Gabe. I just wanted to wish you good luck."

"Thank you. Can you help me with this?" I'm wearing my mother's gift cufflinks, and the right one is tricky. Lily comes over and deftly inserts the silver square and puts it in place. Her hair tickles my wrist as she bends over, and I resist an urge to kiss the back of her head.

"Okay, you're all set now."

"*Tack.*"

I pull on my jacket, and her eyes widen. "Have you been sleeping in that suit?"

"No. But it was at the bottom of my suitcase. Is it that bad?" The dark navy colour won't show the wrinkles too much.

"It's bad. We have a steamer. Give it to me." She puts her hand out.

I take off my jacket and put it in her hands.

"The pants too."

My face reddens. "I'm not taking off my pants in front of you. Is that even allowed?"

Lily rolls her eyes. "It's not something I haven't seen before. Besides your shirt is going to cover up your, um, package."

She giggles as I unzip my dress pants. Getting

undressed in front of Lily isn't as much fun as it used to be. I manage to keep my boxer briefs and semi-hardened cock out of her view. Her gaze lingering on my bare legs doesn't help.

She flashes me a big smile and then disappears with my suit.

I comb my hair, then give my dress shoes a quick polish. I have already cleaned out my equipment bag, and it's waiting in the garage.

There's a knock on the door.

I swing it open. "That was fast—"

Sods is standing there. "You're a little underdressed. Hurry up."

Then Lily brushes by him.

"Here you go. Pressed for success." She passes me the suit, now on a hanger and looking brand new.

Sods frowns. "Lucky bastard. I never get that kind of service."

The odd tension between the three of us only adds to the discomfort in my already nervous stomach. I pull on my pants and then excuse myself to go the bathroom. Flipping my tie over my shoulder, I lean over the toilet and wait. First the taste of bile in my mouth, and then my half-digested dinner lands in the toilet bowl. Although I hoped that things might be different here, my pre-game routine is right on schedule.

I throw water on my face and brush my teeth. When I walk back in the room, both Lily and Sods are staring.

"Did you just throw up?" Lily asks. "Are you okay?"

I nod. "Yeah. It's what I do before every game."

Sods makes a face. "Shit, that's awful. Well, we better go. You're not going to barf in my car, are you?"

"No, there's nothing left."

Lily raises her arms like she's going to hug me, but switches into a pat on the shoulders. "Don't be nervous, Gabe. You'll do fine."

Her touch feels good, but it's not necessary. Vomiting cleanses me. I feel empty, clear, and ready.

This time, the arena is alive with lights and activity. Sods parks in the team lot, and we enter through a special door. We're extra early, so no teammates are here yet. We drop my gear in the room, then Sods guides me to the coach's office. He was at my tryout, but we never spoke.

He's talking to another coach when we get there. Both he and Sods leave once I walk in.

"Leo Gauthier." He shakes my hand. When he focuses his laser gaze on me, I feel like I've already messed up. No wonder Sods fled. "Thanks for doing this."

"No problem. Jesper Larson said I'm supposed to sign something first?"

He pulls out his phone and sends a message. "Yeah, Lucky wants to see you for that. So, I saw you try out, but what exactly is your hockey experience?"

I study the laces of my dress shoes. "I've been playing in a university league in Sweden. But I played competitively when I was a teenager."

"For who?"

"Malmö Redhawks. J18 Elit."

I'm unsure if I have to explain that this is the highest level of junior hockey at that age, but he nods and looks down at a paper. "That's quite a change in only a few years. What happened?"

I shrug. "Family problems. I wasn't able to travel to games anymore."

There's a silence. We both know I'm not telling him everything. But isn't this just one night? Why is the coach interviewing me like it's the real deal?

"Goalies. More than any of my players, their mental game is most important. Are you on top of your mental game, Gabriel?"

I nod. What am I supposed to say to that? I'm a great goalie in my own league, but it's not the AHL. "Uh, I thought I was going to sit on the bench."

He tents his fingers together and stares. Intensity radiates from him. What was going to be an adventure is getting serious. "The odds of you actually playing are probably less than one percent. But you know what they say: if you fail to prepare, prepare to fail. I want my backup to be ready, no matter what. How do you prepare mentally before a regular game?"

"I visualize everything," I tell him. I imagine the chill of the ice, the net behind me, the action in front of me, and shots. Shots coming at me from different places. Even when I got cut and thought I'd never play competitive hockey again, I'd escape into the ice in my head. And here I am—on an AHL bench, something beyond my dreams.

"Then do that. Go through your whole routine as if it's a regular game, and don't treat this like a joke. The best backups are relaxed but ready. You know, like a fireman."

I nod. Despite his manic intensity, I'm beginning to like this guy. His philosophy is one I'd always followed: guard for every eventuality. Because I couldn't control the big things, I tried to control the little things.

"Okay, I'm going to go through a few things about our opponents tonight." He turns his laptop around to face me and flips up some video about the Bakersfield team.

The video is cut to show the best players, and he high-lights their tendencies. "You'll be able to see a lot of this while watching the game, and notice things on your own too. If you go out, use that. And be vocal. You won't even know the guys on your own team, so you'll have to tell your defencemen what you want."

"Jesus, Goats, are you scaring the shit out of Olly already?" Chris Luczak walks into the office with a file folder and a huge grin.

The coach smiles, but his smile is a little stiff like he doesn't use it very much. "I'm coaching him, like I'm supposed to. He's my player now."

"According to this contract, he's your player for tonight. And you've got him looking like he's ready to crap his pants."

I swallow and try to look as relaxed and confident as Sods. "It's okay. I appreciate all this."

Leo nods. "See. The good players always want to learn. They seize every opportunity."

His indirect praise thrills me. This coach is a master of psychological manipulation. He broke me down and lifted me up in a ten-minute span. Sods' mixture of fear and respect make perfect sense now. As the two of them chat about something else, I look around his office. It's tidy and sterile except for a large, colourful landscape painting. The wildness of the art is beautiful but out of place here.

I sign the papers placed before me without even reading them. The defensive coach, Ryan Walsh, appears to take me to the dressing room.

"You look a little nervous," he says as we walk along a cinder-block corridor.

"I'm fine," I reply.

"Don't worry, EBUGs never play."

"EBUGs?" I ask.

"Yup. Emergency Back Up Goalie." He laughs. "One time, Roberto Luongo came back from the hospital just to make sure the emergency backup didn't have to play."

I smile, but my smile feels as awkward as the coach's looked. We push through a swinging door. In the hall, players are warming up. A few guys are stretching, others playing soccer, and some are just chatting. We walk through to the dressing room, where the jerseys and gear are laid out in perfect symmetry.

"Here's your spot."

I recognize my worn gear, but everything else is different. There's a neatly folded t-shirt and shorts below with Property of Vancouver Vice in an oval logo. A brand new jersey shimmers before me: black and silver with my name on it. Olsson, Number 31. I reach out and feel the raised letters. The jersey makes everything feel real.

"Nice. Thank you."

Ryan laughs and smacks me on the shoulder. "It's not a big deal. The best thing you'll get from tonight is the jersey. Smitty's got your skates, he wanted to know how you like 'em."

When I tell him, the coach snorts. "Smitty is not going to know metric. You play butterfly?"

I nod.

"Okay, something sharper then. Maybe 3/8" hollow?"

"Ja, thank you." I'm not sure exactly what I'm going to get, but it will be 100% better than the crabby old man at the university rink who usually sharpens my skates.

"Why don't you change and get warmed up? We'll take some shots at you in the warm-up, so you're all ready for your evening of sitting on the bench." He laughs again and walks away.

Apparently, Leo and I are the only ones taking this seriously. An emergency back up goalie is a joke. But for someone who long ago gave up his hockey dreams, this whole experience is surreal. Maybe Jesper is right: if I work hard, listen to my coaches, and succeed in Sweden, I can make it back here for real. Goalies peak around 27 or 28, so I still have time.

Lily changed my life. No matter what happens between us, she is the catalyst for everything.

Soon I'm in my gear and ready to go out for warm-ups. The other players are in various stages of dressing. Sods introduces me to a few guys, and they're all friendly.

One older player comes over and holds out his hand. "I'm Paul Thiebault. Thanks for helping us out tonight."

"No problem." I notice the C on his jersey. He's taking responsibility for making me feel welcome.

"Don't mind Doughy." He motions to the goalie beside me who has been wearing his headphones the whole time and ignored my attempt at an introduction. "That's his routine whenever he starts. Goalies. You guys are a tribe of your own."

He raises his voice. "Guys, this is Gabriel Olsson. Tonight, he's going to be our back up goalie."

There's a general greeting from the room. Every dressing room has a mood, and the one here is good. There's nervous tension, but there's also camaraderie. The Vice seem like a supportive team, and that eases the final knot in my stomach. We skate out for the warm-up, and there are already many people in the stands.

"Olly, Olly, Olly!" I hear Alexander's excited voice and

look up to see the whole Larson family waving at me. Alexander is jumping up and down. Lily's not waving, but she smiles at me. I raise my stick in greeting.

"Let's go, man." Sods bumps me from behind. I skate back to the bench and begin stretching. The chill of the arena, the comfortable feel of my pads, the swish of skates —all my senses tingle with the familiarity of being on the ice for a game. Hockey is still my escape, and I feel a rush of relief.

43

THE GAME

LILY

"LOOK! THERE HE IS." My brother yells, "Hey, Olly! Olly! Olly!" Luckily, I don't need my left eardrum for anything.

"Is that Gabe?" my mother asks, as if she can't believe he had made it from our house to exactly where he's supposed to be.

"Yes." Gabe looks nervous out there. Well, if his warm-up is tossing his cookies, it's hard to imagine what he'll do on the ice. I smile at him encouragingly, even though I can't tell if he's looking our way. Goalie masks are so deep and dark. Then he waves his stick at us.

"He heard me," Alexander says. "I hope he gets to play. Will he play half the game, Dad?"

My father laughs. "It's not like minor hockey. The best goalie plays the whole game. Although Pillsbury hasn't been great this season."

"How do you know all this?" my mother wonders.

"I've gone to a few games with Lucky. We talk a lot about the team when we're out together."

She shakes her head. "I can't believe how involved you're getting with the Vice. First, Sebastian; then that scouting trip to Malmö; and now, Gabriel. Chris should put you on the payroll."

He squeezes her hand. "It's a hobby. Besides, Gabe didn't pass his tryout, so my record's not perfect."

I wonder if it bothers my father that Gabe wasn't as good as he thought. I nudge him. "Gabe looked amazing in that game back in Lund. Chris would have given him a contract on the spot."

My father flashes me a grateful smile, but he's not fooled. "That was no professional game. Anyone can tell who the best player on the ice is, but only real scouts can figure out how they'll perform at a higher level."

He offers me a stick of gum, and I take it. I'm so happy to be back in sync with my dad again. We both turn back to the ice. Gabe rises from his stretching and goes towards the net. The other goalie skates out, and Gabe skates in. Is he still nervous? It's tough to tell from here, but he's more twitchy than smooth. It's pretty obvious that the players are going easy on him, taking soft shots or even hitting him square in the chest protector, but he's still fumbling.

My throat feels dry, so I take a sip of my water. Poor Gabe. I watch him whiff on a shot that even I could have stopped. My dad sighs. Then Seb skates up, his blond hair flowing behind him, and rips off a high, hard shot. I wince, but Gabe's glove hand whips out and snatches the puck.

"Yes!" Both my dad and I speak at the same time. Hopefully that one good stop will add to Gabe's confidence. The warm-up winds down, and the players skate off.

There are shrieks from one section over, as some of the wives and girlfriends arrive. My mother watches them.

"I remember those days, sitting with all the girlfriends. It was always fun."

"But you were at NHL games," my dad points out. He never spent a day in AHL.

She nods. "Higher stakes and more competitive. I used to spend so much time getting ready. Now I'm lucky if I get matching shoes on."

That is crap since my mother not only looks good, but spends a lot of time getting ready. She turns to me, "You look very put together tonight, dear."

Rats, I hoped she wouldn't notice how much work I'd put in getting ready for tonight. It's not a date, but it's as close as I'm getting right now. Not that Gabe even notices these things. He thinks I look great all the time, which is very sweet, but if all the flirting I get to do is from the stands, then I'm wearing false eyelashes.

The game finally gets underway, and it's a close match. The Vice come out hard and score a goal early, but then the Bakersfield Condors score a few minutes later.

My father scowls at the goalie. "Doughy moves around too much, if he stayed in place, that shot would have hit him instead of going in. Lucky says their goaltending hasn't been great all year."

"Yes, but they've been winning, haven't they?" my mother asked.

"Because they had firepower up front. But now Eric

Fairburn's been called up to the Millionaires, and it looks like he'll be there for a while."

"Seb'll score," my brother said. That's true, Seb is on a scoring streak. He reminds us of this after every game.

"Why can't the Vice call up a better goalie from that Flint team?" my mother asks.

My father sniffs. "There's one on the way, but Flint's goalie situation is not great either. That's why Olly even got a tryout." He's using Gabe's hockey nickname now that he's an actual player.

The score remains tied. Then in the second period, a Bakersfield player drives to the net and the Vice defenceman tries to check him. The two of them fall and take out the goalie as well. With the three of them lying in a tangled heap and the net off its pegs, the ref blows the play dead.

"Damn," my father says.

"What is it?" my mother asks.

"Doughy hit his head against the post there. I hope he's okay."

He's not. He raises himself slightly, but it's clear that he isn't right. Someone skates the trainer over. There's a hushed silence in the arena. After several agonizing minutes, Doughy stands up. There are cheers, but then the trainer and the defenceman both take an arm and move him towards the bench.

The crowd applauds him, then the murmurs begin. It's like everyone is saying, "Oh shit," at the same time.

Gabe is going to play. The emergency goalie—who is really a joke, a backup that you never expect to call on—is coming on. Everything about him says he isn't ready for this, from his shabby white pads to his colour-uncoordinated blue helmet.

The murmurs in the crowd grow louder. Poor guy.

I watch Gabe. He's in his own zone. I remember his routine from the other game I'd seen him play. He skates out to the net, touches both posts with his stick, and then turns and gets into position. He gently stretches out his legs, side-to-side, going lower and lower. Then he stands, shakes out his shoulders and stretches his neck.

"How's he going to do?" My mother's voice is nervous, and my father doesn't even answer.

"He's going to do great," my brother says. "I've played road hockey with him, and he's awesome."

Well, he's probably the only one in the arena who thinks so. But I hope Alexander is right.

Bakersfield smells blood in the water in the form of a shaky emergency backup in net. They start shooting from everywhere. The Vice respond by blocking shots like crazy, but the first shot that gets by them goes high on Gabe's blocker side and straight into the net. He doesn't even move.

There's a collective groan from the crowd. Now the Condors are ahead by a goal.

"Is there a mercy rule in AHL hockey?" my mother wonders.

Thousands of people are thinking the same things: "Is every shot going to go in?" or "What's the most an AHL team has ever lost by?"

Poor Gabe. He can do it. He just needs to relax and not be so nervous.

I stand up and in the hush, scream out, "You can do it, Gabe!"

My brother pops up beside me. "Yeah! Go, Olly! Olly, Olly, Olly!" We high-five each other and sit back down.

Who knows if he heard us or not, but he rotates his shoulders like he's shaking something off and stands taller in the crease.

After the face-off, Bakersfield comes right back and set up in the offensive zone. They're moving the puck around, but no shots yet.

"Ugh, it looks like a Condor power play? Why can't the Vice attack instead?" my mother asks.

"They're collapsing in front of Olly to protect him," my father explains. "But they need someone up high to pressure the points and clear the zone."

He's right. There are five black and silver jerseys around the crease. Plus two white jerseys of the Condor players jostling for position. Could Gabe even see a puck if it gets through?

Zing. A shot comes from the point and hits someone in the crowd. But number 19, one of the best players on the Condors, recovers the puck. I hold my breath as he shoots directly at the top corner of the net.

This time, Gabe's glove flashes out and catches the puck. Cool as can be, he releases it to the nearest defenceman, and the Vice skate the puck out.

"Yeah! Go, Olly!" Alexander yells again.

I release my breath in a happy rush. Surely this is the return of the regular Gabe Olsson, and he'll begin playing the way I know he can.

And he does. Gabe seems to grow taller as he positions himself so that most shots hit his broad chest and bounce to the ice where he smothers them. His glove hand snags pucks that aren't even on the target.

Then the team begins to trust him too. They leave him to make the saves and start on the attack. Near the end of the second period, Seb and Nate Jones manage a two-on-one and when the Condor defenceman moves towards Seb, he slides the puck to Jonesy, who wires it five-hole.

The crowd goes crazy. We've all been on the same rollercoaster of emotions—the despair of seeing an unknown goalie fail and then rise—and the goal is our sweet release. Now the game is tied.

My father exhales loudly. "Good thing that Olly got over his nervousness. He'll be fine now."

"You can really spot talent," my mother assures him.

Watching Gabe skate out for the third period puts my mind at ease. Even from the stands, I can tell he's more relaxed. Then he flips up his mask, and he's smiling. I smile back at him, even though he can't see me.

Both teams buckle down in the third period and push to get the winning goal. They're trading chances and going end to end. Each Condor shot makes me hold my breath, but Gabe is in the right place every time.

"That kid has a natural sense of positioning. Imagine how he's going to be with some real coaching."

My dad sounds as proud as if he'd hatched Gabe himself.

Then, with four minutes left, the Vice pounce on a turnover and speed into the Bakersfield zone. Jones sneakily threads a pass through the slot, and Seb one-times it.

Vice goal! The place goes bananas. This game has been full of emotional ups and downs.

No time to relax. The Condors are coming on, pushing to tie things up again. We're spending way too much time in our zone. And then with over two minutes left, they pull their goalie and the pressure really cranks up. The Vice try to clear the front of the net so Gabe can see, but shots are coming from everywhere. I can see him peeking around the scrum in front of him, just in time to snag an incoming puck with a glorious round-the-world flourish.

"Wow!" Alexander declares. Then he starts cheering again. "Olly, Olly, Olly!"

I chant along with him, and my parents laughingly start cheering too. And then a few more people, until finally the whole arena is chanting and cheering for Gabe. He's the embodiment of everyone's fantasy: the guy who comes out of nowhere and saves the team.

"Olly. Olly. Olly."

His name echoes through the arena right up the final buzzer. Then the team pours off the bench, and he disappears under a mass of happy bodies.

44

THE WINNER TAKES IT ALL

GABRIEL

"HEY, GABRIEL." A radio reporter shoves a microphone in my face. "How did you feel when you saw Doughy go down in the second period?"

"I was hoping he would be okay," I reply. It's only the truth, but everyone laughs. There are three reporters here, and one of them looks quite young.

Nobody wants to see a teammate get hurt though. I still haven't heard how serious his injury is, but he's not in the dressing room, so I assume he's gone to be evaluated.

"What happened on the first goal that got by you?" someone else asks. I've never done an interview before in my life, and I feel really uncomfortable. All I can do is tell the truth.

"Uh, I didn't even see it. There were a few guys in front of me."

"Word is that Doughy is out with a concussion. Are you ready to take over the net now?"

I shake my head. "Nej. Not me. I think the team is calling someone up from the ECHL. I only played tonight because he couldn't get here in time."

"C'mon, after a performance like that? You stopped 24 shots in the last half of the game. You should get the start on Saturday."

"No, I think not. Besides, it's not my decision."

"Where did you play before, Olly?" asks a woman. She holds out her iPhone to record my answer.

"I played for LTH Gripana. Back in Lund. Sweden." I didn't have to add Sweden. My accent tells everyone where I'm from.

"I don't think I've heard of that," she replies.

"It's not the top league." It's many levels below the SHL, but I don't tell her that.

"Then how did the Vice find you?" she wonders.

"Jesper Larson saw me play there. He recommended me to Chris Luczak."

She nods. These are names she knows. "It's a real Cinderella story."

It is. There are a few more questions, but I'm not the kind of personality they need for their stories. They want me to be more excited at the fairy tale nature of the night. But if I were an excitable type, I wouldn't have gotten the win.

Finally, I am free to turn back into a pumpkin. I head for the showers. Afterwards, someone tells me I need to see the coach once I'm changed.

"Don't worry," says Sods. "I'll wait for you." He's in a great mood, with the team win and his own two points.

I walk back into the coach's office. He's sitting there with Chris Luczak and both of them are laughing. It's the opposite of Leo's pre-game intensity.

"Olly! The man of the match," Chris jokes. He has an ease about him that makes me comfortable too.

Coach nods. "You played real good out there. How were you feeling?"

"I felt good," I say. "I tried to treat it as just another game, you know, and not worry about the professional quality of shots coming at me."

Chris laughs. "Yeah, once Bakersfield realized how green you are, they were pissing themselves to shoot from anywhere."

"I could almost see the moment things began to click for you," the coach says. "After that glove save on the shot in tight."

I nod. That was exactly when I stopped being conscious of the crowd, the big game, and all the differences and went into my flow state.

"Mark is under observation for concussion. He won't be playing again right away," Chris says.

"So, we've got practice tomorrow at noon," Leo says.

"Okay, you want me to fill in?" I ask.

They both stare at me like I'm an idiot. "No, we want to give you a trial up here."

"But what about your ECHL goalie? Isn't he coming up?"

"Yeah, but we still need two goalies," Chris replies. "Olly, we'd like you to stay up here and work out with the team."

I stare at them. "But my tryout—wasn't a success."

Chris and Coach Gauthier exchange a look.

Chris leans back in his chair. "Gabriel, let me level with you here. You had a helluva game. You're pretty much the reason that we got the W tonight. So, we'll see what you've got. You're not going to be lights-out every game, but you show much better in a real game than you did on Tuesday. Luke liked what he saw in you: your size, your reflexes, and most of all your ability to take coaching. We just didn't know if you could put it all together, and your track record wasn't giving us any confidence.

"So, what is next?" I ask.

"Well, there's a bunch of paperwork, but that's not your problem. The bottom line is: keep stopping rubber, and you'll stay up here. If you don't, but you still look promising, we'll probably send you to Michigan. Of course, the third possibility is that you get cut altogether."

I prefer the first option. Staying in Vancouver and being with Lily is the dream.

"Will I be paid?"

Chris laughs. "Of course. It's not millions, but I'm sure it's better than what you made before."

"Which was nothing," I reply. They both laugh.

"I'd like to find a place to live here if I'm staying," I say.

"*If* you're staying," Leo emphasizes, but he's smiling. "You'll have to work your ass off to stick. You don't have the reps most guys do."

Chris shakes his head. "Goalies aren't like any other position. They're voodoo. Nancy in the front office can help you find a temporary place."

Leo gives me a schedule of games and practices and a file folder of medical forms. I thank them, then search for

Sods. To my surprise, the whole Larson family is with him too.

This time there's no hesitation; Lily runs over and hugs me fiercely.

"Oh my God, you did an awesome job!" Her face glows in delight. I smile down at her, enjoying that familiar happy energy that Lily generates.

"I scored the game-winning goal," Sods mutters beside me, but all the Larsons are talking at once and nobody even hears him.

"Huh, I'll have to call Chris and see what he thinks," Jesper says. He's clearly proud for having discovered me.

"I talked to Chris. They've asked me to stay here and practice with the team until they figure out the goalie situation."

"Oh, that's wonderful," Dori declares.

"It's temporary," I remind her.

Alexander shakes his head. "You're better than both their regular goalies. You should be the new starter."

"Not after only one game," I protest, and Sods nods.

"You're good. I've seen you play before, and you were incredible then," Lily insists. She's skipping along beside me.

"It's a much harder league though," Sods says. He's pissed off that everyone—especially Lily—is making such a fuss over me. I don't think that he's jealous; it's more that he wants praise too. Sods has simple needs: affection and recognition. From what he tells me, his mother and sisters dote on him, and he expects that all women will act the same way.

"Your goal was awesome! And the game winner," Alexander says, and then Sods is happy again.

Lily keeps bumping into me as we walk. I wish we could hold hands, but I'm not sure what's allowed. This grounding stuff is ridiculous.

She chatters happily. "That save you made at the end was so good. People were standing and cheering. They were chanting your name."

"Really?" I ask.

She laughs. "Did you not hear them?"

I shake my head. "I don't hear anything when I play."

Sods says, "Goalies are so weird. How can you not hear the fans?"

"That's how I concentrate."

"Do you hear the whistles?" Lily asks.

"I hear everything I expect to hear: the other players, the refs, the board sounds."

"Can you hear the coach?" Sods wonders.

"Not a word."

Lily and Sods laugh, and he adds, "I don't listen to the coach either, well, not while I'm on the ice. I listen when I get back to the bench. But you never go back to the bench."

We pause in the parking lot. They're all going in one direction, but my Airbnb is the opposite way. Sods offers to drive me home, and I say goodbye to the Larson family. Lily hugs me again, but nothing more. I hop into the Mustang. When I pull out my phone, I have a couple of congratulatory messages from Johan and Robin, who woke up early and checked the box scores. And there's a long email from my father, who somehow watched the whole game. One line stands out as I skim it: he's planning on telling my mother about my game when he visits today. I can imagine the whole thing, because my mother does respond well to happy news or an excited voice. Maybe she'll understand in some way that I'm succeeding here.

As I'm reading the email, a message pops up from Lily.

I'm pretty sure we can go out this weekend!

"Why are you smiling like that?" Sods asks me.

"Because life is good," I reply. I feel happy about the future—really happy—for the first time in years.

EPILOGUE

SWEDEN IN VANCOUVER

GABRIEL

"I WAS WONDERING, didja want to find a place to live together?" Sods asks me after practice.

I've been on the team for over a week now, and it's going pretty good. I've played two games, and we won both of them. Right now, it looks like I'll be staying in Vancouver.

The other goalie is here from Flint. His name is Felix Lapointe. He's very friendly, and I like playing in tandem with him. I already prefer Felix to Mark Pillsbury, the concussed Vice goalie. Most people think that goalies are in constant competition, but the best ones work together. We help each other improve and share information, and then the team benefits. But Pillsbury is the better goalie. However, I can't worry about partner situations I have no control over. Improving my game gives me the most control over where I play.

"You and me? What will Jesper think of us living together?" I'm not willing to mess up my relationship with Lily's dad.

"It was his suggestion. Apparently, you're a good influence," Sods says.

I'm not completely sold, but it will only be for a few months. We are very different, but he's a good guy. But I have one more concern. "Lily and I are together, will that be a problem for you?"

His lips twist as he considers this. "Lily is great. I really like her, but before you even arrived, she told me we would only be friends. That's okay. Besides, she's a little bossy. No offence."

Sods gets bossed because he needs direction. Lily and I have a more equal relationship. As I guided her in Lund, she will help me in Vancouver.

"Okay, let's live together," I say.

"Phew. Thank you so much." His customary grin flashes. He was nervous about being all on his own.

"I'm not going to look after you though," I add.

"Don't worry. I get that." He starts to whistle.

We go to see Nancy in the front office.

"I've been looking for places," she says. "I guess the real issue is how long the lease should be. Are we going to make the playoffs this year?"

She looks straight at me when she asks this. I notice that her eyelashes are the same bright green as her dress.

"Hey, I am new. Ask him," I reply.

"What you are is the missing link," Nancy says. "Goaltending has been our weakness. Can you keep up the level you've been playing at?"

I nod. Each time I get on the ice with Luke, I learn so much. My skills and fitness improve daily. Whatever happens with the Vice, I'm becoming a much better goalie.

"Okee-dokee. I'll look for a place that can take you into the playoffs. I've already got a line on a sublet that might work. I didn't realize it was going to be both of you though."

"Thank you very much," I say.

"No problem, Gabriel."

Then she turns to Sods and points a long, purple fingernail at him. "Look, Mister, this is your third housing placement this season. If you want to get a rep for being a problem, you are on the right path. And take it from me, problem players subtract years off their careers. Sure, you may be a hot shot on the ice, but if you cause issues off the ice, nobody wants to deal with you. You'll stay down in the AHL longer, increase your chances of getting traded, and get cut sooner."

Sods is shocked. He takes a step back, but she leans forward and pokes his chest. "Next season, you should get your mother to come and live with you. She'll straighten you out. You're young, so you're getting a pass, but believe me, you're causing a lot of trouble. It's time to straighten out and fly right. *Capisce?*"

"Sorry?" Sods stammers. "I don't understand."

"Are. You. Going. To. Stay. Out. Of. Trouble?" She stares him in the eye like a snake charmer, and he nods slowly.

Then her emerald eyelashes flutter, and she adds, "Keep it in your pants, Sebastian. I mean that. This team is close to the playoffs for the first time, and it means more than you even know. If I find out that you're still messing around, I will hunt you down and cut it off."

"Uhhh," Sods hunches over like he's trying to protect the part in question. "Ja, sure."

I'm trying hard not to laugh. Nancy is the toughest teacher you ever had, multiplied a hundred times. But maybe Sods needs to be scared straight.

"Thanks again, Nancy," I say and nudge Sods out the door.

She smiles sweetly at me. "No problem. I'll let you know as soon as I hear something."

NANCY FINDS us a furnished apartment that will last until June 30th, well past the finals of the Calder Cup—if we even make the playoffs. It's close to the rink, and we can move in right away. And even though there is some furniture, we need more home supplies. Since it's the weekend, Lily offers to borrow her mother's large SUV and drive us to IKEA.

"You are not grounded?" I ask, when she comes to pick us up.

"It's a loophole. We're going out during the day and Seb's with us, so it's not really a date."

But we still kiss. Lily's lips taste like honey. Is this a cosmetic or her natural sweetness?

"If you're gonna make out, I need a woman too," Sods grumbles from the back seat.

"Don't let Nancy hear you say that," I warn him. He winces and crosses his legs.

We drive along a busy highway, and Lily points out various sites we can visit later. Then we arrive at IKEA.

"Wow, this looks exactly like the IKEA at home," Sods says. I nod. It looks exactly like the one in Malmö as well.

When we get inside, Sods is even more excited. "Look at the food! I can get Kalles here! He starts loading the cart with tubes of fish paste. And then he adds crisp-breads, jams, and even frozen vegetable balls.

"Calm down," Lily says. "There are two IKEAs in town. You can always—oh my God! Look, Gabe!" She pulls me over. We are already holding hands, so it's not difficult. I can't stop touching Lily.

She holds up a frozen package. *"Kanelbullar*! They're frozen, and you bake them. And they look exactly like the kind we ate in Lund."

The ones on the package do look like the proper Swedish type.

"I can bake real ones for you once we get flour and sugar," I offer.

Lily beams at me. "Oh, I forgot what a perfect guy you are."

"This is true." I wrap my arms around her waist and pull her close to me. And then we kiss again. Her mouth is both firm and yielding, and a rush of emotion comes over me. It's desire, but more than that. When the kiss ends, I lean my forehead against hers. "You make me happy."

She smiles. "You mocked my cheerfulness, and now look at you. Now that you're in Canada, you're all about the happiness."

I chuckle. But it's not the place, it's the person. Lily and I are happy here. And in the summer, we can go back to Lund. Lily will finally meet my mother. All that matters is that we are together.

Sods calls out to us, "Guys, look! *Salmiaklakrits*! They have salty licorice too!"

Lily goes over to see. "Oh, that stuff is nasty. But look at all the candy. We can celebrate *lördagsgodis* today."

"Maybe we can do cozy Fridays too," Sods suggests. They both turn to me.

"Why do you look at me?"

"Can you cook tacos?" Lily asks.

"You don't have to cook tacos, you assemble the ingredients," I reply. "Any idiot can make tacos."

"I will learn," Sods says. "I find out my family recipe."

Lily reaches for my hand again and squeezes it. "I've been missing Sweden so much. But now we can have the best of Sweden here in Vancouver."

I nod. Sods tells Lily she can bring her girlfriends over. Perhaps we will make our own group of friends, similar to my life-long friends in Lund. I'm excited to experience life in Vancouver and see the similarities and differences. All I have to do is keep playing hockey well. But instead of pressure, this idea gives me strength. So many things in my life have been out of my control, and at last I determine my own path.

As she argues with Sods about one of her friends he's interested in, Lily makes a crazy arm motion and accidentally knocks a candy scoop off the wall.

I bend down, catch the scoop before it can hit the floor, and replace it on the hook.

"Wow. Good reflexes," says Sods.

Lily wraps her arms around my waist. "Thanks for the save, Gabe."

"I'm here for you," I tell her. After all, saves are what got me to this very moment. I'm living in a new country. I'm making saves for the Vice—a team I couldn't imagine playing for even a month ago. And I'm with Lily—a woman who inspires me to enjoy each day to the fullest.

ACKNOWLEDGMENTS

I hope you enjoyed *Coast to Coast*. If you would like to leave a review on your favourite book site, I would really appreciate that. Your opinion helps other readers to discover new reads.

This book took a year to write and the first draft was a bit of a mess. So, there are many people to thank for the polished version you're holding.

First of all, I'd like to thank my editor, Jodi Henley. She's worked with me on every book in the Vancouver Vice series, and she's always brilliant and kind. She really worked her alchemy here.

Secondly, my copy editor, Amy J. Duli, worked hard to polish *Coast to Coast*. (Commas, what are they?) But she also gave me a ton of positive feedback at a time when I really needed it.

I had two new beta readers for this book: Samantha Wayland and Stephanie Kay. Both are hockey romance authors whose books you should be checking out. Thanks also to Daisy, who has been my beta reader from day one.

Finally, setting a book in Sweden meant getting the European parts right.

Thank you to Helen Foster for tweaking my British slang and making the character of Sally Lloyd properly authentic.

And Annika Einarsson gave me the gentlest notes ever to correct my many mistakes about Sweden and my terrible Swedish spelling. If I had a krona for every accent I missed, I'd be rich. Annika, thank you so much.

ABOUT THE AUTHOR

U.S.A. Today best-selling author Melanie Ting writes, watches hockey games, and binges on Nordic noir dramas in beautiful Vancouver, B.C. She visited Sweden but left without meeting any tall Swedes or eating *kanelbullar*. She now makes up for that lapse by eating cinnamon buns at every opportunity.

Please visit www.melanieting.com to learn more.

ALSO BY MELANIE TING